WHETSTONES OF THE WILL

Book III Lords of Order and Chaos Series

R. J. Hanson

Hanson Publishing

ISBN-13: 9798638104283

Cover design by: MiblArt
Library of Congress Control Number: 2018675309
Printed in the United States of America

CONTENTS

LORDS OF ORDER AND CHAOS

Part III: Whetstones of the Will

By: R.J. Hanson

This work would not have been possible without the support and advice from my wife, Michelle, and input from my son, Alex, my daughter, Kaity, and son-in-law, Riker. I would also like to extend my thanks to Una, our friend from across the Atlantic, for her distinguished contributions to the refinement of this tale. As always, I would have none of what I have if it weren't for the Lord. I am richly blessed. -RJ

Bloodlines Reforged Saga by R.J. Hanson

PROLOGUE

The Death of a City, the Birth of a Curse
Part I

One brother carried another, his own wounds seeping and dripping blood onto white marble that would one day be a street of the great trade city of Moras. King Ivant, never one to lead from behind, now labored under the pain of his injuries and the weight of a noble brother in arms. Their long black hair, identical in its respective obsidian waves, mingled together in loose tangles. The crimson flow of blood tinted their dark locks and stained their white and red tunics.

Now he ran from the coast and ruined docks farther inland, hoping to escape the reach of the dreadful beast. Ivant, more than seven feet tall, had a great stride that lent to his speed. However, burdened with Truthorne's weight and dodging hatchlings and collapsing buildings made for slow progress.

"I can make another stand," Truthorne grunted as Ivant's shoulder pounded into his gut while he jogged along. "Put me down and let me stand!"

Ivant had hastily thrown Truthorne over his shoulder before running for the protection of the vast stone citadel of Ivory Rose.

"I can see the bone sticking out of your leg," King Ivant barked, perhaps harsher than he intended. "It's in its death throes now, I'm sure. I have to get you back to a priest or a healer."

As he spoke, a black tentacle struck a chunk of stone the size of a five-masted ship from the top of a nearby temple.

The ground beneath Ivant's feet trembled with the force as the mountain-size steeple loomed over them, blocking out the sun.

Ivant frantically scanned their surroundings and the doom that toppled above them. Seeing what he hoped would be a route of escape, Ivant charged up the steps of the magnificent cathedral from which the stone was being dislodged. He hit the gilded door with his shoulder, and both warriors were knocked to the ground when the door gave not a bit.

Ivant scrambled to his knees and pulled his Shrou-Hayn, Swift Blood, from his side. As he moved to the bottom edge of the cathedral's door, Truthorne called out.

"No," he cried. "You'll break her!"

"Not her crosspiece, I won't," Ivant said, not looking up. "Her crosspiece is dragon-forged Roarke's Ore."

Using his considerable, and in fact, legendary, strength Ivant wedged the crosspiece more than four inches under the door and heaved. Truthorne's surprise was complete when the sectot wood cried out along its hinges, and the door rose. With great effort, Ivant pried the door up and off its hinges. As the door tilted in, Ivant was already dragging his sword and his friend through the archway and into the holy place.

Ivant then rolled violently to the side with his cargo, bringing a scream of pain from Truthorne's throat. Just as they reached the sanctuary of thick timber and crafted stone, the steeple struck the street outside. Debris shot past them with vicious indifference to the sanctity of the holy building.

"Death throes?" Truthorne managed after easing his leg to one side.

"Well..." Ivant began but couldn't finish.

In spite of their dire situation, both men began laughing. That laugh was cut short when the huge steel church bell crashed through the ceiling, destroying the beautiful murals, and slammed violently into the marble floor. Both rolled to the cover of Truthorne's upraised shield, but the terrible collision of the bell only filled the air with choking dust and a ring that would deafen both warriors for several minutes.

Ivant rose and hauled Truthorne up once again, this time much more careful of his tender wound. Ivant started for the opposite door and into a courtyard rapidly filling with hatchlings. The creatures were tiny when compared to the size of the leviathan. However, they were still more than thirty-six feet tall at the shoulder, covered in an almost impenetrable exoskeleton, and each possessed eight of those powerful black tentacles with a reach of more than sixty feet. A single tentacle of one of the hatchlings had easily crushed Truthorne's leg already.

"No," Truthorne huffed between painful breaths. "The passage through the priests' nook; that's the path we should take. It should lead us safely in-land."

"I'm not wearing the right cloth for that," King Ivant said, also trying to regain his breath but still managing a bit of sarcasm. "They won't forgive anyone that's not part of the clergy passing through their nook."

"Then let their forgiveness be cursed," Truthorne said through gritted teeth.

Another loud burst of titan against stone stole all other sounds from the air for several long moments.

"I'll take this oath," Truthorne said, his lips red with blood from his lungs. "I'll never raise a hand against you or your kin, and, if the church demands otherwise, then let them be cursed!"

Ivant took another look at the courtyard and had to admit to himself that, in truth, there was no other option. Only certain death at the hands, or tentacles and pincers, of the hatchlings awaited them beyond those doors. Several hatchlings were already trying to bash their way through the arched doorways and windows of the cathedral. The last thing his kingdom needed was more trouble with the churches, but this was unavoidable. Thus, he turned them both toward the altar and ran. They were within a stride of the altar when another loud burst shuddered the very stone beneath their feet, causing them both to sprawl to the floor. Ivant heard the sickening sound of Truthorne's exposed bone scrape against the gold and silver gilding of the marble floor.

Ivant turned and saw the last bout of pain was more than the valiant Truthorne could bear. He lay a few feet away, unconscious. Ivant grabbed the black and white tunic, bearing the Hourglass of Father Time Truthorne wore, and began dragging him toward the altar. As he pulled him along, Ivant saw the black onyx ring bearing Truthorne's family crest; a two-headed dragon backed by crossed spears, fall from the necklace he wore concealed under his tunic. Knowing how much his crest meant to him, for his family and lands had been lost to them all, Ivant carefully tucked it back into place.

Ivant struggled to crawl under the altar of marble and gold just before another loud crash signaled the collapse of more ceiling. He grabbed Truthorne and pulled him under the protection of the altar as well. Choking on blood and dust, Ivant grabbed the chalice of holy water from beneath the altar and drank deeply. Then, with a prayer to Bolvii, he used the remainder of the water to wash dust and blood from Truthorne's mouth.

After what seemed like an eternity of searching, Ivant found the hidden catch that opened the concealed door beneath. Churches had been building these escape hatches for priests since the old days of the wars between the crown and the faiths. Now this one might save the King. Ivant smiled at the irony of it.

Ivant began down the gentle slide, pulling Truthorne with him slowly, not wanting to make a bad wound worse. The passage was free of cobwebs, and there was no smell of rot or decay, which Ivant took to be a good sign.

Once within the tunnels beneath the cathedral of Time, much of the sounds of destruction from above were muted. Ivant didn't realize just how loud the havoc of the monsters above had been until he moved into the quiet dark of the underground network. The silence was a relief at first. However, gradually it became more ominous.

He fumbled at the sidewall of the tunnel until his fingers found the raised edges of the ward that would trigger the magical lights. He traced his thumb over the lines, and a soft blue glow, one that seemed to come from all around them, lit the small room. As the glow grew, it traveled along the two tunnels leading away from them, one toward the nearby docks and the other toward the mountains inland.

Ivant, who was always a soldier first, scanned the room for threats, then supplies. He smiled when he found the healer's bag hanging from a peg on the wall alongside several waterskins and a sack of dried fruits and cheese. Ivant rummaged in the healer's bag for only a few moments when he found the herbs he needed. He put two roots in his mouth and began to chew. It wasn't the approved method of making a paste with them, but his time was short. While he chewed, he set three leaves out on a shaving basin, and then took hold of Truthorne's twisted and broken leg.

With a quick and violent jerk, Ivant pulled Truthorne's leg back into place, which started the blood flowing again. He spit the root paste into his hands and smeared it on the wound. Then he laid the leaves over the gash and wrapped it with the hem of a priest's robes he found hanging on another peg.

Now, with Truthorne's wounds treated, Ivant took up a silver platter from the small table next to them. The dish had been polished to a high shine and made for an excellent mirror. Ivant removed his heavily enchanted armor and tunic and examined the puncture wound on his left leg and the slash on his lower left abdomen. Using the mirror, he eyed the slash that ran from just below his chest muscle down to his belt line. They needed stitching, badly. He checked the cut above his right eye and noticed the blue glow of the light made his light blue eyes appear almost white. He looked to the herbs again but decided it would be best to save them for emergency use.

He pulled the leather satchel from his weapons' belt and found his curved needle and thread. Then he took a waterskin, specially marked with three black 'x's, from his pack. It contained a clear spirit the Great Men of Elgellund, the frozen plains in the far south, made from honey. Not to be confused with their meads, this stuff was at least ten times more potent. This was not Ivant's first field dressing.

He uncorked the waterskin, poured a mouthful down his throat, and then sprayed the burning liquid into the wounds on his side and his leg. The pain stole his breath, but it was a pain he well expected. He took a few moments to get his breathing back to normal, and then took up the polished platter and his needle and thread. It took several long minutes, but he finally managed to close both wounds. He tore more lengths of cloth from the priest's robes and wrapped his torso, his leg, and his head.

He needed to get back to his men but couldn't leave Truthorne behind. After all, his plan to attack the leviathan was to be a one-way trip. It likely would have been had it not been for Truthorne disobeying his paladin and coming to his King's aid.

Ivant decided that he must trust in his generals and get the rest he needed. The leviathan was down, but the battle to secure the city was far from over. Ivant took another drink of the burning spirits those in Elgellund were so proud of, and then let sleep take him.

"Well, come on then," a gruff voice he knew well startled Ivant from sleep. "Will ya' be napping all the day long?"

"Vech, King Vech of the dwarves, is that you?" Ivant mumbled and squinted his eyes. "The great beast's venom, my eyesight..."

Vech ran to his friend, Ivant, and dropped to the floor next to where he lay. He leaned over the Great Man King, examining his eyes and digging through his own herb pouch at the same time, all the while beginning a feverish prayer to Roarke, the god of all dwarves.

Ivant slipped a hand up and grabbed a handful of Vech's coarse, wiry dwarven beard and gave it a jerk. Vech, so surprised by the sudden move, and the immediate pain, jerked backward and fell to his rump.

Ivant burst into laughter, much to the complaint of the stitches in his side, and was so loud that he woke Truthorne, sleeping only a few yards away.

"If it'd been any other than yourself doin' that sort o' thing to the King o' the Stonebeards, you be sure they'd be tastin' me knuckles!" Vech roared.

"What are you doing sitting in the hall?" Truthorne asked, trying to hide the beginnings of a smile taking shape at the edges of his mouth.

That sally sent Ivant, always one to enjoy a good joke, into another gale of laughter. Vech huffed and scowled at Ivant as he struggled to get up from the floor. Finally, with a kick of his leg for momentum, Vech managed to roll over and get to his feet.

While Vech continued to scowl at them, Truthorne tested his leg by bending it and then, after rising, slowly putting weight on it. Ivant checked his bandages and saw the bleeding had stopped and hadn't entirely soaked through the cloth. He deemed that a good sign.

"How did you find us?" Truthorne asked as he began gathering his gear and taking from the stores left in the small alcove by the church.

"I'm a dwarf, ain't I?" Vech grumbled. "You're under the stone, ain't ya'? Who's knowin' the stone and what she hides better than a dwarf?"

"How fares General Willock and our troops?" Ivant asked. "Casualties?"

He had enjoyed his gibe at Vech, but now it was time to get back to the business of saving Ivory Rose. He had also carried a lot of worry in his heart for his good friend and advisor, General Willock.

"It was lookin' pretty bad, morale wise, and there was some rough words between some of the clerics and your General Willock," Vech said as he brushed dirt from the floor out of his beard. "But that stunt of yer's, we'll be talkin' about that by the way, but that stunt of yer's shut them all up."

"I meant the work to secure the city," Ivant clarified. "I meant how many men have we lost."

"I know what ya' meant," Vech said, patting the air with his thick, hairy hands. "They're doin' good work up there and got a bunch o' those hatchlings pushed out. My count is... well, it looks like about one hundred and twenty dead, another thirty or forty to be joining them before morning, and another three hundred that won't be getting home without being carried."

Ivant nodded as the pall shadow of a grim look drifted over his face. Vech shuffled from one foot to the next, looked away, and began fiddling with one of the many gemstones braided into his beard.

"What else?" Truthorne asked.

"It's yer own brethren," Vech said in a low tone. "They... they wouldn't let the Kingsmen get the orphans out. Said it was church property and wouldn't let anyone sworn to serve the crown inside."

"A bit foolish to turn down the help, but I don't see why..." Truthorne began, unconsciously wiping the dirt and grime from his templar's tunic.

"Turns out the priests didn't get them out either," Vech said with a heavy sigh. "Thought the whole thing was a ploy of the crown to make them abandon their riches. We haven't taken back that part o' the city yet, but none have been seen to have made it out."

"If they let those children die because they were more worried about their gold and their silver..." Ivant began but couldn't finish.

The trouble with the churches had been building for some decades now. First it was just the Cathedral of Time led by Most High Cleric and Supreme Pontiff Lynneare, but now there were more and more priests succumbing to the temptations of corruption.

Ivant had to admit to himself that he shared part of the blame. When the whole issue began, he should have handled it more diplomatically. When the church started to force tithing on the congregation, and many who weren't even members of the church, Ivant responded by arresting the templars and paladins who were going door to door to 'collect' for the 'welfare' of others.

As those things tend to do, what should have been a simple arrest escalated. The templars and paladins had no authority to act anywhere other than church grounds, or within the confines of the King's Law, so the arrests were binding and just. However, that meant nothing compared to a young templar pulling his sword on a King's knight and paying the price with his life.

Of course, the problem had been building for decades. Slights against authority, over-reach by a priest or a reeve, taxes versus tithing; they had all contributed to the crossroads Ivant's kingdom now faced. But he knew the real problem. The real problem was vanity.

Life had been easy for the peoples of Stratvs for generations, and an easy life makes easy people. Ivant, a close friend to the famous philosopher and general Arto, had discussed the topic with the great thinker on many occasions. It seemed that kingdoms were not immune to the cycles that nature imposes. Hard times made hard men and women who grew strong enough to stand up to those trials and learned to appreciate what they had. Their struggles made life more comfortable for their children, which, in turn, caused people to be less appreciative and more demanding. When their consumption outweighed their production, people starved and began to murder for food and basic shelter.

It was only natural for a man or woman to want their children to live better lives than they had led. However, none are immune from the harsh realities of the world. There will always be men willing to kill to take what is not theirs. There will always be those who are hungry and cannot feed themselves. Thus, there must always be those that will stand for the weak and feed those who are hungry. As Arto had put it, 'the villain does not create the hero, but he does reveal him.'

"Be careful what you say next, my King," Truthorne, in an uncharacteristic tone of seriousness, warned. "I know you are angry. I, too, am angry. Do not let the fiery nature of our blood cause you to make an oath you should not make, much less fulfill."

Ivant shot Truthorne a hard look, and the templar replied by only holding his hands out wide. Neither noticed, but King Vech placed his hand on his trusty leiness hand axe and watched Truthorne for any false move.

Vech had no dog in the hunt, as the saying went, when it came to the troubles between the crown of men and the churches in their cities. Nothing beyond supporting his good friend who happened to be the King of the Great Men and maintaining a flow of trade between their peoples. However, his support for his friend was absolute, and he would even readily strike down a templar, or surrender his own life, for Ivant should a situation call for either.

"We worked for centuries together to unify many peoples into a kingdom," Truthorne continued, hoping he was planting seeds of reason that would choke out Ivant's temper. "Let not all that bloodshed be destroyed by a few years of discord and a few hastily spoken words."

Ivant opened his mouth to reply but bit the words back. A scream in the distance broke the tension and drew the attention of each of the three experienced warriors.

PART II

"That was the cry of an elf," Truthorne whispered.

"Aye," Vech responded, nodding. "Brought a few of yer royal scouts with me, and they were to watch the entrance to these tunnels. That scream was too close, though. They must have been..."

Vech didn't finish, but he didn't need to finish. All three knew what the only reasonable conclusion must be. The elves had been pushed into the tunnel by assaults from something, or someone, from outside.

Truthorne drew his holy shrou-sheld and his mercshyeld dagger and moved to the left. Vech drew his black leiness axe, which to the dwarven kings and people also served as scepter and orb and record of their history, and shouldered his shield fashioned from the scapula of a firedrake. King Ivant took a moment to gather the healer's pack, extra waterskins, and other items of use, and slung them over his shoulder. He smiled at how his friends had instinctively moved, one to the right, the other to the left.

Ivant removed his storied helm, made of mercshyeld and possessing a magical gem of lexxmar in the forehead, from his pack and strapped it on. It was rare that he wore the helm, for he preferred his enemies see his face, his eyes, during combat. However, the helm provided faultless vision through the gloom of the underground caverns and protection against any mental attacks. Ivant picked up his Shrou-Hayn, Swift Blood, a greatsword six feet in length, and stepped between the Templar and Dwarven King to lead in the vanguard position. The tunnels would make for close work, so Ivant took a specially mailed gauntlet from his pack. Then, holding the mid-haft of Swift Blood in one hand, he took the top third of the blade in his gauntleted hand and held the sword more like a staff than a sword.

The three moved silently and swiftly through the soft blue glow of the tunnel light. Occasional screams and scrapes of metal against stone could be heard from up ahead of them. They passed a few side chambers where some of the wealth of the local churches was secreted and noted that each of those passages was warded against entry. They also noted the dust drifting down from whatever tumult was taking place on the streets above them.

They rounded a corner as one, sorrowfully in time to see something terrible. If they had been a bit slower, if the templar had been a bit more merciful, if the elf had died of his initial wounds... If and if and if. Yet, none of those things happened, and thus the fate of future generations, of peoples and nations, was sealed.

Each of the three warriors watched, helpless and speechless, as a templar wearing the Hourglass of Time upon his tunic, slowly pressed the point of his longsword into the eye of an elven scout, an elven scout bearing the sigil and crest of the Kingdom of Great Men. The execution was enough to make inevitable the templar's fate, but the smirk he bore as he extinguished the life of that faithful servant set the temper of King Ivant ablaze. Truthorne caught a sigh that was more a whimper in his throat, for he perhaps better than the others understood the weight of what had just transpired.

Ivant roared a battle cry that Vech had only heard once before, a battle cry that Bolvii, the god of war on high, heard clearly. This would be the first time the King shed the blood of a servant of the churches. It would not be the last.

Vech, shocked by the callousness of the templar's executing blade and the rage of Ivant's battle cry, was startled into action by Truthorne's cry.

"My King, no!" Truthorne pleaded.

Truthorne's cry, not to mention Ivant's roar, drew the attention of more than just the templars of Time standing over the elven scouts. Vech sprinted, for dwarves are natural sprinters, in hopes of catching up to his friend. Vech saw there were too many templars in those tight quarters for even the mighty Ivant to manage on his own.

Ivant charged forward with fire burning in his veins and his eyes. Truthorne, much quicker and more agile than his good friend, still struggled to keep pace with the maddened King Ivant. Vech, huffing and puffing, followed close behind. Ivant thrust Swift Blood forward before Truthorne could catch up. The magical speed of the storied blade sent it piercing the air almost as a lightning bolt.

The templar of Time smiled, thinking he now had an opportunity to remove King Ivant as an obstacle once and for all. Truthorne saw the templar lifting his longsword to parry Swift Blood, following the blade with a dagger concealed in his off-hand. The templar clearly intended to knock Swift Blood out of line and then drive the dagger forward, hiding the attack beneath the other crossed blades. Truthorne whispered a quick prayer for the soul of the templar, a brother he did not know.

Swift Blood thrust in as the templar's longsword rose, but the parrying blade rose far too slowly. Swift Blood darted like the tongue of a viper slicing through the templar's chainmail shirt and then into heart, lung, and spine. The templar of Time dropped to the stone, dead before his corpse could feel the coolness of the marble beneath him.

Ivant whipped his greatsword back as quickly as it had struck and caught the top third of the blade in his off-hand as he spun toward the next templar of Time. Truthorne had seen this move a number of times and knew exactly how the King would execute it. Truthorne arrived barely in time to knock Ivant's powerful slash upward, forcing Swift Blood's edge just above the helm of the next servant of Father Time and Supreme Pontiff Lynneare. Ivant, undeterred, continued the move and spin and came around to strike the templar hard in the face with the pommel of his greatsword, knocking the templar to the stone floor, too stunned to speak.

Another templar thrust at Ivant's side and Truthorne forced that attack low and wide with his own longsword as he rebounded from Ivant's momentum. Another spear came from the darkness to the left, bound for King Ivant's unprotected thigh.

Just as the spear came in, so did the powerful Vech. The dwarven king caught the haft of the spear in the crook of his axe and pulled it down hard against his upraised forearm, snapping the head off and leaving the ambushing templar holding only a broken stick.

Ivant kicked the seated and stunned templar in the head for good measure as he moved past him and on toward the rest of his number gathered in a chamber only a few feet away. Truthorne dove and stretched out his considerable frame, launching himself not unlike an arrow past Ivant and into the gathering templars.

Many of them raised a sword or mace but paused upon seeing the holy Hourglass symbol emblazed on Truthorne's armor, tunic, and weapons. Without pause, Truthorne hopped from the ground, spun, and faced Ivant to knock wide the next attack from Swift Blood.

"Please!" Truthorne pleaded.

Ivant hesitated a moment, but only a moment, for a templar to the side threw a spear at the King of the Great Men, aimed for his neck. Ivant spun on a tilted axis that brought his greatsword up to slap the spear high of its mark. Ivant, maintaining his momentum, continued the spin, reversed his grip on his sword, and slid toward the templar on one knee. Holding the pommel in his right hand, he drove the top third of the blade up with his left, slicing through mail, then guts, then ribs. Ivant, continuing the motion without pause or hesitation, pulled Swift Blood free, locked his leading foot into place, and pushed himself up into the stance of the Raven Wing, which secured his right arm close to his ribs while his left remained high and out to the side.

The templar staggered back, grasping with both hands to put back what had not been disturbed since Father Time put it there. The templar slumped to the ground, his hands full of his own entrails. His eyes locked with Truthorne's for a moment, and then saw nothing more.

"This treachery by the crown will not stand!" one of the templars cried as he charged toward Ivant but was cut short by Vech's axe swipe. "You have violated a holy place!"

"You've killed kingsmen," Vech replied as he pushed the templar's longsword wide and punched into his abdomen with the head of his axe, knocking the wind from the man. "How'd ya' think that will go over?"

Vech and Truthorne managed to force themselves between Ivant and the remainder of the templars. Ivant circled as a hungry lion might, trying to get around his friends to those that had, in his opinion, abandoned their rightful duties to kill his scouts instead. Dust drifted down into the chamber, a result of the terrible battle raging above in the streets of Ivory Rose.

"Wait!" Truthorne pleaded again. "Please, hold! This doesn't have to get worse..."

"You took an oath not a few hours ago to never stand against me and mine," Ivant reminded Truthorne, his voice taking on a dangerously cold tone. "Do templars forget their oaths so easily?"

"Now you hold too, Tall Walker," Vech cautioned, hoping the dwarven nickname given Ivant would jar his mind enough to make reasoning with him possible.

It was not lost on Truthorne how desperate times had become that a dwarf was the voice of reason among them.

"There be a time and place for hashin' this out, but this ain't either," Vech said, hoping his words were finding purchase in the hearts of the men around him. "You maybe ain't hearin' them o'er the sound o' the blood in yer ears, but there's women and kiddos screaming an' cryin' above us. They be needin' us, every one o' us."

"I have ever been true to my oaths," Truthorne said. "I will forever honor my oath to you, good King Ivant, but I must also honor my oath to Father Time. Please listen to the wisdom of the dwarven king."

Ivant, much to the surprise of his friends Truthorne and Vech, nodded his head in agreement. Ivant lowered his head, closed his eyes, and gave a great sigh.

"Remove yourselves from our path so we may be about the duties of the strong administering to the needs of the weak," Ivant said in a low tone to the small gathering of templars. "I pray thee."

The remaining nine templars moved to the sides of the chamber, out of the path of the King, and Ivant started forward. Truthorne and Vech saw the doom of them all, but with no time to react or intervene. A spear, thrown from amidst the ranks of the templars of Time, flew through the air, bound for King Ivant's exposed side. Ivant also saw the hurled spear, but not even the enchanted speed given him by Swift Blood enabled him to move out of its path. Ivant had only enough time to wonder at Truthorne's culpability in his assassination.

As the three friends watched the head of the spear knife through the air with deadly accuracy, they also instinctively crouched as the stone above them gave way. They realized that the sounds of the grating stone had been in their ears for several moments, yet none of them registered the significance until now. The ceiling of the chamber collapsed as the street above fell in upon them; the debris swallowed the hurled spear.

King Vech shoved a large piece of what he presumed was once a wagon off his sturdy chest and then began to cast about in the dust, dark, and screams. He saw Swift Blood's pommel and knew Ivant's hand would not be far from it. He crawled through the rubble, comprised of the remains of this chamber, the street, and what must have been at least two buildings above them, to the sword of his friend.

Vech pushed aside stone and dirt to find the gloved hand of King Ivant. Vech moved around, paying no attention whatsoever to the blood coursing from his own brow, and latched both of his thick hands around the wrist of his friend. The first pull brought the helm of Ivant within sight, and Vech took great relief in seeing the puffs of dust from under the helm, indicating that his companion still drew breath. The next pull brought Ivant's top half out from under the pile, leaving only his legs still buried. Vech took a moment to catch his breath, and then leaned into the third pull, straining with all the considerable power of his shoulders and arms.

As Ivant's leg came free from the rubble, another spear flew in, striking Ivant's side and sinking in deep. Vech looked up, thinking to haul his axe out and give it a throw at whoever had struck his good friend. Instead, he watched, a bit horrified, as one of the hatchlings wrapped a tentacle around a smiling and unsuspecting templar. The templar's smile transformed to a scream of terror during a single heartbeat as the hatchling ripped away one of his legs and stuffed it into the maw situated between its great pincers.

Vech pulled Ivant farther from the feasting hatchling and along a side tunnel. Two more templars were pulled from the rubble by another hungry beast that dropped into what was a subterranean chamber. There was no sign of Truthorne or the other templars. Vech thought it likely, given the size and quantity of the stones that fell in on them, the templars and Truthorne had been crushed to death and buried in one swift stroke by the gods.

Vech decided that it might be best for Truthorne, a way to die with his honor and his soul secure. Vech liked the Master Templar but had known for years that one day he would face a choice between his friendship with King Ivant and his blind loyalty to an over-reaching church. Vech knew, should that day come, it would likely end with catastrophic results.

Vech was no priest but had spent decades if not centuries in one battle or another, and he knew wounds. Now he checked Ivant's and determined he was likely only knocked out and perhaps had a few broken ribs from the falling stone. Vech thought to himself that Ivant's remarkable smoke-colored breastplate had saved him again, for the stone that cracked those ribs would have crushed an angry bear. It was Ivant's other injuries that worried him. There were deep cuts that had been bandaged and stitched but were now seeping blood once again. There was also the puncture from the spear, which had caused unknown internal injuries.

Vech ran for several hundred yards through the now darkened tunnels underneath the great coastal city. The magic of the light Ivant had activated had been shattered when the chamber collapsed, but Vech's dwarven eyes, eyes that were no stranger to the dark places of the world, showed him his path clearly. After many twists, turns, stairs, and ladders, King Vech smelled the salt air of the sea near at hand.

"Is that you, good dwarf?" came from an elven voice in the distance. "Although I don't see you yet, your distinct smell is unmistakable."

"Julian, get ya' in here and bring ya' back o' magic plants!" Vech roared at the always joking elven scout. "Yer king's hurt!"

Vech heard Julian's signal horn call for aid. He heard it clearly as had General Willock and the remainder of King Ivant's armies, no doubt. Vech did not often envy anything crafted by another race, but Vech envied Julian's signal horn. Helldjern it was called.

Julian, a tall and rather thin elf with long black hair and eyes that tinted from brown to gold, sprinted down the tunnels toward them, toward his King. As he ran, he dropped his sectot bow from his shoulder and nocked an arrow. Vech, stunned and confused, could only throw himself over Ivant's prostrate form as Julian ran at them, drawing his bowstring.

Julian's bowstring sung, and Vech instinctively twitched in anticipation of the pain that would soon follow. However, much to his surprise, he heard the arrow strike armor, or bone, above and behind him. Vech turned in time to see one of the hatchlings; he had no idea they could have ever been so stealthy, less than ten yards behind him and crumpling. The giant beast collapsed in a heap, dead instantly from Julian's expert marksmanship, and his Roarke's Ore tipped arrow.

"Glad you could finally catch up," Vech huffed, trying to maintain his composure. "Thought I was gonna have to kill another o' those cursed things."

Julian began to smile but stopped when he saw the blood on Vech and his King, Ivant. In one swift and fluid motion, the tall elf dropped to one knee, slung his healer's pouch to hang before his lean stomach, and worked with both hands independently to select herbs. With his left hand, he passed two different types of leaves and a moss to Vech, who only just then noticed the blood coming from beneath his breastplate. With his right, Julian pressed another moss on Ivant's forehead and then worked to unstrap his smoke-colored armor.

Julian found a few older wounds poorly treated and a host of new injuries when he examined Ivant. His efforts and every action were efficient and quick. The elven scout expertly cut the cloth strips from Ivant with a slim dagger in one hand while applying an enchanted leaf and fresh bandage with the other. In the time Vech had removed his own armor, stopped the bleeding from a stab wound he was unable to recall, wrapped a bandage around it and his head wound, and get his armor back on Julian had finished healing King Ivant and he was coming around.

"Truthorne?" Ivant asked in a groggy voice.

"Buried in the rubble... I think," Vech said. "There was only a few what stirred once the roof, meaning also the street, came down upon us. Those few got et by one of them wee krakens."

"Julian," Ivant said and needed say no more.

"My King," Julian responded. "Before I go, I signaled for General Willock. He should be near the end of the tunnels just there," the elf scouted pointed toward the soft glow of early evening light, "within half an hour or so. We have the city, the damage has yet to be assessed, but it is secure."

With that, Julian hopped to his feet and sprinted down

the tunnel toward the last known location of Master Templar Truthorne.

A short time later, Vech and Ivant sat on a low stone bench just outside the tunnel's concealed entrance and were sharing what little remained of Ivant's strong drink from Elellund, the frozen lands to far south. The sounds of General Willock and his vanguard's armor and horses could be heard for several minutes before they actually arrived. King Ivant climbed to the top of an up-tilted foundation stone and waved to them in hopes of slowing them. He wasn't confident what their next move would be, but he was sure they would want horses as refreshed as possible.

"My King!" Willock called as they approached. "My King, your injuries?"

Willock's relief to see his King alive and in the company of his friend, King Vech of the Stonebeards, was splashed across his worn and scarred face. Willock swung down from his horse, pulled his waterskin from his saddle, and offered it to his King.

General Willock, also of the Great Man race, was a bit more than six and a half feet tall with black, short cut hair in the style of the Silver Helms, and hazel eyes. He was clad in well maintained and highly polished white alloy steel armor engraved and inlaid with powerful magical runes and wards. Few knew it, but Willock's armor made him all but immune to any wizard's bolts of fire or lightning or any changes the climate might have to offer. He also carried a beautiful white alloy shield of matching design and craftsmanship. He wore a black bladed shrou-sheld at his side that was also heavily enchanted.

"Seen to," Ivant responded with a wave of his hand.

"But your fall," Willock said, undeterred by Ivant's reassurances. "Few saw it, but I was among them. The sight of you falling from Merc's Road thrusting your lance before you into that great beast... I can't believe that worked and that you survived it! I was heartsick that you might..."

Willock paused, taking a moment to put those fears behind him. Ivant looked at Willock, his expression making it clear that any conversations about a lost lance and past dangers were over.

"My King," General Willock continued. "You should know that the churches, all of them, withdrew some time ago."

"How far back did they withdraw?" Ivant asked in a dangerously quiet tone.

"They didn't… they teleported away, vanished, my King," Willock said. "Lord High Paladin Maloch showed up with Master Templar Truthorne and met with the Supreme Pontiff, Lynneare. They mustered over five hundred men around a large black pearl, about the size of a horse's head, and then Lynneare cast some spell. No spell of a cleric either. This was arcane magic. The pearl exploded, and they all just disappeared, teleported away."

"That's a mighty spell indeed to move that many men," Vech said. "And an expensive component to burn up just to cast it."

"They must be on their way to Nolcavanor," Ivant said as his eyes stared off over the seas.

Vech had often seen Ivant stare off into the distance like that when he was thinking. It was as if he could see with his eyes the thoughts, the logic, as it fell into place while he reasoned.

"We are here with only a small contingent holding the capitol," Ivant continued, slowly as the plans of their enemy became plain to him. "I think Lynneare means to move on the Keep of Nolcavanor itself. He'll bring his mount as well. We'll need to be ready for a battle with a dragon."

****

"Truthorne, seize Lord Ivant, for he is no longer a king of anything. The kingdom that was, is no more," Supreme Pontiff Lynneare commanded.

When the Master Templar hesitated, Lynneare raised a single eyebrow that transformed his whole face into a sneer. King Vech and General Willock, Julian's bow hanging from his shoulder, stood to either side of Ivant, and both slid their feet to blade their stances to Lynneare and those sworn to him.

They had caught up to Lynneare and his entourage exactly where they expected to find them. They were in the highest tower of the cathedral dedicated to Time in the capital city of Nolcavanor. It had been a bloody fight, and there was still so much left that must be done.

"Your command would cause your Master Templar to violate an oath he made to me before Father Time, and in Time's cathedral," Ivant interjected. "In the once great temple of Ivory Rose, he vowed never to raise a hand to me or my kin."

"That is blasphemy!" Lynneare roared, on the edge of losing control. "Blasphemy, and it will be added to your Scroll of Charge and Accusation! Your blood will be required to atone!"

Ivant curled the edge of his mouth into a smile; a smile that confused all present except for King Vech. Vech knew that smile well.

"You don't get to decide what is or is not blasphemy," Ivant said coolly. "You are to teach the word of Time, the way of Time, and heal and care for those in your charge. The power of command is not given to you in His laws, nor mine. The power to call for blood is not given to you in his word, nor by mine. I am the ruler and protector of our nation of Great Men. I am the one who will seek justice for Julian and my other slain scouts, dead at the hands of your murderers! I call for blood, and I now call for yours! You are not welcome in this house! Get ye hence!"

Thunder seemed to come from the distance and from within each stone of the magnificent structure. Every eye, except those of Ivant which never left Lynneare, searched their surroundings for the source, the potential threat that sound might herald. The air charged with palpable primordial energy. All in the room felt the weight, the power of banishment from the rightful king.

The Lord High Paladin, the elf known as Maloch, instinctively drew his magnificent paired shrou-shelds. Lynneare, his skin beginning to lose its color and black curly locks of hair of which he had been so proud fallin in clumps from his head, screamed in defiance and wrapped a boney hand around a pillar of the Hourglass. Truthorne, acting out of habit to support and defend his Supreme Pontiff, reached to support Lynneare, lending him his strength and will.

The banishment, the curse, traveled along the Hourglass as a visible blue/black light poured out of Lynneare's eyes and mouth, swam down his shriveling arm, and rushed across the Hourglass. Once the whole of the curse washed within the Hourglass, it then reverberated and magnified as it burned back into the raw flesh of the Most High Cleric and Master Templar.

Thousands of years and leagues from that terrible scene, young Roland jerked awake, his body sheathed in an icy sweat. He could still feel the effects of the Hourglass, a powerful totem he had only ever touched but the once, stirring in his soul, as he awakened from a dream he struggled to understand.

CHAPTER I

Dark Strangers

Four dark figures crouched on a rocky ledge hundreds of feet up and watched the Blue Tower with their long-glasses. It was late fall of the year 1650 of the Age of Restored Great Men Kings. Although spring, violent and icy winds still cut at the four and caused their cloaks to whip frantically at their unsecured edges. Lord of Chaos Silas Morosse, Lady Dru, Warlord Verkial, and Field Marshal Hallgrim, promoted from Captain for his work in bringing Wodock to heel, each studied the stones and mortar of the Blue Tower. Each hoping some vulnerability would reveal itself.

"An assassin would be a better choice, a Shadow Blade even better than that," Verkial said as he took the long-glass from his right eye and collapsed it down to a six-inch tube and slid it into his leather pouch. "Yes, I have troops, but sending them against the sorcerers of the Blue Tower would be like shoving the hands of a child into a sausage grinder. I need an army to hold western Tarborat and Wodock. I don't *need* anything in the Blue Tower."

"We're not proposing a direct assault, nor are we suggesting a protracted battle," Silas said as he put away his long-glass. "We should only need your men for transport. I believe we can move the item much like shipwrights move vessels over land. I think..."

"It would fail," came from a deep and rich voice behind the four conspirators.

They all turned, Verkial hauling out a barbed Shrou-Hayn and Hallgrim slapping a second hand to the colossal battle hammer he carried. At the same time, Dru and Silas began to silently prepare spells. They all looked upon a tall figure concealed within the folds of a heavy cloak of black wool. The character extended one boney ring finger and pointed toward Hallgrim.

Dru barked the final command word of her spell, but as she did so, her mouth was slammed shut by some outside force. Silas reached within himself to access the powers of Shezmu and found a stranger sitting on the throne of his mind-keep. Verkial took a single, faltering step, and then, when the dark figure stuck out his king finger and thumb, found himself bound by invisible chains of magical power. Hallgrim's eyes rolled in his head, and he collapsed to the stone. Verkial, in spite of himself, worried for his Field Marshal until he saw the steady rise and fall of Hallgrim's chest and heard him begin to snore.

"As I was saying, it would fail," the dark figure said again as he lowered his pale hands and clasped them before him within the folds of his black coverings. "You seek the Drakestone, and it cannot be found by going from room to room, looking in closets and pantries, and so forth. Furthermore, gaining entry into that citadel is possible by the skills and magics you possess or command, but it would be costly. Might I suggest an alternative?"

The magical bonds and restraints of mental domination relaxed enough for Verkial to stretch his neck and Dru and Silas to organize and think coherently once again. Of course, this creature's message, and Silas was sure he was a creature and no mere man, was emblazoned in their minds. They wouldn't be able to forget his words for days, if ever.

Silas could smell the sea on the mysterious figure's clothing; he and Shezmu could smell human blood on his breath. Silas wondered, deep within in his thoughts to avoid them being easily read as Dru tended to do, just how much power this person could command. He also wondered if such powers could be taught and learned.

"I will assume by your silence you are willing to hear me out; I thank you for your courtesy," the dark shape within the cloak whispered. "And, to answer your question Chaos Lord Silas... Dreg Zylche."

To Silas's complete shock, and horror, Shezmu's magical blade fashioned of an ice drake's claw appeared in the thin and pale right hand of their visitor.

"You see?" the stranger asked. "If I wanted you dead, you would be dead. I understand that is difficult for any of you to accept, for none of you would have gotten this far on your various journeys had you been willing to accept such concepts with such little evidence. Therefore, let me say this..."

He gestured with his hand and dismissed the wicked blade back to the ethereal plane from whence it came and continued. Silas conducted a quick mental inventory to find the blade returned to his possession. Silas decided it best he keep his teeth together, as his brother Dunewell used to say, and hear what this man/beast had to say. Also, he didn't want his words to give away even more than his plainly read thoughts already had.

"I assure you, I mean you no harm and am interested in your success," the dark figure said as he turned to look past the four and toward the Blue Tower. "None of you would take that at face value, nor should you. Thus, I offer this explanation; there is a wizard in the Blue Tower; perhaps you're familiar with him. His name is Eljen Unglau. I have decided it is time for him to pay for his offenses toward me and mine. I have decided he will pay with his blood and soul. Furthermore, there is another coming. He is rising against you as we speak, although some of you do not know of him yet. Some of you do."

It was at this point that the mysterious creature's eyes, only his eyes, became visible and gleamed with a bloodred glow within the deep cave that was his hood. They locked with Dru's exotic eyes and lingered for several heartbeats.

"The Drakestone will do you little good against him when he comes, but there is another whom he fears, and rightly so."

"Another?" the words popped from Dru's delicate, if vicious, lips before she could catch them. "Who? Please, who?"

Her naked desperation shocked Silas and, he had to admit, frightened him a bit. Anyone the powerful and skilled Lady Dru feared was someone to walk a wide path around.

"In time," the dark figure said with a wave of his hand. "In time. Warlord Verkial does not trust me. I don't believe he will come to trust me either, but I do believe he will come to believe what I have to say and that I mean him no harm."

"You've talked all around it, and yet you've actually *said* nothing," Verkial spat. "Now, get to the point or get out of my business."

"Just so. I know where the Drakestone is kept, and I know how to get to it. It is held in a dimensional rift on the three hundred and forty-second floor of the Blue Tower. Now, before you begin your detractions, there are more than one thousand levels of that venerable tower; however, magic is the only way to reach most of them."

As the stranger spoke, Silas noted Dru nodding her head in affirmation. "There are vast levels of the tower that are only accessible by different magical means. That much is true," she said.

"I am aware your alliance is in its infancy," the dark figure continued. "What I need from you is for you to form a lasting bond. Very soon a great power, a great evil, will be released on the world, and I will need your help to stop it."

"You want us to believe that *you* seek to prevent the release of great evil?" Verkial asked, his incredulity plain.

"Is it so hard to believe that, if for no other reason, I wouldn't desire any competition?" the creature retorted.

Verkial shrugged at that and nodded.

"Of you three, only Lord Verkial could enter the room where the Drakestone is held, for it is heavily warded against evil," the stranger continued. "Of you three, only Lady Dru of the Disputed Isles could hope to shield her mind against the rebuking waves of mentalist energy that assail all who enter the secret chamber. None of you three know how to transport the

Drakestone once access is made. I can make arrangements for all those requirements to fall into place."

"So, we're to sit here while you go get this Drakestone, a rock I'm not even sure I want, and trust that you'll bring it to us once you have it?" Verkial asked.

"Ah, this complicates things a bit," the dark stranger said as he waved one boney finger back and forth at Dru and Silas. "You didn't tell him about Isd'Kislota, did you?"

Verkial shot a glare at Dru and Silas. A glare Dru did not bother to return and that Silas answered with only a shrug and a smile.

"He's within the mountains of Wodock," Silas did finally say. "If he is to be owned, he belongs to me, per our arrangement."

Lady Dru tilted her head and raised a single eyebrow.

"Of course, when I say he belongs to me, I mean in such a way as I, and all that I own or control, is the Lady Dru's to do with as she pleases."

"Very well," Verkial said, surprising them all with how well he took such news. "What is an Isd'Kislota, anyway?"

"He is an ancient and powerful acid drake," the tall, dark figure replied. "He fought against the gods during the Battles of Rending."

That information raised Verkial's eyebrow but garnered no further response.

"Soon, you will be sorely pressed by Ingshburn's forces," the stranger continued. "You will need Isd'Kislota and the support he can offer. Thus, whether you wish to admit it or not, you, Lord Verkial, will need the assistance of Lady Dru. A dangerous villain is pursuing Lady Dru. She will need your help very soon. Other things are in motion that I will not tell you about because you wouldn't be able to understand them."

"Try us," Silas said, his devil-may-care smile twitching at the edge of his mouth.

"Very well, I'll re-phrase," the stranger said, his voice growing above a whisper and seeming to resonate in their bones. "I am Lynneare, Warlock of the Marshes. I will tell you what you need to know, when you need to know it. You *will* do something for me, and you *will* allow me to retrieve the Drake-stone for you. I am the Original Betrayer, I am OathBreaker, and I am not asking for your help; I'm demanding your service."

As Lynneare spoke, his hood, as of its own accord, flew back from his shaved head to reveal his pale visage. His words were heavy with magical power, and his eyes burned with an intensity that caused them all to inadvertently gulp air down their suddenly dry throats.

All eyes went wide at that declaration. This dark figure, Lynneare, had shown his absolute power over Silas and what he thought were considerable defenses. He had shown his strength in binding both Verkial and Hallgrim, in spite of the wards placed on them by Verkial's witch, with ease and deft speed. He had stilled Lady Dru's tongue, and her mind for that matter, against any chance of casting a spell or uttering an incantation. His power had been demonstrated, but none had guessed the person in black robes before them could be the legendary Lynneare.

"I will assume your silence is indicative of your appreciation of the grave nature of your circumstances," Lynneare said pleasantly. "That is good and will save *you* grief and *us* time. I will retrieve your Drakestone for you and properly arm you against the Blue Tower. In fact, I will assist you when the time comes to assault it. You, young Lord of Chaos, will speak with Lady Evalynne of Moras. An assassin is coming to Moras. He will attempt to bribe the Lady for some *considerations* while operating in her city. She needs to understand it is imperative that she agree to whatever conditions he sets, but then communicates those conditions to you immediately. Furthermore, if he should ask her for any information, she is to relay that to you as well. Make sure she understands that when you say imperative, it means that you will tear down her house and her soul, stone and muscle, iron and bone, piece by piece over decades if your will is not heeded. You will not use my name, none of you will, nor will you mention to any that are not here any word of our arrangement."

Silas nodded slowly; his devilish smile gone like the snows of winters past.

"Lady Dru, you think you know the nature of the one that comes for you," Lynneare said as his eyes, those deep-set and ominous eyes, shifted from holding Silas to rest on her. "I tell you now that you do not. The drow queen, Jandanero, is in possession of a Dark Guardian."

Silas had to admit to himself that he enjoyed seeing Verkial's reaction to that announcement. Verkial was not one to ever look surprised, much less fearful, but both emotions flashed across his face at the news that the drow controlled a Dark Guardian. Silas was also a bit surprised to see it was news to Lady Dru. He caught the tell-tale sign of her lovely eyes widening a bit at the mention of the deadly creation. Silas hadn't actually known, not for certain, but he had suspicions since noticing the unusual nature of one of her constructs that carried her throne. Suspicions that were now confirmed.

"You need to convince her somehow to allow you to *borrow* the being for a short time," Lynneare continued. "I would imagine she will not agree to such an arrangement without significant recompense. You are a capable woman. I leave that to you to negotiate. I will meet you at Isd'Kislota's cave with the Drakestone when you have possession of the Dark Guardian. I will require it for a period of no more than a single month."

Lady Dru, feeling no confidence whatsoever, nodded without hesitation, or the appearance of any doubt.

"Lord Verkial, I need you to sever your ties with Lord Kyhn, Engiyadu, and Daeriv," Lynneare said after a brief sigh.

The Warlock's posture told Verkial that Lynneare expected an immediate and violent reaction to that declaration. The old vampire was right to expect it.

"You deign demand of me the company I keep and the allies I make?" Verkial asked as his jaw muscles tightened, and his voice took on a dangerous edge, even in light of Lynneare's commanding presence.

"I do," Lynneare said simply. "Lord Kyhn seeks to betray you as we speak, throwing his support and loyalty to the mage, Daeriv. Under other circumstances, I would leave you to fight that battle on your own and learn the hard way, perhaps even in your death, of Kyhn's betrayal. However, I have need of your army and your services. Thus, you will cut ties with them. You will say that it is to ensure, when Ingshburn turns on you for seizing Wodock and western Tarborat, it will keep him from suspecting them or acting against them. You will gain all the confirmation you will require of Kyhn's disloyalty when you tell him and Daeriv of your decision to split from them. If they respond understandingly, but suggest you leave some back door open for them, then you will know they plan to betray you. If their response is one of puzzlement, anger, and suspicion, then I have counseled you wrong, and they truly intend to stand by your move to seize your own kingdom. Learn for yourself which of the two is the case. Once you realize the truth of what I say, I will need you to begin building underground fortifications in the mountains of Wodock, and subterranean reserves of water and shelter throughout the western Tarborat desert."

Silas opened his mouth to say something but wisely closed it again when Lynneare raised a single king finger.

"The mountains, per your agreement, belong to Chaos Lord Silas and thereby to Lady Dru," Lynneare continued. "They will gladly permit you to house troops and supplies there, for it may be the only place of refuge for them, depending on our fortunes. Furthermore, Queen Jandanero and Warlord Rogash will contribute to the construction of the stronghold in exchange for some of what the mines yield."

Lynneare turned his eyes, those eyes that were at once terrible and sincere, on Silas. Silas responded with another dutiful nod of his head.

"Why?" Verkial asked defiantly.

"Because dark times come," Lynneare said mildly and unperturbed at Verkial's impudent tone. "Dark times, dangerous times are ahead of us all. We will make strange allies and un-suspected enemies. We will need a strong fortress, a network of underground routes, and enough stores to feed armies for at least seven years. You have your father's mind for tactics and military organization, and that is why I want you in charge of building the defenses and securing a mountain stronghold."

Verkial was clearly stung by Lynneare's words and his mention of Verkial's father, but it was a reaction Silas and Dru did not understand. For, how could they understand Verkial's abject hatred for a man that had so abandoned him? Abandoned him to the whims of the evils of this dark world?

"How will you get the Drakestone?" Silas asked. "How can you? You are, if you will forgive my saying so, not exactly qualified to stroll past holy runes."

Lynneare, Warlock of the Marshes, the Original Betrayer, and OathBreaker, allowed the ambient light to penetrate the air about him to more clearly reveal his shaved head, pale skin, strong bones, and charming smile. The red glow of his eyes fell away and was replaced by a softer, almost human, set of light blue-gray irises.

"I have my ways, o' Lord of Chaos," Lynneare whispered, and then disappeared.

Lynneare's sudden disappearance surprised and slightly shook Dru and Silas; however, Verkial did not miss a moment before asking, "So, what is a Dark Guardian?"

Hours and leagues later, sitting by a fire under the over-hang of a cliff, two of the four ate wild pheasant taken by Hall-grim with a bow. The other two shared the still bloody remains of a huntsman they'd encountered in the forests east of Stam-don and north of Nolcavanor.

Dru teleported them four different times in three differ-ent directions before they arrived in this remote part of the forest, hoping to disguise any magical trail that might be sniffed out by the sorcerers of the Blue Tower. Once arriving, they walked for several hours through the forest so, if they were followed, they would have a chance of hearing any from the Tower coming up on them.

"I'm not convinced," Verkial said, tearing meat from the pheasant still impaled and roasting on the spit. "We should be cautious in our dealings with... with him."

"Lord Verkial, please don't get me wrong, but there is a reason you hesitate to say his name aloud," Silas said. "Furthermore, he offered you a perfectly reasonable and sound means of learning the true intentions of your cohorts in Lawrec."

"I don't get it," Hallgrim interjected.

"He means we can read their plans in their response to a tactical move on my part," Verkial began to explain but stopped when Hallgrim started shaking his head.

"I mean, well, what's a Dark Guardian?"

"Fantastic creations!" burst from Silas's mouth.

He was ever eager to explain, to teach, and the trait was beginning to bore Dru and Verkial as signaled by their eye rolls. Yet, Hallgrim, who seemed ever interested in new ideas or tales, found him quite amusing.

"You see, an alchemist must construct a suit of armor," Silas continued, very excited to once again have the opportunity to explain the combination of what he had read and what he believed. "The better the material, the greater the Guardian. So, once an alchemist has made the armor, with the help of a skilled blacksmith, of course, a sorcerer imbues it with animation. He basically gives it energy and alters its inert state. Now, you could stop there and have your basic construct. However, if you then find a cleric with powerful prayers, you can summon a champion, or fallen champion as the case may be, to inhabit the suit. The cleric and the sorcerer have to work together to bind the champion to the armor. It is a costly and time-consuming endeavor. Then, if successful, you have a creature that even dragons have been known to fear."

"They're not real," Verkial broke in. "If they were, Ingshburn would have scores of them. It's just a fanciful tale."

"Perhaps he has no need for them," Dru put in. "Perhaps

Ingshburn is content letting the lands around him kill as many men and women from Lethanor as his armies do. Perhaps he waits for the crown and the church to once again draw blood against each other, allowing him a window of opportunity."

Verkial and Silas both opened their mouths only to close them again and recede into deep thought. After several moments, Silas took in a deep breath in preparation to launch another barrage of information. Verkial and Dru both sighed.

"Perhaps Ingshburn spends his resources more wisely than that," Silas began, to himself as much to anyone listening. "The materials cost alone would be astounding, and he could field a thousand soldiers for a thousand days for the cost of one Guardian. In terms of line breakers, great warriors such as yourselves reserved for difficult missions, he has, or had, you two, Lord Kyhn, Engiyadu, and the elf warrior mage, Gallis Argenti. I've no doubt there are others I'm not even aware of."

"There are others," Verkial said as he tossed the bones from his meal of pheasant into the fire. "Gallis Argenti isn't among us... them, though. He's never been a part of Tarborat. He's just a vicious criminal. The crown uses his name and ties it to Tarborat to keep the taxes flowing in, I've no doubt, but he has never been part of Ingshburn's plans."

"Interesting," Silas replied, tapping his king finger on the point of his chin.

"Not really," Verkial said, tearing another piece of meat from the spit.

"My Lady, I should be departing for Moras in the morning, with your permission and help, of course," Silas said, changing the subject. "Unless you'd prefer me at your side when you speak with the drow queen?"

"That won't be necessary," Dru responded as she mentally turned over the prospect of negotiating with the drow. "You should take some time and think over how you will approach Lady Evalynne. Our contact with her thus far has been largely to her benefit, and you had the advantage of significant surprise before. You will not enjoy such an upper hand again.

Not with her and not with her mage."

"Yes, my Lady," Silas said with a bow.

"So, you do plan to tell Daeriv and Kyhn that you are splitting from them?" Dru asked, watching Verkial's facial features closely.

"I do," Verkial said simply.

"You don't think his recent defeat in Lawrec will cause suspicion?"

"I was clear when I told him putting all his efforts into such an army of undead was unwise," Verkial said.

"I've heard tales about the knight responsible for Daeriv's defeat," Dru said, feigning an innocent tone. "You know him, I think."

"Who?" Hallgrim asked, missing all the nuance of the conversation.

"No one," Verkial spat, the blood rising to his face in an instant. "That is a subject you'll not speak of in my presence again, or I'll take your head, and the head of your Chaos Lord here."

Verkial's words were carefully measured, and his tone was deadly and even. The rage burning behind his eyes was plain to each of them. Dru was satisfied that she had identified a weak point in Verkial's emotional armor and let the point drop.

"See to your business and send me the workers, dwarves, and ogres, you promised," Verkial continued, unapologetically changing the subject. "No slaves. If one creature arrives in Wodock in chains, I'll kill the lot of you."

"You speak very confidently," Silas said, allowing the edge of his mouth to quirk in the hint of a smile.

"Because I am."

"Thank you for coming," Lynneare said as he extended a hand, one cloaked in illusion, to wave for a waitress. "I've made extensive use of your services of late. I understand how taxing that must be."

"Of course," Ashcliff said, taking a seat opposite Lynneare.

They sat in a small tavern called the Whaler's Rest in the southwestern quarter of Modins on the west coast of Lethanor. The sun had been down for over three hours now, but the city still bustled with not only those seeking entertainment, but those conducting business as well. The business wasn't cotton, or wheat trade, nor was it the trade of silks, furs, armor, or weapons. It was the most lucrative, and most dangerous, trade in Modins. The trade of information.

The girl, a young blonde creature with an accent Ashcliff recognized, brushed past their table. She dropped two mugs of ale, ale they had not ordered, along the way, and said something about if they wanted wine they were in the wrong tavern.

Ashcliff smiled to himself. She did an excellent job of acting disinterested. She would certainly bear watching. Ashcliff had made it his business to monitor the affairs, all the affairs, of Sir Roland of Lawrec. This young lady, Marnie was her name, was running the weapons shop Sir Roland had established in Modins, and was investing his coin in many other ventures as well. From everything he'd seen, Ashcliff was quite impressed with the young girl. Ashcliff did find it a bit amusing that he thought of her as a 'young girl' given that he was no more than three years her senior.

Of course, she didn't have a hope of recognizing Ashcliff, not that they'd seen each other much anyway, but this evening he appeared thirty years older, forty pounds heavier, and wore the furs of a Slandik sailor.

Ashcliff wasn't the only one disguised this evening. Lynneare, the Warlock of the Marshes himself, wore the outward appearance of a noble from Moras. His skin appeared a normal tone, he had reduced his height to no more than six feet and had cast an illusion of long and luxuriant black hair that hung in loose curls down past his shoulders.

"Shall we go see the furs tonight then?" Ashcliff asked in a thick Slandik accent after he quaffed his mug of ale.

Lynneare pushed his mug, still full, toward the center of

the table, and smiled and nodded. Ashcliff thought it a good idea that Lynneare's disguise be one of a noble. For Lynneare seemed to have an air about him, an aura of gentile upraising, and an aristocratic behavior that Ashcliff thought would be hard for the ancient vampire to hide.

Ashcliff, in keeping with the role he played this evening, reached across the table, took Lynneare's mug, and drained it as well before stepping away from the table. He tossed a bronze coin over his shoulder that bounced, rolled, and finally settled on the tabletop. His casual behavior in the presence of one such as Lynneare set his nerves on edge, but he hoped the powerful vampire would not take offense.

Ashcliff led the way to a Slandik vessel he had arranged to use for the night. He'd purchased the entire cargo, bought the sailors aboard several rounds of drinks, and hired a few mercenaries he knew well to stand guard.

Ashcliff strode along the gangplank and noticed Lynneare hesitate briefly at the dock. Ashcliff turned a concerned look to Lynneare, who responded with a casual wave of his hand.

"There was a freshwater current flowing through just now," Lynneare said, smiling. "It has passed."

They proceeded below deck among the bales of furs, barrels of salted fish, and casks of whale and bear oil. Once in private, Ashcliff bowed low, and Lynneare dropped his magical illusions.

"You have paid very well in the past, and thus, I am ever at your service, sire," Ashcliff said.

"I offer you coin," Lynneare said as he studied Ashcliff's expressions carefully. "However, I offer you something more than that, as well."

Lynneare could easily read the young Shadow Blade's mind, if he chose to. However, he also wanted to gauge the skill of this fledgling assassin as well. He had proven himself valuable to Lynneare in the past, but what Lynneare had in mind for him now would require remarkable precision and excellence without flaw.

Ashcliff maintained a passive expression. He knew that many who sought the services of the Shadow Blades hoped to barter with them after a fashion, knowing they couldn't afford the high fees demanded by the assassins' guild. However, Lynneare, the First Cursed, the Original Betrayer, the Warlock of the Marshes, was not just anyone. If he offered something of value, it would indeed be intriguing.

"Your master will be approached about a contract, if his services haven't already been engaged," Lynneare continued in his rich, smooth voice. "It will put him in a position to work contrary to my interests. Will that be a problem for you?"

Ashcliff had great respect for Lynneare, for he'd seen him accomplish amazing feats in addition to his well-established reputation. Yet, he'd seen nothing to indicate Lynneare had the ability to spy on One of the Twelve, on a Shadow Blade Master.

Ashcliff started to open his mouth but froze. He prayed he had not given anything away in face or posture. Lynneare could read his thoughts, of course, but Ashcliff would know if he were. The realization of what Lynneare must have done to divine his Master Ashdow's plans struck Ashcliff like a blast of freezing water to the genitals.

Ashcliff had been the one to retrieve the Hourglass of Time from the ruins of Nolcavanor in Lynneare's service in the first place. He had been the one to return the mighty artifact to the vampire; however, he had no idea Lynneare would have found a way of using it, and so quickly.

Roland, the boy who had actually touched the Hourglass, had aged decades in seconds, and he was, as far as Ashcliff could tell, pure of heart and purpose. The event had given Roland some sort of precognition, some ability to glimpse near future events, but nothing the likes of what Lynneare must have done to spy on a Master Shadow Blade.

For a moment, a brief moment, Ashcliff wondered if he might be able to learn how to manipulate the potent tool of the gods. He dismissed that thought the moment it occurred to him. He had survived thus far by being very pragmatic. He intended to continue his survival for as long as possible.

"Are you asking me to act directly against him?" Ashcliff asked although he thought he knew the answer.

"No," Lynneare said as he began to stroll about the cargo and absently examine the facets of the Slandik vessel. "Nothing like that. It is your custom, I believe, that you cannot act directly against a master until such time as you seek to unseat him."

"That's not exactly correct, but close enough, yes," Ashcliff replied. "And, to answer your question, it is not a problem for me unless you find that you do need me to act against my master."

"Excellent," Lynneare said with a smile as he produced a black leather pack from seemingly thin air. "You will need these. We will be burglarizing the Blue Tower."

"The Blue Tower?" Ashcliff asked, trying to keep his voice steady. "The same Blue Tower south across the channel from Broken Time? The same Blue Tower occupied by the greatest, and most dangerous, wizards and sorcerers of the last thousand years?"

"Yes, that one."

"We?"

"Yes. My daughter will be joining us. I believe you've met."

Ashcliff did not hide the curl of his lip into a sneer as Dactlynese entered the hull.

CHAPTER II
Strange Bedfellows

"You failed to mention your friend, the inquisitor, was so tenacious," Jonas said as he rummaged through his pack for the last of their jerky.

"He's a Silver Helm and a King's Inquisitor," Dunewell responded. "What did you expect?"

Jonas rode their single mount, a horse stolen from a farmhouse six days prior, while Dunewell walked along next to him on the trail. Technically the horse had been purchased, for Jonas had left a few gold coins in place of its feed sack in the barn, but Dunewell was quick to point out that, in absence of consent, the removal of property was indeed theft.

Split Town was several months behind them now, and Ranoct had quite effectively, and literally, loosed the hounds upon their trail. They were a few hundred leagues north of Ostbier, home to the palace of King Eirsett, and moving northeast to skirt the wildlands. The night before they spent in a campsite last used a few years prior when three boys chased spies toward the ruins of Nolcavanor.

"Yes, yes," Jonas said, not looking up from the pack. "Ranoct Siege-breaker, Arrow-eater, Dragon-slayer. I get it, but I had hoped, being that you two were friends, he might not pursue with such vigor."

"Have you truly been at your skulking and skullduggery so long that you have forgotten what it means to uphold an oath?" Dunewell asked, as the irritation that had been mounting in him made its way to his tongue. "Have you forgotten what it is to be a Silver Helm?"

Jonas jerked his head around to Dunewell but caught his bitter words in his mouth before they escaped it. He remembered his first years on the road in pursuit of Slythorne and his assassins. He remembered those lonely days of doubting the nature of his soul and his disgust at his own actions and thoughts. He remembered the drunkenness that almost consumed him, and the severe bouts of rage. He remembered feeling lost, feeling alone, and feeling angry that his life as a soldier and a knight had been stolen from him. That had been over eighty years ago, and here he was, still on this course to avenge her death.

How long had it been since he'd really spent any time thinking of her, of his Giselle? Of course, Jonas thought about her daily, but only to keep the fire of rage alive in his heart. He rarely thought about all the wonderful things that made Giselle who she was, likely because he had no one to talk to about her. *Who could understand?*

Velryk, of course, would understand, for he'd lost two wives, but Jonas had burned that bridge long ago.

"Perhaps..." Jonas began but then paused.

The pause was brief, but Dunewell, a trained interrogator, noted it.

"Perhaps I'm just lost in the woods," Jonas said as his hand folded the top of the pack closed and then came to rest upon the dagger at his waist. "Perhaps, because my heart no longer points true north, I have come to find myself deep in the shadows of dying trees."

"Very poetic, Lord Jonas," a baritone voice said from somewhere a few yards to the south of them. "Inquisitor Dunewell, you'll have no need of that hammer you so cleverly drew and now conceal under your cloak. I mean neither of you any harm."

Dunewell took a few steps to the side of the game trail they'd been following. Jonas turned in the saddle so that his body hid his dagger and the hand that hovered near it, from the voice in the shadows. Both watched the shadows for several heartbeats, but neither saw more than the shadow of a tall man wearing a cloak that blended well with the dark recesses of the thick wood and underbrush. They both noted the dark figure hold his hands out far to the side which revealed the shape of two sword hilts at his waist. Dunewell and Jonas both checked the other trees nearby, and a rocky outcropping almost one hundred yards away, for others that might be preparing to ambush them.

Jonas had not taken the time to reforge his longsword, his WarriorBlade, and the pieces of it had been left behind in Bolthor. Forging a new one would take time, materials, and there were spells he had to prepare and cast. He had planned on having the materials brought aboard ship and taking his time during their sea voyage to make a new weapon that would respond to his particular set of spells and enchantments. Unfortunately, thanks to Ranoct's pursuit, that was not to be. Now Jonas desperately wished he'd taken the time or risked going into a city to forge a new blade. He did not take great comfort in the short sword and lone dagger that he now carried.

"There are no others," the voice from the shadows said. "I will step into the open, but I think we should converse for a moment first."

"Why is that?" Dunewell asked, genuinely curious.

Dunewell thought the dark figure could be stalling and waiting for friends to get into position, but he was confident, in this dense forest, they would hear them coming. Furthermore, he was sure they could escape them, however many there were, in the underbrush and wild country around them.

It's beginning to happen to me, Dunewell thought. *I'm starting to think like HIM. I'm thinking about escape and evade rather than confront and capture!*

That is the path we are on now, Whitburn thought/said in reply. *Nothing remains the same. All things change. Do not be afraid of the growth that comes with it.*

"You may find my appearance upsetting," the shadow said. "Just the same, I hope to assure you that you may trust me."

"Then you waste your breath and our time," Jonas said evenly. "Step forward, speak your piece, and let us get on with this whole matter."

Several slow moments passed as the shadows deepened with the waning of daylight. A breeze stirred the dead leaves of the ground, and the sound of leather creaking resonated through the air as Jonas's stolen horse shifted its weight from one leg to the other.

The dark figure within the shadows moved slowly, deliberately, from under cover of the trees; his hands still held wide.

"I come to ask you to help me in Nolcavanor," he said as he continued to move forward. "In return, I will help you find and destroy Slythorne."

Jonas had been bothered that this chap had managed to get as close to them as he had without him knowing. Jonas had been even more perturbed when this stranger, whoever he was, called Jonas by name. As far as Jonas knew, there were only three other people in the world that knew he hunted Slythorne. Slythorne, the assassin Slythorne had used, and Dunewell. As Jonas was coming to grips with the disturbing fact that the man in the shadows also knew about that, the man stepped forward.

When Jonas saw that he was no man at all, but a drow, he became even more concerned.

"I am Maloch, no longer of the Black Lance," Maloch said with a slight bow.

As Maloch bent forward, his long white hair spilled out of the hood he wore. He raised one hand slowly and pushed back his cowl to reveal his ebony skin and shining white eyes. Dunewell twisted his war hammer in his hands and scanned their surroundings once again. He'd faced drow in Tarborat and knew they were fond of their tricks, deceptions, and ambushes.

Why did I not sense him? Dunewell thought/said.

He isn't evil, Whitburn replied. *Perhaps he was once, but he no longer bears the aura. I'd like to kill him too, but I think we should hear him out. He has the scent of Father Time's power and will.*

"I bet you have an interesting story to tell," Dunewell

said, hoping his tone would help to calm Jonas.

Dunewell did not miss the fact that Maloch's shrou-shelds bore the symbol of the Hourglass on their hilts in purest Roarke's Ore. It could be part of the deception, but if that were the case, it was a very expensive prop.

"I do," Maloch said, nodding. "I also have a few fresh rabbits, potatoes, and carrots if you would prefer a fresh stew to more... trail food."

The drow said the words 'trail food' with obvious disdain for the dried fruit and scraps of jerky remaining in their pack.

"I don't think I'll be eating anything a drow brings me or prepares for me," Jonas said. "I know of the Black Lance, and I know your name. You've been on the front in Tarborat. I understand you once crossed swords with Ingshburn's captain, Verkial, and with Lord Bessett's general, Lord Velryk."

"That is true," Maloch said. "I have crossed swords with many, including your nephew, the young Sir Roland. I also attended his wedding as a guest this past summer."

Jonas and Dunewell both scanned Maloch for signs of deception, and both were unnerved when they noted none. Both thought it more likely meant the drow had lied to them, and they were unable to detect it rather than him actually telling the truth.

"I suppose that means Roland is no more honorable than his older brother," Jonas said. "For who else would have a drow attend a goat skinning as a friend, much less his own wedding."

Maloch sighed. He had known this would be difficult. In fact, he'd argued with Lynneare about it for days. Yet, no one had drawn blood thus far, and that was much better than he'd expected.

Dunewell, already guessing some relation, now had the proof his inquisitor's mind sought. Jonas and Velryk were brothers. Jonas was Verkial's uncle and uncle to this Roland, whoever he was.

"In truth it was honor, his honor, that has brought us to the unusual set of circumstances and has given us a chance to avoid almost certain doom," Maloch said. "I will not tell what that doom is, nor will I entertain any questions about it save to say this, it could be the end of all goodly kingdoms. I am here to offer my help and ask for yours."

Dunewell and Jonas exchanged a curious look and turned back to the drow paladin. After a few moments, Maloch came to realize the odd look was the only response he was going to get thus far, so he continued.

"I once ruled the Black Lance of Nolcavanor. I faced Sir Roland, before he was knighted of course, in the ruins of that long-dead city a short time back," Maloch said, looking to the mountain range to their west. "He challenged me to a duel under the terms that I allow him and his friends to leave if he should win and offered himself as a slave to me if he should lose. Some of his maneuvers were, shall we say, creative and, in the end, he bested me. I fully expected him to take my life. He did not. He offered me mercy, and I accepted. I spent long hours thinking about that exchange afterward. It showed me... it made me realize how dark my heart had truly become. I decided to make a change in my life. That decision has brought me here, to you."

Dunewell and Jonas remained unmoved and offered no signs of response other than to listen and wait. Thus, Maloch continued.

"You seek to destroy Slythorne and pursue him to Moras even now. You have likely assumed he would have hired or enthralled help. I tell you that he has, specifically a Master Shadow Blade, among others. You will need help in Moras, and that is something I offer. I ask for your help in striking a blow against the drow that remain in Nolcavanor in exchange for my help with Slythorne."

"That's a bit mercenary for a paladin, isn't it?" Jonas asked.

"A paladin?" Maloch replied simply.

"I know who, or rather what you are Lord Maloch," Jonas said. "You are a dark Paladin of the UnMaker and his servant of blackest evil. 'His is the hand that wounds,' and you are that hand."

"I was," Maloch said, surprising Jonas at the mild nature of his tone. "I am guilty of many sins. Sins that go beyond a person's capacity to forgive. Sins that should doom my soul. For reasons I do not understand, I have been given an opportunity. I have been given a chance, a slim chance, at redemption, but that is not why I am here. I am here because I owe a debt. One that I must find a way to repay."

"You would sacrifice your life for this redemption; to satisfy this debt?" Jonas asked.

Maloch responded by pulling his heavy tunic aside and unbuckling his mercshyeld breastplate. Maloch lowered the breastplate to the ground, kneeled, and pulled his shirt collar open to expose his bare dark flesh.

Dunewell had a moment to think Maloch was likely bluffing when Jonas called that bluff. Dunewell may have been the only one in the small glade surprised when Jonas, with a quick twist and jerk, hurled a dagger for Maloch's chest. Maloch did not flinch, did not cast a spell, and did not turn away. The dagger struck with deadly accuracy, bringing blood forth from Maloch's lips and the wound in his breast.

Jonas and Dunewell were both surprised to see the look of serenity that bloomed on Maloch's face and the smile of contentment that spread across his mouth. As that look spread across his face, Maloch's body collapsed back to the tangles of dead grass and brown leaves surrounding them.

Dunewell rushed to Maloch's side, jerked the dagger free, and placed his hand over his wound that was now gushing with drow blood. Dunewell concentrated for several heartbeats and, as he did, a light blue glow emitted from his hand and Maloch's wound. As the moments slid slowly past, Maloch's wound closed in on itself, and his eyes fluttered and reopened. Dunewell held him as he began to cough and then sat up. Dunewell helped the drow paladin to his feet.

"That was a risk," Dunewell said, looking up to Jonas,

who still sat his horse unmoving. "It has been some time since I last drank from a river or stream. There's no way you could have known I would have enough power to heal him."

"Actually, I forgot you could do that," Jonas said flatly.

Dunewell clenched his teeth, then opened his mouth to respond but was interrupted by the sounds of baying dogs in the distance. Ranoct was much closer than they thought.

"It would seem turning to the west, toward Nolcavanor is your only sound option," Maloch said as he wiped blood from his lips. "If you go north, you only move out onto the open plain where they will surely run you down. If you turn east, the outcome would be the same. They come from the south."

Jonas cut his eyes at Maloch.

"West it is," Dunewell said, not wishing to face Ranoct or any of his men.

Dunewell had taken an oath, three actually, to never take an innocent life. Ranoct and his men were innocent and only sought to carry out their sworn duty. That meant his only options were to escape and evade or be taken to Moras or Ostbier in chains for execution. Dunewell cared for neither of those options.

Dunewell picked up Maloch's breastplate and handed it to him. Maloch offered him a brief smile and began strapping it in place. As Jonas and Dunewell started westward, they both paused and turned back around at the sound of Maloch casting a spell.

Maloch produced a Roarke's Ore Hourglass symbol from his gauntlet, kissed it, and began to pray. As he did so, a shimmer in the air, much like the heat rising over the desert stretches of western Tarborat, began to form to their south. In moments, that shimmer ran beyond their vision in a semi-circle covering the north and east as well.

Jonas had seen that sort of enchanted prayer only once before in all his exotic and lengthy travels. In laymen's terms, it was a time trap. Only those in tune with the will of Father Time were reputed to be able to cast it. Jonas still held to his suspicions of this drow but had to admit the power of that spell, if only to himself.

"Will that hurt them?" Dunewell asked.

"No," Maloch said with a bit of a wounded look on his face. "I would not hurt them, for they only seek to honor their oaths, oaths given to serve justice. The prayer will only delay them. When they leave the area, no time will have passed as far as they will know or be able to tell, however, four days will have come and gone."

"So, this gives us a four day lead on them?" Dunewell asked.

"Yes."

"I have no problem killing drow," Jonas said as he eyed his stew and then watched and waited for Maloch to eat a spoonful from his own bowl.

Jonas sat with his back against a large tree, and his packs stacked up high to his right. To the casual eye, it appeared an arrangement so that he could recline and have a windbreak. Dunewell and Maloch were not casual observers and knew Jonas had arranged things just so to provide some basic cover should they be ambushed in their encampment, perhaps by drow conspirators. The smell of the stew caused Jonas's undisciplined stomach to growl loudly, for it had been weeks since either he or Dunewell had eaten a hot meal or enjoyed the warmth of a campfire. Tonight, they had the opportunity to savor both.

"Clearly," Dunewell interrupted, still perturbed at Jonas for trying to kill Maloch earlier.

Dunewell squatted next to the fire. He made sure to remain in a position so that he could intervene between Jonas and Maloch if the situation called for it. He gulped his stew with the mechanical habit of a career soldier.

"As I was saying," Jonas continued, unconcerned with Dunewell's disdain. "I have no problem with that, but what I don't understand is why we're only weakening them and not killing them all."

"It is part of a larger plan," Maloch said after swallowing

his bite of rabbit stew. "If we kill them all, then others will become suspicious and may change the course of events. But we cannot leave them at full strength either."

"Course of events?" Dunewell asked.

"Father Time," Jonas put in. "Priests and paladins of his are always worried about the 'course of events.'"

"He does grant some glimpses of possible futures to a chosen few," Maloch said as he ladled another bite of stew from his bowl. "You know this to be true."

"And this assistance you offer regarding Slythorne?" Jonas asked, still clearly suspicious.

"I was there when he committed his act of betrayal," Maloch said as his white eyes drifted up toward the stars and looked back over thousands of years. "I knew him then, and I know his heart now. I understand his curse, for I was in the room when Father Time smote him. I was there when the Master Templar, Truthorne, died, and the creature, Slythorne, was created. You have hunted him for a few decades. I have known him for millennia. I know the name of the assassin he hired, and I know his tactics. I know why you hunt them and can tell you now the name of the one that killed your Giselle."

Dunewell started at the revelation, but Jonas did not even bat an eye.

"What makes you think I would believe anything you had to say?" Jonas asked coolly.

"I have earned your mistrust; your abuse and derision even," Maloch said. "Perhaps in time I will be blessed with the opportunity to show you."

"I suppose we'll see," Jonas said as he took a small bite of his stew.

"You fought Velryk and survived?" Dunewell asked, hoping to both change the direction of this conversation and to gain more information. Information that Jonas would likely not part with easily. "Then attended the wedding of his son?"

"I faced Lord Velryk in battle, yes," Maloch said, nodding and thinking back to his days in Tarborat. "I also fought General

Verkial. They were both strong, and skilled. However, I wielded the power of the UnMaker at the time and was a formidable foe, not without my tricks."

"Your friendship with his son, Sir Roland, that is why you were invited to his wedding, even in Lord Velryk's presence?" Dunewell asked, pleased with himself.

Dunewell noted Jonas's twist, as if he were sitting on a sharp pebble or a stick gouged at his back. Every time the words 'Lord Velryk' were uttered, it drove a bur under Jonas's saddle. Dunewell thought Jonas could do with a bit of discomfort. Dunewell's observations of Jonas were interrupted by Maloch's pause and sigh. Dunewell had inadvertently hit upon something. *But what?*

"I was invited by another," Maloch said. "Neither Sir Roland nor Lord Velryk knew I would be attending. When I arrived in the company of another guest, I approached Sir Roland and told him I sought redemption. I offered him my friendship, and he accepted. It is interesting that you, both of you, wear a totem of the white rose. Sir Roland was knighted for rescuing Shrou-sheld Blancet and gifting it to Prince Ralston. He also gifted him the armor of Lord Mandergane. I'm sure you both know the significance of Lord Mandergane's colors, the crest of House Ozur, and the white rose. I'm surprised neither of you has a feather of a red raven to accompany such a totem."

"What *guest*?" Jonas and Dunewell asked in unison.

Maloch had attempted to move past this part of the conversation and onto something he hoped Jonas and Dunewell might find intriguing. Maloch knew a good deal about both of them but did not appreciate their skills as trained interrogators.

"Let us put the answer to that question aside for another time," Maloch said with a plea in his eyes. "Please."

Dunewell looked to Jonas, who only shrugged. It seemed that Dunewell was the only one genuinely interested in the answer to that question, for Jonas had written off anything Maloch had to say as just another lie from a drow.

"There is a forge in the Black Lance caverns of Nolca-vanor," Maloch said, moving once again to another subject. "I assume you would wish some time to forge a new Warrior-Blade?"

"You're a Lanceilier?" Dunewell asked of Jonas.

Dunewell was well aware of the special rank of Silver Helms. They were very rare, but he had seen one once in Tarb-orat. They were Silver Helms chosen for special training in the magics of mentalism, imbuing them with spells and enchant-ments useful to a professional soldier and commander.

Among those special skills and spells was the ability to forge a Shyeld-Hayn. A special weapon that would only heed the call of its maker, and that was inscribed with potent magical runes. The lanceilier had to be tied to the forging of the blade, in some way binding his blood or his flesh to the weapon. *Had the silver longsword broken by Jonas in the fight against the skinshifter been a shyeld-hayn? Could that have been why he was so deeply wounded?*

"What I am is tired of this drow running his mouth about matters that are not his business out in the open," Jonas said with a noticeable edge to his voice.

Perhaps nettling him with the Lord Velryk talk wasn't such a good idea, after all, Dunewell thought.

Perhaps not, Whitburn replied.

"We are unwarded and unprotected," Jonas continued. "Sorcerers or assassins could be scrying our campsite this very moment, listening in on every word you utter, and you carry on as though we were as safe as in mother's womb."

"You wear your totems of the white rose, and Daeriv wouldn't know to search for us, any of us anyway," Maloch said, hoping to set Jonas's mind at ease.

"So, it's Daeriv, that wizard in Lawrec; you're worried about?" Jonas said, satisfied that his trap had worked so well.

Dunewell, now seeing precisely what Jonas had done, had to appreciate the guile of the man.

"Yes," Maloch said with a resigned sigh. "Yes, and no. He

is on a path, a dangerous path, that will threaten many."

"That's the necromancer Sir Brutis was traveling to Lawrec to put down," Dunewell put in. "He was going to advise Prince Ralston and aid General Maddit."

"Brutis is a good man," Jonas said, a little more at ease now that he had more information with which to work. "Prince Ralston is as well, for all that's worth."

"Sir Roland, your nephew, also stands with them," Maloch said. "Shall I get back to the forge?"

"Please," Jonas said. "It would seem I will be needing a new shyeld-hayn sooner than I had thought."

Two days of travel brought them to a clearing where several rotten giant heads were mounted on pikes in a circle around an old campfire. Jonas guessed the camp, and the heads, to be at least a year old, and perhaps two or even three.

Three days after that, they arrived at the source of the mighty Whynne River. The sound of the waterfall had been in their ears since the day before their arrival. Dunewell remembered the river well, for it had saved him and almost killed him.

"There's a stair that begins behind that grove of trees," Maloch said, pointing across the great waterfall and wild river to its opposite bank. "Any thoughts on how we should get across?"

Maloch had to yell, for the roar of the waterfall was so loud regular conversation was impossible. The sound of crashing water even penetrated their bones, causing their frames to vibrate with the force of it.

Dunewell yelled for Maloch to repeat himself. He had followed Maloch's finger to the grove across the river but had heard none of what he'd said about it. Maloch began again but stopped at Jonas's upraised hand.

Jonas took a moment to focus his thoughts and called forth a spell he'd not used in decades. In moments the thoughts of the three were linked together in an ebb and flow of telepathic communication.

Jonas had been considering this possibility since agreeing to travel to Nolcavanor. The advantages offered by the telepathic link were apparent on the battlefield and could easily be seen by any observing the perfectly coordinated movements of small squads led by lanceiliers. However, given they would be facing drow in their own territory, the black dark of undermountain, Jonas decided the ability to communicate without having to speak or even whisper outweighed the drawbacks of allowing Maloch limited access to his thoughts. It also offered each of the three a bit more protection against magics that would seek to read their minds or influence their actions.

Ah, that is much better, Maloch thought.

Yes, much, came from Dunewell.

This will prove to be quite interesting, Whitburn interjected, shocking both Maloch and Jonas.

You hear the voice of that... of your champion? Jonas asked.

Of course, Dunewell replied. *How did you think it worked?*

I don't know that I had thought about how it would work, Jonas replied, unable to mask his regret at casting the spell. He also thought he recognized something about Whitburn, but nothing he could put his finger on. Furthermore, he certainly didn't want to think on it too long while his mind was connected to the other two... the other three actually.

I was saying there's a stair beyond that grove of trees on the other side of the river, Maloch thought. *It leads up to a cavern entrance behind the waterfall. It's over twenty years since anyone has been in that cavern or that part of the tunnel complex. There's a secret path that will lead us from there to my private forge. I don't know how much of the materials there would have been looted, but there should be something there worthy of a Shyeld-Hayn.*

Even if there's good steel there, it would take days, several days, for me to forge a proper Shyeld-Hayn, Jonas thought.

Maloch smiled.

Oh, that's a great idea, and truly amazing, Dunewell thought. *A spell that somehow halts time around us so, even if it's several days within the spell, only a few hours pass in the rest of the world.*

I didn't realize that was 'out loud,' Maloch replied. *This will take some getting used to.*

You two are getting too far ahead, Jonas began.

The stair is on the other side of the river, Whitburn finished for him.

How much rope do we have? Dunewell asked.

We only have about forty feet in our kit, Jonas replied.

I have almost eighty feet, Maloch thought.

Do something with the horse and then tie a harness for your-selves, Dunewell thought to them without taking his eyes from the sheer mountainside. *Secure anything we won't need here as well, so we are carrying only what we need.*

Jonas and Maloch moved as one, Jonas leading the horse into the forest in search of an area where he might be safely hobbled and Maloch checking large stones nearby for clefts that might hide their packs. Of course, they already knew what Dunewell was thinking.

Dunewell walked to the mighty river that roared out of its womb nearby. The great and powerful Whynne that had saved him, and nearly killed him. Dunewell laid flat on his stomach, plunged his head into the freezing waters, and drank deeply from the replenishing torrent. He could feel Whitburn swelling within him as his strength was renewed, and his muscles, physical and spiritual, surged with power.

Dunewell tied the end of Maloch's rope around his own shoulders and chest and began his ascent up the sheer rock face, driving his fingers into the stone when no ledge or other purchase could be found. Maloch watched Dunewell's climb in amazement. Maloch had known of the Lords of Order, and had known those of the Old Code reputed to be bound with champions, but he'd never witnessed the power of one before. Now he stood in awe.

Jonas, who'd witnessed Dunewell's feats firsthand, still stood next to Maloch and marveled at Dunewell's climb. Jonas knew, just knew, if he could only get Slythorne trapped in a room with him and Dunewell, he would have him. His revenge would then be complete.

As Dunewell passed seventy feet from the beginning of his climb, he looked back to see Maloch and Jonas secured in their harnesses and those were tied to the other end of the line. Dunewell searched for and found a ledge that would hold both Jonas and Maloch a little more than twelve feet to his right. Dunewell, in one great swing, hurled his weight up from his handholds to land on that ledge. Once in place, he began hauling his two companions up the side of the mountain hand over hand almost as fast as either would have been able to rappel down the same cliff.

In just a few heartbeats, Dunewell had pulled Jonas and Maloch up to the ledge where they both grabbed hold as soon as they were within reach. Just as Maloch and Jonas were getting their elbows onto the ledge, Dunewell leapt back toward the waterfall and traveled thirty feet with ease before catching an outcropping of stone. Dunewell swung back and forth on the small outcropping two times and then launched himself out of sight from his two companions underneath the blanketing mist of the waterfall.

Jonas and Maloch had heard, or rather saw, Dunewell's thoughts clearly. The river was wide, far too wide to cross, at the waterfall's terminus but narrowed dramatically the farther up one traveled. Here, only about one hundred feet off the ground, the distance across the waterfall was less than eighty feet. It just required that someone make the climb in the dark roaring world that existed between the falling water and the slick black stone of the mountain behind it.

There was a heartbeat of time when the sun disappeared from view, and Dunewell's whole universe became a thundering blackness of icy stone. Then Dunewell saw through Whitburn's eyes, and the shadow of his surroundings evaporated to reveal his environment in remarkable detail. The telepathic connection between the four was so strong that Maloch and Jonas saw it too.

Dunewell had no trouble hurling himself from one hand-hold to another as he rocketed across the mountain face. In only a few brief moments, he was across the waterfall and standing on the stair Maloch had described. Dunewell wrapped his end of the rope around his forearm twice and then took hold with both hands. Just as his grip tightened, Maloch and Jonas leapt for the waterfall.

The weight of the two warriors, combined with the force of the waterfall occasionally striking them, was considerable. No man, nor any group of three men, could have remained fast against that pull. Yet, Dunewell was more than man. He hauled on the line as Jonas and Maloch swung clear of the water and past the stair, halting the momentum of their pendulum swing and bringing them back to the hidden path.

Dunewell paused for a few moments then, not because he needed to catch his breath but because it looked to him as though Jonas and Maloch did. He gave them a slow count of ten and then began hauling them up the stair to the landing where he now stood. Then, without a word for none was needed among them, Dunewell started up the stair at a rapid pace while Maloch and Jonas worked their slow way up behind him.

As Dunewell reached the end of the length of rope between him and his two companions, he would stop on a landing and haul them up to catch up to him. Then he would continue his quick ascent. Dunewell continued this routine until they were all standing on the top landing where King Lucas of the House of Thorvol had lost the first of his men to Nolcavanor two decades prior. A place where a man once called Kelmut the Fierce had killed the two Slandik standing with him and disappeared into the dark places of the mountain.

CHAPTER III

Dark Deals

"Will we discuss Slythorne now?" Silas asked from deep within his heavy winter cloak and blankets.

Dru's only response was to turn her head only slightly, just enough to pin him with one slitted eye. She sat on a prominent outcropping of rock overlooking the river Olithyn and the huddled city of stone and liars known to the world as Moras. His dark silk gown flapped against her toned legs and hips, driven violently by a harsh winter's wind. The chill did not bother Lady Dru, however, and she let the wind have its way with her dress and lush black hair.

Her eyes scanned the mountainside and plains below them for any sign of Slythorne or his scouts or assassins. Of course, none that Slythorne would employ would be so unprofessional as to be spotted from such a vantage point, but she sat sentry just the same.

Silas, not immune to the ravages of the environment as his mistress was, was wrapped in his winter cloak and a few extra blankets. A fire would have been out of the question, even if they weren't watching their back trail for the infamous Slythorne. However, it was not the first discomfort Silas had weathered, nor would it be his last. He accepted the chill stoically and allowed himself to be glad he would be returning to Moras.

Dru had prepared a letter for him, or rather for Cambrose of House Wellborne, to stay at House Morosse. The letter also offered access to all the House and grounds had to offer during his stay. For Cambrose was in Moras to negotiate a trade deal with House Morosse and would need to travel freely from the manor to the mines. Furthermore, this trade deal would involve Lady Evalynne in so much as she would handle some of the shipping issues for the two Houses. The cover was solid enough to keep from arousing any suspicion from the watchmen or inquisitors. Not that they couldn't have been easily bought for the most part, but Silas had always felt bribery the tool of the unskilled.

"If we are not going to discuss him, then might I enumerate my concerns for your safety?" Silas continued when he saw that he would receive no verbal response from his Lady.

"We have discussed your concerns."

"If it please, my Lady, we have not. I have told you about them, yet you seem unmoved by them."

"Then perhaps you should stop trying to move me."

"My Lady, your wellbeing is tied directly to my own," Silas reminded.

"Your concern for my safety is born solely of your own need to protect your own neck?" Dru said with a scowl.

Silas averted his eyes, opened his mouth to say something, then thought better of it and closed his mouth again. Dru regretted the words the moment she spoke them. She knew, absolutely knew, that Silas loved her. She also knew that she loved him. Nothing romantic had passed between them, but they shared a love that only those cast out by all others could share. A love that recognized the only people they had in this world were each other. Yet, it was not in her nature to apologize, nor would it be in Silas's to expect one.

"I care for you, my Lady," Silas finally managed. "I care for you and wish to know you, to truly know you. I understand how hard that must be to believe, but I understand your inner loneliness. I foster my own variety of that loneliness. Forgive me if I go too far, if I offend."

"You do not offend," Dru whispered in a much softer tone, but she could not bring herself, couldn't allow herself, to turn and look at him. "Put your mind to the task before you.

You have a difficult negotiation to navigate. You are adept, but still a novice at a game that Lady Evalynne mastered before you were born. On the other front, you must convince Rogash of our plan. I know you two seem fond of each other, but there is still a fair chance that he may decide to eat you."

"I wouldn't say we were fond of each other, not exactly," Silas replied, working to keep his teeth from chattering as he spoke. "I think it is just that we understand each other on some level, which is a rare thing, for there are not many like us."

"I'm sure the priests and clerics are glad of that," Dru said, managing to interject a bit of humor into this dour conversation. "It has been long enough. If anyone had tracked us from the last point of teleport, we would have seen them by now. Get yourself to Rogash's clan, and I'll do whatever I must with the drow."

"Do you think you will be able to convince Queen Jandanero to *loan* her Dark Guardian?" Silas asked. "I suspect she will be quite angry that anyone even knows of its existence, much more so that they should want access to it."

"The Queen is not unreasonable," Dru said, still scanning their back trail. "I just have to find a way for the proposal to benefit her position."

Dru rose, made one more scan of the entire horizon, and began down the broken trail to the drow caverns. Silas stood up behind her and bundled his pack and blankets into one large mass that he tucked under his arm. Then, after she was several steps away, he turned to watch her leave. He stood for several long moments watching her, watching after her, before her voice reached into his mind.

You have much to do, Lady Dru's voice resonated in his head. *Be about it.*

Silas smiled and started down his own rocky and broken trail toward a different cavern. Not quite four leagues away was the entrance that led to the caves of clan Jett Hammer and the home of Rogash the Warlord. Rogash, commander of ogres and giants, wielder of Time's End, a mighty battle hammer, and hopeful progenitor of a race of half-dwarf and half-ogre peoples, was also a friend to a certain Lord of Chaos.

As he approached, Silas moved to the side of the rough pathway and turned within himself to access a power, a new power, that merited further experimentation. Silas's body, and all that he wore and held, slowly began to melt into shadow. That shadow flowed into the dark corners at the edge of the trail around him, adding only slightly to the shadows already there. His physical self was still present, yet virtually impossible to detect with the human eye.

Next, he focused his mind on his body temperature. Silas knew that elves and dwarves, along with a few other creatures that haunted the dark places of the world, were able to see someone's body heat as well. There were entire sects of drow that solely relied on infravision, abandoning *normal* sight altogether. He reached out with his nerves to sense the cold stone around him and drew that chill into his skin. It was a slow process, but he had no doubts that, after some time practicing, this maneuver would take place much quicker. After several long moments of concentration, he appeared no warmer than the rock on which he stood.

The final component of this attempted act of stealth was to focus on his movements, making each step deliberately slow, deliberately silent. Silas had developed his ability to teleport from one memorized location to another; still, he imagined a number of scenarios in which infiltration would be required of him. The Blue Tower came to mind.

Silas was no novice to the art of stealth, having practiced it for years in recording his observations of nature in the areas surrounding Moras. However, never before did he have access to a means of literally changing his form to something similar to shadow or completely masking his body heat. He was, however, very familiar with the patient approach, the slow pace, such a maneuver required.

He approached the outer guard, two ogres, and watched them for several minutes, observing their habits and patterns of motion. Just as he was beginning to move, Silas caught another sight that caused him to freeze in place.

There, on a ledge, just a few feet from the ogre guard, crouched a drow concealed in shadow with a heavy crossbow close at hand. He realized he had been a fool not to have scanned the area with his other ranges of perception before beginning this 'exercise.' Silas watched for several more heartbeats, but the drow did not move against the ogres, nor did he attempt to move deeper into the cavern beyond them.

After Silas was satisfied the drow was not going to move any time soon, he elected to continue into the cavern. He had not committed himself to either side of the Rogash/Jandanero equilibrium and hoped he wouldn't have to, not any time soon, at least. Thus, he decided his best course of action was to enter and try to subtly discern from Rogash how relations were with the drow coven.

Silas moved silently, and virtually invisible to just about everything that walked or crawled on or in Stratvs. He negotiated several occupied hallways, dining rooms, and caverns serving as barracks. He admired Rogash's cunning in arranging his clan in such seeming disorder. Giants and ogres were not exactly social creatures and, thus, were likely to cause trouble with one another if quarters were too... crowded. Rogash had organized his clan into several much smaller groups that seemed to operate independently from the others in their day to day activities but could be called to serve with others as need be.

He had also arranged a system, not precisely of rank, but rather a notoriety among the rabble. Those that made a name for themselves on the battlefield, carefully chosen and recognized only by Rogash, found their exploits, regardless of how mundane, chanted, and worshiped. They found themselves the recipients of larger food rations, better treatment, and associated with Rogash much more frequently. These same 'heroes of clan Jett Hammer' found themselves happily enforcing the word and will of Warlord Rogash.

Silas made his way through several more carved rooms and natural caverns before his winding path finally put him in front of the doors to Rogash's private chambers. As Silas approached the imposing doors of iron and wood, he wondered at the fact that Rogash did not bar much less lock the portal to his chambers. These thoughts led him to wonder how he might have navigated that problem had Rogash employed some locking mechanism. Silas decided the design, and defeat, of locking mechanisms was another field of study he must pursue.

Silas slipped inside the inner chamber and discovered Rogash, his back to the large doors, bent over his desk, with a piece of black chalk in his left hand while his right scratched his lush beard. Silas slid along the smooth stone wall, just at the edge of the torches' reach, until he was within a sword's thrust distance from the exposed neck of the mighty Warlord.

Smiling to himself, Silas eased his star iron dagger, the gift from Rogash, from his bracer and crept forward. Silas gently placed the tip of the dagger to the top of Rogash's spine, causing the warrior to halt all motion, including his breath.

"Perhaps you should consider establishing a personal guard," Silas quipped as he tapped Rogash's thick green skin with the tip of the deadly blade.

Just as he was finishing this statement, Silas felt gentle but steady pressure applied to the underside of his groin. Silas looked down to see the tip of a black blade, also star iron, protruding from between his legs. He noted that the edge of the blade was against the inside of his thigh and near his femoral artery.

"Perhaps he has," Hellmog said from behind Silas.

Silas sheathed his dagger and began to chuckle, which was quickly overshadowed by Rogash's full-bellied gale of laughter. Hellmog did not laugh, nor did he remove the short sword. Rogash rose, turned, and clapped Silas on the shoulder with one hand, waving Hellmog back with the other. The much smaller creature bowed dutifully, sheathing his own blade and stepped back in one fluid motion.

"He did spot the drow at the entrance," Hellmog said once Rogash and Silas's laughter began to die down. "That is commendable."

"So, you're aware there's a drow watching the entrance to your caverns?" Silas asked, clearly perplexed.

"You think Hellmog here would let them just rove around our caves without givin' 'em a good look-see first?" Rogash asked.

"Is trouble brewing between the Hammer clan and coven?"

"No, no, nothing like that," Rogash answered, patting the air with his meaty hand. "There's word that some drow from the old days is on the move, Maloch they called him. Seems the little dark queen doesn't much care for 'im and has cause to think he might be on the road to seek his revenge against her. Apparently, they had themselves a falling out a while back."

"He hasn't been known to travel with vampires, has he?" Silas asked, wondering if this information could be tied to the news they'd received about Slythorne.

"Vampires, no," Rogash said. "Why?"

Silas silently cursed himself. He would certainly need to sharpen his tongue and his wits if he were to treat with Lady Evalynne, for just in this relatively simple banter with Rogash, he'd let precious information slip. However, Rogash was not a mere warrior or common Warlord. He was much shrewder than he let on.

"Say, how did you find and follow me?" Silas asked, turning to Hellmog and hoping to deflect Rogash's line of thought.

Hellmog, changing his expression not a bit, simply pointed at his nose, or rather, at the smudge of flesh that served him as a nose.

"Ah, of course," Silas exclaimed. "I didn't mask my scent. How foolish of me!"

"Often overlooked," Rogash said, nodding thoughtfully. "Now, about this vampire."

Silas smiled his trademark smile, and Rogash returned

the grin.

"Hellmog, be about your business," Rogash said at length. "My friend and I have many matters to discuss."

Silas turned to watch Hellmog go and was surprised that the small creature had already managed, without any form of magic as far as Silas could tell, to disappear.

"He's quite slippery, that one," Silas said out of genuine appreciation.

"He's not the only one," Rogash said.

He turned his chair, a stump from a colossal tree carved into a solid seat to accommodate his enormous frame, to face Silas and sat down. Now, being at eye level with Silas after sitting down, Rogash began again.

"So, about this vampire," Rogash said as he began to twirl the thick king finger of his right hand in a 'go on' motion.

"Someone from my mistress's past," Silas began with some trepidation. "Reputably a dangerous foe. We have word that he may be coming to Moras."

Rogash looked every inch the unthinking brute the churches and lords believed him to be. His thick muscles, hard hands, and the massive weapons he preferred all spoke of a warlord that ruled through a system of despotism. However, Silas knew there was another Rogash beneath that camouflage. There was the Rogash that had repeatedly defeated Silas at Scepters and Swords, the age-old strategy game used by kings for millennia to gauge their generals and advisors. There was the Rogash that had designed, with no education whatsoever, a schedule to manipulate the hereditary structures of two races to combine them into one. There was the Rogash that had devised a means of smithing a material alien to Stratvs, the so-called 'star iron,' into weapons and pieces of armor of great might.

"What are you not telling me?"

Silas took a moment to reflect that he'd actually had an easier time in his conversations with Dunewell, the King's Inquisitor, about Silas murdering their mother than this conversation with Rogash.

"There are a number of factors in this situation that I don't..."

"What, are, you, not, telling, me?" Rogash repeated the question, emphasizing each word.

"Understand that, if what I tell you in any way harms my mistress, I will kill you."

Rogash took a moment to look Silas over. He noted no quickening of the pulse, no dilation of the pupils, no dry gulping signaled by a bobbing of the knot in his throat; in short, no signs of fear and nothing to indicate a lack of confidence.

"You have my word that nothing you tell me now, or ever, will cause your mistress harm in any way."

"Very well," Silas said, completely comfortable with the concept of taking the half-ogre warlord at his word. "We parleyed with Lynneare, the Warlock of the Marshes. He warns against the arrival of some vampire of the name Slythorne."

Rogash's green skin concealed much of the effect of the blood draining from his face. Yet, Silas was still able to note a slight ashen tone present in those deep green hues.

"The Warlock of the Marshes? The OathBreaker?"

"One and the same."

"Who... where... what did you discuss?" Rogash finally managed.

Few knew it, but dwarves were remarkable historians. Rogash had read everything he could find penned in the dwarven language hoping to learn all he could about the art of smithing. Dwarves, however, didn't group their writings into different subjects. Dwarven works were all based on individuals. Thus, if you wanted to learn about smithing, you had to read about the life of a great smith. That meant learning about what era he lived in, who was king at the time, what wars he fought in, and so on. Thus, Rogash had read much of the history of Stratvs without even trying.

Furthermore, it was a little-known fact that ogres were possessed of lifespans that nearly rivaled the elves of the deep woods. The issue with an ogre's remarkable length of years was a combination of the facts that they tended to get themselves killed in one foolish act or another, and their abilities to reason left them at the level of most seven-year-old humans. They had an incredible capacity for remembering details; they were just unskilled at using those details to extrapolate outcomes that others would have easily foreseen. Rogash knew two ogres that were well over a thousand years old; this based on the fact that they remembered the names of lords that hunted them that had been dead for centuries. Neither of those ogres appeared any older than any other he'd encountered.

In fact, Rogash had devised the concept of combining the races as a form of everlasting legacy. Rogash had studied enough of history to know that kings rarely left any mark worth remembering unless it be some colossal failure. This new race of dwarves and ogres would be his legacy, his living mark upon Stratvs.

Thus, Rogash had discovered some ogres in his clan to be invaluable sources of information. The fact that they could remember events accurately was helpful, but most importantly, they lacked the imagination to embellish on what they'd heard. They also lacked the imagination to draw erroneous conclusions. They simply repeated what they remembered.

Having exploited this source of information, that so far remained undiscovered by others, Rogash had availed himself of much of the history of Stratvs, even if viewed through the eyes of dullards.

Consequently, Rogash was well aware of the reputation of the Warlock of the Marshes, the Original Betrayer, Oath-Breaker, First Among the Cursed, and so on. This knowledge also, and very unfortunately Rogash thought, coincided with the news that Maloch, the Knight of Sorrows, rode once again. For Rogash knew Maloch's reputation as well, which, of course, is why Hellmog was scouting the areas around the cavern entrance and why Rogash was so welcoming of the drow scouts. Rogash didn't know, not for certain, but suspected Maloch's roots were tied to the Warlock of the Marshes, somehow, as well.

"He offered to help us," Silas said, working to choose his words carefully in spite of his trust of the warlord. "He said a dark time was coming and that we would need our allies and should work toward that end."

"The First Among the Cursed said that 'dark times' are coming?"

"It was not lost on me that he seemed concerned about what the future held," Silas said, nodding as he pulled up his own chair to sit across from Rogash. "I have been given a few tasks. I must work out a means of supplying Warlord Verkial with a skilled mining force for Wodock. I must also strike a bargain with Lady Evalynne for an exchange of information regarding a few unsavory sorts bound for Moras, and I must prepare for this Slythorne without any sort of understanding as to what he is capable of."

"Warlord Verkial?"

"Yes, he's split, or is going to split, from Ingshburn and a few others to establish his own lands in Wodock and western Tarborat."

"The mining workforce will be no trouble," Rogash said confidently.

"No slaves," Silas said as his eyes moved from the map on Rogash's wall to meet those of the leader of Clan Jett Hammer. "Warlord Verkial was very specific on that caveat."

"That does make for an unexpected obstacle," Rogash said, stroking his thick red beard thoughtfully. "Thoughts as to why?"

"Beyond the fact that he enjoys being obstinate, no. I assume the ogres and giants follow your command and would voluntarily travel to Wodock to establish holdings there," Silas paused until Rogash responded with a nod. "Very well. The dwarves are the ones we must... convince."

"There is a fine line between slavery and wage work," Rogash said as he rose to begin pacing the large chamber. "There is a fine line between convincing an individual and coercing one. Of course, Verkial would not question the labor force, but they must have the option of walking out on whatever project is to be undertaken..."

With that, Rogash stopped, turned to Silas, and raised a single wiry eyebrow.

"The construction of an underground fortress, the mining, and processing of another of Merc's chariots, your star iron, and another more delicate project."

Rogash continued to stare at Silas, his expression unchanged.

"There is a dragon, Isd'Kislota, trapped by a mountain top that may topple and crush him," Silas said with a sigh. "He promises to serve us if we free him."

"Us?"

"My mistress, of course. However, her gratitude toward Clan Jett Hammer would be expressed in terms you find agreeable."

"These mountains, who mines them now?"

"No one," Silas replied. "They are inhabited by ogres and the like only. No dwarves or drow. Pristine and unspoiled."

Rogash nodded his head, smiled, and resumed his pacing. Silas was a bit taken aback that Rogash seemed nonplussed by the news Silas had hoped to withhold until a more proper, more advantageous time.

"Dwarves it must be then," Rogash said after several quiet laps around the large central bed of hides and hay. "Come."

Silas rose and followed the large warlord from his chambers and down a winding corridor to the caverns where the dwarves Rogash held worked and slept. It was a short walk and heavily guarded. Silas noted the only ogres and giants wearing armor and carrying weapons in all of Rogash's complex were those who stood guard here. He now realized in the other chambers where the creatures lived, ate, and slept none carried a weapon or wore any armor, although both were kept close at hand. He made a mental note to ask Rogash if that was a result of their comfort among the clan, or a policy instituted by the deceptively wise warlord.

After only a short walk, Rogash and Silas arrived at the large, iron-bound doors that secured the caverns where the dwarves were kept. Four giants stood guard, and Silas noted that it required the strength of all four to haul the great doors aside. Apparently, Rogash had found a simple means of securing the door without the need for lock and key.

Silas could hear many sounds from within that reminded him of the smithing quarter of Moras. The sounds of hammers ringing on steel and the churning of large bellows filled the air along with the distinct smell of soot, burning coal, and dwarven sweat. As they entered, all work, all activity, came to an immediate halt.

"I call for your anvilmen," Rogash said, referring to the term for reliable workers, which the dwarves had also assigned the meaning of leaders that could be counted upon.

The cavern was a large complex in and of itself, with forges and kilns to the left of the entrance, a large area rowed with tables and benches occupied the center, and individual homes and dwellings had been carved into the stone to the far right. Silas saw that it resembled more a small town rather than the slaves' quarters he'd imagined.

Rogash moved to the large area in the center of the cavern and waited while seven dwarven males, although Silas had to admit that the determination of gender was an assumption on his part, gathered around him. The rest of the dwarven population remained near where they had been when Rogash entered the room.

Of course, these people had been brutalized by the warlord in his way. However, it seemed to Silas that, beyond the taking of a female now and again for his breeding experiments, Rogash had been somewhat reasonable regarding the treatment of the dwarves. Silas moved through the gathering to stand next to Rogash. Oddly enough, the dwarves seemed comfortable with Silas, likely owing to the fact that his input in Rogash's breeding experiments had brought a halt to the use of dwarven females in the process.

"Hear me, think on my words, and give your reply when I come this time tomorrow," Rogash began. "I come to offer freedom by means of a contract. I am in need of workers to travel to a far land and build me a fortress there. I'm in need of skilled hands with hammer and pick that know steel and stone. My offer, that for ten years of good service, you'll go free with a gold coin in your pocket for each year."

The dwarves began to murmur at that, and the noise of their chatter rose until Rogash held up his broad hands.

"You'll not travel there with your family," Rogash continued. "They'll remain here, where I can keep them... safe. But, come ten years' time, you'll walk free alongside your family with coin in your pocket. There is a mountain range that remains untouched since the time of the Battles of Rending. There are great treasures there, and each one of you that is willing to accept my rule can have your own mine after that ten-year time."

Silas opened his mouth to protest but stopped at Rogash's upheld finger and hard stare.

"Think on this, speak to your people, and have your answer and any volunteers ready this time tomorrow."

With that, Rogash walked from the room. Silas, still stunned at the offer to the dwarves made by Rogash, had to run to catch up to the half-ogre warlord.

"Warlord Rogash, we might have discussed ownership and future contracts before you made such a grandiose offer to your slaves," Silas said as he caught up to Rogash in the corridor outside the dwarven caverns.

"We might have," Rogash replied with a nod. "But then I would not have garnered such a genuine response from you. They noticed your strong desire to protest the offer. That will give it more value, more credit, to them than anything I said. They'll have a few questions tomorrow, and that's when we'll square away the details. I think you'll have quite a large workforce when we're done negotiating."

"One question, if you'll allow," Silas said.

After a few more paces, Rogash nodded.

"Those mountains, and everything that's in them, belongs to me, and thereby my mistress," Silas said. "How do you plan to pay us for what you've just claimed?"

"Your mistress's gratitude would be, 'expressed in terms you find agreeable,'" Rogash said. "Those were your exact words, were they not?"

"I think you know that they were," Silas said, a bit angry at himself for allowing this to transpire as it had.

"Relax, young Chaos Lord," Rogash said with a smile that curled around one upwardly turned tusk. "Taxes will be paid to me, and I will pay my share to you, or your mistress. As to the dragon, I have no need for such a beast, and thus make no claim on one of the greater treasures to be found in Wodock. This star iron, though. That is another matter."

Silas felt much better the following day, largely thanks to the meal offered by Rogash. Apparently, one of Rogash's patrols had happened upon a priest in the forest outside the Suthiel. Of course, the priest was there to meet with a prostitute, but he was not the first soul to go missing outside that fabled wooded land.

He met with Rogash, as they had arranged, and returned to the dwarven caverns to see if any among their number were willing to sign such a contract. Silas did have to admit that the proposal was a clever one.

Rogash once again made his way to the center of the large gathering area of the cavern. There he stood and awaited the seven anvilmen of the dwarves. The dwarves gathered about, many looking to one another for support. Not the anvilmen, though, Silas noticed. They were clear of mind and purpose. Or, at least, they appeared to be.

"When you say serve you, what do you mean by that?" one of the younger dwarves asked unceremoniously.

"You are?"

"Kentooc, hinge-master of clan Iron Knee," the young dwarf responded.

"Well, Kentooc, I mean the same as any lord, warlord, or king would mean," Rogash said in response. "Worship whoever you like. Govern yourselves however you like. You'll pay me a twenty percent tax on what you produce, and you'll fight for me when called. However, unlike the King of Lethanor, I give you my word now that you'll never be called to arms for a cause other than to defend your own homes and our lands."

"What value does your word have?" Kentooc asked plainly.

"No more value than you assign to it, I suppose," Rogash replied bluntly. "I've taken from you, stolen from you, years and blood—no doubting that. There's not one among you that I don't owe, and I could never repay you for what's been taken. I don't propose to even try. This isn't a deal for us to get even. This is a deal for me to get something I want, and for you to get something you want. No more, no less. I've enslaved you by force of arm and plan to keep you so. This deal is your chance out. That simple."

"How can you know we'll not rise up against you once we have our freedom, families, and own mines in this distant land?"

"I don't. I am, however, convinced that your prosperity there will far outweigh any grudge you feel against me. If I'm wrong, then so be it. You can try your uprising, and I'll kill every single one of you. If I'm right, then you'll be too rich to care about old grudges."

There was a good deal of murmuring at that, and some quiet discussion among the seven anvilmen. Soon enough they nodded some silent agreement and addressed Rogash and Silas once again.

"How many?"

"All who wish to sign on," Rogash said.

"So, we could all accept the deal?"

"That's what I'm offering."

"Done," the seven said in unison.

"Meaning how many?"

"All," Kentooc said.

"When will they be ready to sail?" Silas asked as he and Rogash were once again walking back up the corridor to Rogash's chambers.

"As soon as you have a boat ready," Rogash replied.

"Technically, if it's a sea-going vessel, it's referred to as a 'ship,'" Silas corrected out of habit.

Silas looked up to the warlord that was two feet taller and untold stone heavier and took note of the lack of humor in that face.

"Boat, boat is fine," Silas said. "I'll have it ready within a week. Move them through the drow caverns to the mines of House Morosse. From there, we'll move them through Moras and to the docks. There is one more thing I must ask of you. The star iron, do you have enough left to make a longsword?"

Six days later, Silas, posing as Cambrose of House Wellborne, was summoned into the throne room of Lady Evalynne of Moras. The harsh clip of his boots striking the polished black/white checkered marble floor resounded throughout the corridors of the Keep. Silas entered the room to find Lady Evalynne sitting in her throne flanked by two guardsmen, Uriel-Ka standing behind and to the right of her. Silas noted that Uriel-Ka was attempting to look confident and imposing. Silas also noted that Ka had managed to replace or regrow the ring finger Silas had snatched from that hand and eaten in this very room. Clearly feeling Silas's eyes upon the hand, Uriel-Ka tucked it behind his back, trying but failing to maintain a threatening posture.

Lady Evalynne wore a sea-green gown that barely concealed her more intimate curves and lines, clinging and sheer in some places, and hanging almost too loose in others. Her hair hung in large, loose curls about her tanned shoulders, and paints had been skillfully applied to her eyes and lips. Silas recognized she had clearly not given up on plying him with her wiles.

Silas stopped the appropriate distance from her throne, offered a curt and professional bow, and then turned his gaze to the guards. With a bit of a sigh, Lady Evalynne flicked her hand toward the guards, her arm never lifting from the throne. These men were well-practiced and well trained. They recognized the subtle signal immediately and marched from the room without the slightest hesitation.

"It was very kind of you to allow me to enter with my ceremonial rapier and dagger remaining on my person," Silas said with a slight bow. "I'm glad to see that we are building trust."

"I think my wizard can attest that those obvious weapons are far from the most dangerous in your repertoire," she said as she rose and strode toward a table of maps and ledgers nearby. "Our new trade routes are proving successful; I take it?"

"They are," Silas said as he also approached the table and set a large bag of coins before her. "Very successful, I believe. So much so, in fact, that we may have to make other arrangements for your *tariffs* to be paid. I fear semi-annual meetings like this will require large and quite heavy chests of coin. I shudder to think of what such weight might do to my poor back. With your permission, I would suggest your percentages be paid to your sea captains per shipment. I think we've established the route such that the men involved have come to understand the procedure, and the nature of those they serve."

"That sounds like a fine suggestion," she said as she tossed the sack of coins to Uriel-Ka. "On to new business?"

"New business, my lady?"

"You want something," she said, allowing her lips to brush the edge of her teeth in what Silas was sure she believed to be a seductive gesture. "I can always tell when a man wants something."

"If you'll pardon my saying so, I believe the lady desires something as well. However, I was not raised in the absence of manners or etiquette. Thus, I'll *show my cards first*, as the sailors say. My lady is no stranger to steel or the use of a blade. With your permission?"

Silas gestured to the dagger on his belt, the one made for him by Rogash, and she nodded her consent. Silas removed the dagger and noted Uriel-Ka seem to tense from eyebrows to toenails. Ka had made a quick count of the coin in the bag, and it now rested on the throne next to him, leaving both of his caster's hands empty and ready. Silas also noticed, using his other senses, that Ka concealed a wand of twisted copper and steel within the sleeve of his robes and that he was prepared to drop it to his skilled hands in the flash of one swift movement. Silas smiled at that. Once upon a time, he had considered the wizard supremely dangerous, and to discount him now would be a perilous mistake, but Silas now saw him merely as a man who possessed a few common tricks. Deadly tricks, to be sure, but tricks, nonetheless. Silas now had a much better understanding of true power.

Silas drew the star iron dagger; its black metal shining in the trace rays of sunlight gleaming through the nearby windows. He gestured toward another dagger, one of steel that lay on the map table currently holding the corner of a map in place. Upon her nod, Silas took up the steel dagger in one hand and placed the edge of the star iron blade against the crosspiece, his thumb opposite the edge in the same manner one might slice an apple. With only a little more effort than needed to slice an apple, Silas cut through the crosspiece, handle, and blade of the steel dagger, dropping the upper end of the hewn blade onto the table.

Both Lady Evalynne and Uriel-Ka were practiced diplomats and courtiers, skilled in the arts of deception and misdirection. Silas was pleased to note the reaction, although subdued, from both. Clearly, they were intrigued.

"House Morosse has made claim to the mountains of Wodock," Silas said, rather bluntly. "I assume that information is not news to the Lady of Moras."

Silas was glad to see this revelation was not news to either of them. In fact, he observed that Evalynne and Ka both seemed a bit deflated, indicating this was news they were hoping to somehow ambush him with and use to their advantage.

"Material such as this is very limited," Silas continued. "But there is some to be had."

Silas sheathed his dagger and clapped his hands loudly. Upon his signal, two dwarves were admitted into the throne room, walking side by side. They each carried a black silk pillow, the hilt of a longsword wrapped in a silver chiffon cloth rested on one pillow while the blade of the sword, also wrapped in chiffon, rested on the other. The silver and black were colors of Lady Evalynne's crest, but she noted they were the colors of House Morosse as well. Walking in step with one another, the dwarves approached Silas and stopped, as practiced, ten paces from him and bowed.

Of course, the blade had not been crafted by dwarves; in fact, it had been crafted by the greatest bladesmith Silas had ever known. However, the fact that the bladesmith was a half-ogre might taint the perception of the gift. Thus, the presence of the dwarves allowed Silas to imply something without having to say a word.

Silas placed his hands under the blade and hilt and lifted the longsword from the pillows. He then turned and took a knee before Evalynne as he offered the sword up to her. She approached, skepticism and excitement warring for control of her facial expressions. She was a lady of court, but had spent many decades with longsword in hand conquering small pieces of the world one at a time. Lady Evalynne of Moras was now enamored with those days of battle as memories of hardships often do return in a kinder light.

Evalynne took up the sword, a masterful work of this black metal inlaid with silver, and examined the hilt closely. She noted large white diamonds at each end of the crosspiece, complemented by an even larger white diamond on the pommel. She also saw her sigil, the symbol of a sword cutting the waves of the sea, engraved on both sides of the shoulder of the blade and inlaid with shining silver.

In one fluid motion, Evalynne rolled the hilt over her hand and flipped the magnificent blade full circle. She then retracted the blade, spun, and reversed her grip to thrust it out behind her into the empty air. She pulled the sword back to her middle once again, reversing her grip, switching hands upon the hilt, and thrust the tip of the blade several inches into the thick wood of the large map table. The blade slid through the hard wood as though it were no more than a mound of hay.

This was the sort of weapon Lady Evalynne truly appreciated. It was stunning in its beauty and craftsmanship, and it was as deadly as it was attractive, much like its new wielder.

"Did the craftsman dub it with a name?" Evalynne asked after several more moments of close examination.

"No, my lady."

"I will call her *Helleka Toongall*, Queen's Tongue," Evalynne said.

"My Lady, perhaps that would be a bit presumptuous," Uriel-Ka put in from his place near the throne. He had been careful not to take a single step closer to Silas.

The threat that flashed in Lady Evalynne's eyes was clear and beyond alternative interpretation. Uriel-Ka lowered his eyes immediately and took a half step back.

"Queen's Tongue, excellent moniker, my lady," Silas said as he rose from his kneeling position.

"What would you have for it?"

With a wave of his hand, the dwarves tucked their pillows under their arms and exited the throne room with haste. As the doors closed behind the dwarves, Silas turned to Lady Evalynne and offered her a knowing smile.

"If you have not been approached yet, then you will be," he said as he began the words he'd rehearsed over the past few days. "An assassin of uncommon skill and reputation is coming to Moras, intent on moving against Stewardess Dru and myself."

"If he has such a reputation, perhaps he's not as skilled as you say," Uriel-Ka dared to say.

Silas favored Ka with a slight smile and ran his tongue briefly over his teeth. The small act carried a significant threat, as far as Ka was concerned, and thus he lowered his eyes once again.

"And?" Evalynne said, returning her gaze to the sword in her hands.

"And, he will contact you to let you know that he will be operating in your city," Silas continued, barely able to resist the urge to pace as he spoke. "He will do this as a courtesy to you, I'm told, in hopes of avoiding any entanglements with watchmen or inquisitors of Moras. He will likely not divulge much; however, much might be learned from scrutinizing the little bit he does offer. I ask that you simply inform me of each and every detail gleaned from what he says and does during that meeting, and in any other communications he has with you or your lieutenants. It would also be wise to avoid any set of circumstances that would indicate to him that we have the arrangement that exists between us."

"And for this, I receive..."

"Continued prosperity with the promise of a very bright future."

"That seems a bit vague," Evalynne said, her attention returned fully to Silas and this negotiation.

"A dagger to match Queen's Tongue, then," Silas offered.

The excitement in Evalynne's eyes was unmistakable. Silas had known she preferred the sword and dagger style of fencing and had hoped this enticement would be enough to secure her cooperation.

"How will you return here to learn of this assassin if he will be hunting you?"

"I will not, but an emissary will. The drow have moved rather freely throughout Moras, remaining unnoticed thus far. It should be no trouble for one of their number to visit you from time to time. Of course, those visits would, by necessity, be unannounced and unbidden."

Uriel-Ka opened his mouth to respond to such an outrageous suggestion. However, he held his tongue when Lady Evalynne raised a single finger and returned her gaze to her long-sword.

"Agreed," she said with a smile.

CHAPTER IV

Damaged Souls

They had avoided seven traps thus far, three spotted by Maloch, two others by Jonas, and the other two by Dunewell. According to Maloch, the drow had as much to fear from other covens of drow as anyone else in the outside world. Given that Maloch was leading Jonas and Dunewell into this coven for a punitive expedition whose only goals were to diminish their number and create chaos among their leadership, Dunewell had to agree with that notion.

In using Whitburn's divine sight, Dunewell had noticed a faint glow about the white rose that he wore. He noted the same aura around the totem Jonas wore. It didn't give off any light that the normal eye could perceive but a soft, magical hue. He still did not understand what had transpired that moonlit night when he and Jonas had witnessed the struggle between the red raven, the great snake, and the wolf pup amidst the white rose bush. He had not taken the time to consult a shaman or a witch hunter, but he had no doubt the event was somehow significant.

Dunewell was no novice to the use of stealth and had, in fact, led several successful scouting missions in Tarborat. Maloch also proved to be remarkably quiet when he wished to be, passing through the darkness like a black feather through a moonless night. Yet, neither of them held a candle to Jonas's capabilities. Had it not been for abilities borrowed from Whitburn, Dunewell would have lost Jonas completely. Dunewell considered the decades Jonas had spent hunting the greatest assassins ever to walk the low streets and dark alleys of Stratvs. He supposed that when you made that your business, you either learned to be quiet, or you weren't around long enough to learn much else.

After almost an hour of negotiating tight turns, blind tunnels, deadfalls, windlass traps, and false floors, the three arrived at a wall of masonry that appeared to be a partially buried segment of wall from the Nolcavanor that was. Maloch looked it over carefully and finally found the triggering device for which he'd been searching. Dunewell heard a series of light clicks behind the wall, and a portion of it swung away silently to reveal a hidden passage.

Maloch paused at the entrance and noted a single strand of long white hair that had been disturbed by their passing. He also pointed to another tripwire and pressure plate just within the portal.

This is good, Maloch thought to the others while holding up the single strand of hair. *None have passed this way since I last secured it.*

Personal escape route? Dunewell asked.

No drow is comfortable with three exits when he may have four, Whitburn and Jonas thought in unison to the group.

This caused Maloch and Dunewell to turn as one to stare at Jonas, for Dunewell couldn't very well stare at Whitburn.

It's a common saying, Jonas said.

Whitburn was peculiarly quiet.

Among who? Dunewell asked.

Seeing that they weren't going to get an answer to Dunewell's last question, Dunewell and Maloch turned back toward the hidden pathway.

To answer your first question, my people knew my chambers, and many of my better thieves and rogues thought they knew my other routes as well, Maloch thought. *However, when one is the leader of a drow coven, one can never be too careful about listening in on the barracks or at the wine cask about budding coup attempts. Thus, this passage.*

They stalked through the tunnel for less than one hundred yards. Yet, due to the many twists and turns, they didn't cover more than perhaps a third of that as the raven flew south to north. The final turn brought them to three concealed door-ways.

Two are decoys and are heavily trapped in case someone had discovered this tunnel and sought to murder me in my sleep, Maloch thought to the group. *The one on the far left is the true pathway into my private chambers. Chambers which are very likely to be inhabited.*

And your plan is to kill whoever is in charge of your coven and, in doing so, create instability? Jonas asked.

Yes, Maloch replied.

Wait here, Jonas said. *Don't make a move without me.*

Dunewell was discovering that mental communication conveyed even more emotion, tone, and connotation than ver-bal speech ever could. Jonas's tone was one of command and absolutes. Dunewell and Maloch, both soldiers in their hearts, knew an order when they heard one. They waited for several minutes, monitoring Jonas's travels through the tunnels via the telepathic link they all shared. Something changed then, and Jonas was there but no longer *there.* Dunewell started at that, worrying that something might have happened to him, but Whitburn held him in place.

Do not fear, Whitburn imparted to Dunewell. *He has moved into a silent place, but he is not injured in any way.*

Maloch picked up on the thoughts from Whitburn and nodded, still not comfortable with the idea of Jonas alone in the depths of Nolcavanor. Dunewell had never liked the under-ground places of Stratvs. The idea of millions of tons of stone hanging above him and waiting to crush him, never to be heard from again, was not an idea that comforted him. It surprised Dunewell to learn that Maloch, after so many centuries under-ground, actually took great comfort in the same sensation that caused Dunewell such unease. The open places of the surface world, particularly the plains and flatlands, troubled Maloch. He had the feeling that Roarke's anvil, Stratvs, might just let go of his soul, and he would drift up from the world and into the darkness beyond the clouds, alone in the vastness of that empty black place.

Then Jonas's thoughts, but not his presence, returned to their minds.

I'm coming up the tunnel, Jonas imparted to them.

Gradually Jonas's presence also returned in their unusual mind/hive. Moments later, he came back into actual view carrying a drow dagger marked with the broken hourglass on its hilt. It did not escape Jonas nor Dunewell that Muersorem's symbol, the UnMaker's mark, was a broken sword. Yet, in the forming of this coven, Maloch had chosen to instead defile the Hourglass symbol of Father Time to mark his soldiers, weapons, and property. Maloch, sharing in their thoughts, hung his head in shame.

Stand aside, Jonas thought to them. *I'm going to use this dagger to kill your friend in there. Then we'll let the madness of drow versus drow play itself out for a bit. Do you have any good trackers? I mean really good?*

There are several in the ranks of this coven, Maloch replied.

Good, Jonas replied as he palmed the dagger and quietly padded toward the door on the left.

You're not going to murder the person in the next room without call or challenge, are you? Dunewell asked.

But of course, he already knew the answer to that question. It was in Jonas's mind as plainly as if it were in Dunewell's own. Jonas paused, both he and Dunewell wondered for a moment if they were going to have this argument about the virtues of murder, and then Jonas continued toward the door. Maloch, due to his mental tie to the other two, absorbed every argument these two men and brothers-in-arms had ever had about the cause of chivalry versus the pragmatism of what must be done to save lives. It was an argument Maloch knew well, for he had often faced the same internal struggle.

Jonas crept into the master room of the underground chamber on feet quieter than any cat's. The room was dimly lit by a single candle whose light only came to the main chamber after reflecting from the polished stone wall within. The paltry light would not have been enough for anyone to see by properly; however, these three were not just anyone.

Across from the portal was a bed large enough for an ogre and plush enough to satisfy even the most foppish of royalty. Amid the silks and feather stuffed pillows of the bed lay their target, a large and well-muscled drow. Though almost all drow took great pride in their long, flowing white hair, this one wore his hair cut very short in the style of the Silver Helms. He slept soundly while the two scanning the room could read the road map of pain and battles past in the scars on the drow soldier's arms and upper back.

Next to the bed on the right was an armor tree that held a beautiful set of black steel plate. A mercshyeld tipped spear, and short sword hung in a weapons belt on the same tree. Farther to the right was a washbasin, mirror, and the door to the rest of the living quarters.

The coppery smell of blood was thick in the air and mixed with the odor of urine. Those scents stood in dramatic contrast to the luxurious décor before them.

To the left of the bed was a passage that led around to an alcove. That alcove served as a closet from whence the candlelight trickled. Across from that passage was a whipping pole. Dunewell looked past Jonas to see two young human girls, perhaps fifteen, certainly no more than twenty years old, chained together on that pole. Blood had scabbed at their noses and busted lips. Their clothing, little that there was, was soaked in urine. Their arms were pulled above them while their heads drooped in the sleep of exhaustion.

That was when Maloch discovered that emotions, as well as thoughts, could be communicated through their telepathic link. Dunewell's reaction to seeing the captives was so loud, so profound, in Maloch and Jonas's head that both jerked and feared the entire complex had heard them. Of course, outwardly, Dunewell didn't so much as twitch an eyelash.

There is a pattern on the carpet to the right side of the bed, Maloch communicated to Jonas and Dunewell. *It looks like a flash of black lightning. Follow it carefully for the floor is heavily alarmed and trapped.*

Dunewell, his emotions pulling him one direction and his morals another, watched as Jonas crept over the carpeted floor to the sleeping drow. Jonas eased each foot down in slow succession, testing the surface for the slightest resistance of a tripwire or pressure plate. As he moved to within a single stride of the bed, Jonas flipped the dagger around in his hand so that it was now poised for a thrust. However, Jonas discovered that the bed was too large for him to reach the sleeping drow from its edge, meaning he would have to climb onto the bed as well. Jonas knew that move would almost certainly alert the drow soldier turned commander. So, with another quick flip of the dagger, Jonas reversed his grip again and hurled the blade with a deft and practiced jerk of his arm and snap of his wrist.

The point of the blade sunk deep into the soft flesh between the top of the drow's spine and small opening at the base of his skull. The drow spasmed only once and then fell still, forever. Jonas climbed onto the bed then, removed the dagger, and twisted it violently against bone as he did so. This deed caused a small piece of the blade to break free of the dagger and lodge into one of the drow's vertebrae.

Dunewell and Maloch went to the two young girls who, now awakened, sat with their eyes wide and vacant. Jonas moved to the chamber door and ensured the inner bolt was secured.

"You're safe now," Dunewell said to the two girls. "We are here to rescue you from them."

Both girls stared blankly at Dunewell, responding by only shifting their eyes to Maloch and then turning them back on Dunewell.

They've seen too much violence, Dunewell imparted to his two companions. *I've seen it before. We need to get them out of here and to safety.*

Maloch moved off toward the closet and returned a few

moments later with silk shirts and heavy wool cloaks for them. When they saw the girls would not be responding, Dunewell and Maloch moved to remove their stained and soiled clothing and replace it with what Maloch had brought from the closet. However, when Maloch moved to help them, one of the girls twitched violently and let out a small gasp. Maloch nodded to Dunewell and stepped to the door where Jonas stood.

Dunewell helped the two girls out of their clothing and into the silk shirts. Although it was warm in the chambers of the master, both girls drew the cloaks around them tightly and shivered beneath them.

Leave me their soiled clothing, show me to that forge, and then cast your spell, Jonas thought to Dunewell and Maloch. *You two will need to get them back to Ranoct.*

Ranoct? Maloch and Dunewell responded in unison.

Yes, Jonas replied. *He'll have no choice but to get them to safety, which means he'll either have to divide his force or divert his route altogether. Either of those possibilities is good for us. You'll need be crafty about it, though. I'd leave those two in an open glade and, when Ranoct and his men approach, sneak around them and be prepared to steal... commandeer three horses. At least three horses.*

Dunewell, you get them back to the waterfall, Jonas commanded.

Dunewell replied with a quick nod.

Maloch, while he's doing that, you show me to this forge of yours.

You'll be in here alone, out of your element, and against a coven of drow, Maloch thought to Jonas.

You have no idea what my element is, Jonas replied. *I've handled worse.*

I get the dagger, but why the soiled clothing? Dunewell asked.

Was there something in my tone that invited questions? Jonas asked, although it was clear he wasn't interested in any answer.

Can you bring them into our mind-link? Dunewell asked as he nodded toward the two young girls. *We could reassure them...*

NO! came from Jonas's mind with the force of a fist to the nose. *Now move.*

Dunewell put an arm around each girl and stood them up with him as he rose. He moved silently to the hidden doorway and disappeared into the black throat of the tunnel. Jonas moved over and took up the soiled clothing left behind by the captives and then nodded to Maloch.

Now, show me that forge.

Dunewell worried about the traps and alarms he would encounter on his way back to the large cavern behind the waterfall. He worried that the two young girls would wander about, fidget, or stumble along. He was correct in assuming their absence of agility; however, they did not move without his say-so. Each time he approached a trap or trigger and whispered for them to stop, they did so without hesitation.

Twice he heard drow patrols approaching them from an adjacent corridor. The taller of the two girls, the one with red hair, stayed perfectly quiet and presented nothing but a blank affect. The shorter one, perhaps a bit younger, but it was hard to tell amid the blood and dirt, began to tremble at the sound of the patrols drawing near. A slight whimper escaped her mouth, and she began to shake as though she might fall to the ground.

Dunewell had seen these symptoms before. Fear, and other extreme emotions, would bring on bouts of the Vile Twitch in his younger brother. Dunewell wrapped one great arm around her while the other girl put her hand over the mouth of the younger captive. They held together like that in the absolute black for several long moments, waiting to see if their presence had been detected.

Once Dunewell was confident the patrols had continued on their way, he and his two charges continued their trek toward the outside world. Dunewell, who'd always had a head for mazes and a nose for true north, had little trouble retracing their steps back to the large cavern. He moved the girls down the sharply carved staircase to the floor of the cavern and the mouth of their exit. He helped each girl past the final trap, a windlass trap and alarm, and then moved into the tunnel behind them.

The two captives moved through the tunnel ahead of Dunewell while he remained behind them as watch and ward for any drow that might have picked up their trail. As they moved closer and closer to the waterfall, the roar forced both girls to place their hands over their ears. It occurred to Dunewell then that it had likely been a long time since either of them had heard anything louder than the sound of a leather strap striking their flesh, for Dunewell knew well that drow preferred a quiet if not silent environment.

As light began to filter in from the tunnel's entrance, Dunewell turned back one last time to ensure they weren't being followed. As he looked to the rear, Dunewell suddenly heard a mewling sound blurt from the direction of the waterfall, the direction of the girls. Dunewell turned and ran. He was bound for the corner that would lead him to the landing at the top of the stair. As he approached, he saw the shadows of figures moving about just beyond that turn.

Dunewell rounded the corner just as the two girls ran screaming toward him. Only they weren't quite screaming. Their mouths were open, they were clearly terrified, but there was something... Dunewell then realized what was wrong. The drow had cut their tongues out.

The two captives ran past him, and Dunewell could only hope they would slow or stop before they arrived at the trap that lay at the end of the tunnel. Ahead of him, running toward him, were three drow soldiers.

With a thought, Dunewell's hammer leapt to his hand. The holy symbols of Bolvii blazed from his grip up the shaft and encircled the head of the hammer. The three drow, clearly practiced in fighting alongside one another, spread themselves out. The leading drow hoisted a broadsword for a high attack, while the one right behind him was already sliding to his knees and bringing two short swords in line for slashing attacks at his legs. The third quirked the edge of his mouth in a smile and leveled one of their deadly crossbows. The third drow triggered his crossbow and launched a dart, very likely poisoned, that skimmed through the air directly toward Dunewell's exposed neck.

Dunewell, moving quicker than the drow could have anticipated, punched out with his hammer knocking the broadsword high and out of line. In the same move, he stomped down with a powerful kick that caught the second drow's upper arm and drove it down into the lower, parallel arm. Dunewell attacked with such force that both the drow's arms were slammed to the floor, the bones within shattering under Dunewell's boot.

The poisoned dart flew past both the parry and the stomp, however. The poisoned dart jetted through the air and drove its tip against the exposed skin of Dunewell's throat. To the absolute shock, and horror, of the drow, the dart splintered as if striking flat stone, not even marring Dunewell's tanned skin. Skin hardened by his will and the power of Bolvii through Whitburn, his champion.

Dunewell continued to move forward and drove the broadsword of the first drow high into the air while at the same time pivoting his hammer underneath that parry. The drow moved to draw a dagger from his waist but could not lay a hand to it before Dunewell struck him in the chin with the pommel of his war hammer. The force of Dunewell's blow split the drow's jaw and drove the haft through the roof of the drow's mouth and deep into his brain.

Dunewell's stalwart legs, pushed on by Whitburn's will, drove him forward toward the third drow with incredible speed. The last drow hauled out a morning star and was just swinging it back when Dunewell reached him. The drow shifted his arms in hopes of a parry when Dunewell simply struck out with his boot again and kicked the drow square in the chest. Dunewell's momentum, as well as the remarkable strength of his legs, shot the drow back and launched him off the landing and into the killing path of the roaring waterfall. The third drow disappeared from sight, never to be seen again.

Dunewell turned back to the remaining drow, the one with two broken arms, and found one of the girls, the one with red hair, standing over him with one of his swords in her delicate and bloodied hands. As Dunewell stepped toward her to comfort her, the drow began to plead his case, although in a language Dunewell doubted the girl understood. When the drow's mouth opened to form his next word, she slipped the end of his sword into the space between his teeth.

The drow stopped speaking and tried to gesture with his hands by holding them out to the side, indicating his surrender. Clearly the drow soldier assumed she was trying to scare him into silence or submission. Dunewell did too. The look of shock on the drow's face matched the one on Dunewell's when the girl continued to push the tip of the sword into the drow soldier's mouth. She did not thrust it quickly, and she did not slash or hack at him with rage. Her face remained emotionless as she slowly forced the blade through his tongue, the edge separating teeth and prying several loose. The drow began to scream, a scream that was lost in the roar of the waterfall and the gurgle of blood.

For several moments, long after blood had ceased flowing from the drow's neck and mouth, the girl twisted and rocked the blade back and forth, gradually hollowing out the grisly wound as one might drill a hole in a flute with a dagger point. Dunewell, who had witnessed many battles and many deaths, understood the actual injury before him. This girl's life had been changed forever, and it would require great fortitude for her to let this strengthen her instead of destroying her.

Dunewell walked past her to check on the shorter one with dark brown hair. He found her crouched just beyond the corner, huddled with her arms wrapped tight about her pulled up knees and rocking back and forth. How many times had he found Silas in this very same pose doing his best to battle another bout of the Vile Twitch?

Without warning, his heart contorted in his chest for his

brother that was, and the creature he had become. Dunewell had pushed Silas far from his thoughts for many months now only to find his love and his regret renewed in the vision of this tortured girl. Dunewell prayed in his soul then; prayed to Father Time. He begged for the chance to return to those days so many years ago. He begged for one more opportunity to tell his mother, Helena, what she was doing to her son. He begged for one more moment with Killian when he could either turn his heart with his words or pierce his breast with his sword.

Dunewell picked the younger girl up and carried her back down the tunnel. Back toward the waterfall and back toward the outside world, hoping her soul was coming with them.

When he managed to get both girls to the landing, he took up the harnesses originally made for Jonas and Maloch. As Dunewell was tightening them to fit the two captives, Maloch approached from behind.

"Here to cut us off?" Maloch asked, gesturing to the drow dead at his feet.

"I don't think so," Dunewell said. "They weren't expecting us. I think they happened upon the rope and harness that we left behind and were just beginning to investigate it when we three arrived."

"Just the two?"

Dunewell shook his head and jerked a thumb toward the waterfall rushing only a few yards away. Dunewell looked Maloch over then and noticed a new pack and a few other items.

"The pack?" Dunewell asked.

"The drow here are evil," Maloch replied with a nod. "Their food is not. I grabbed some waterskins as well."

"Your breastplate?" Dunewell asked.

"It is with my greaves. They are becoming a longsword, a Shyeld-Hayn, in the hands of a Lanceilier as we speak."

"That's a generous gift."

"Would you believe it only made him more suspicious?"

"Yes," Dunewell replied. "Yes, I would."

"Thoughts on getting them past the river and back toward Inquisitor Ranoct?"

"I think I have that worked out," Dunewell said as he took up the rope. "You climb down behind us, just in case. I'll lower them down, eighty feet at a time, and leap from landing to landing myself. Once we're down, I'll start to work on a raft. I know we'll have to move a good distance downstream before the waters will be calm enough to navigate, but I think that is our best bet. I haven't worked out how we'll get Jonas across though."

"Don't worry about him," Maloch said. "I told him what I knew of the upper caverns, and we arranged to meet on the northeast face of this mountain. I only hope he can make it through those caverns alone."

"You know a great deal about Jonas," Dunewell said as he gathered up the last of the rope. "Far more than he would like, I've no doubt. But, did you know that he made a practice of hunting Shadow Blades?"

"That's true?" Maloch said, doubt plain upon his face for Maloch had heard the stories of the Gray Spider.

"True."

Dunewell grabbed the two dead drow, one in each hand, and walked to the landing where he hurled their bodies into the chaos of rushing water. Then he moved the two girls to the edge of the landing and explained to them again how he planned on getting them from one landing to another. If either of them understood his words, they didn't show it with an outward response. Dunewell reached again for the drow short sword the girl with the red hair still held. She pulled back from him, dangerously so on the high ledge, so he decided to surrender that battle.

The descent down the stairs went much quicker than the climb up. It didn't hurt that the young girls together didn't weigh a quarter of what Maloch and Jonas weighed. In short, easy work, Dunewell arrived at the bottom of the stair alongside his two charges.

The taller girl, the one with the red hair, draped one arm

around the shorter one while holding the looted drow short sword in the other. They leaned against a nearby tree and watched the stair with sharp eyes.

Dunewell removed their harnesses and set about looking for fallen trees that would serve as raft material. His champion-enhanced strength served him well, and, in the time it would have taken ten men, Dunewell had seven large logs together. He didn't bother stripping away limbs other than those that would interfere with ensuring one log sat next to another with as small a gap as possible. To his thinking, the remaining limbs would serve as excellent handholds should they be needed.

As Dunewell was tying the last lash to secure the logs together, Maloch was taking the final steps down the rocky climb. Dunewell herded the two girls onto the makeshift raft and then took up the end and began to pull it along the land, moving it downstream to calmer waters. Maloch paced along next to Dunewell keeping his eyes, and his ears, on the forest around them and the stair behind. Maloch took a moment to note the sheer strength Dunewell possessed. In his estimate, it would have taken a team of at least two oxen, and perhaps four, to pull that raft. Dunewell was doing it with one arm while carrying his war hammer in the other hand.

After another two hours, the sun, although not close to the horizon, was still down enough that the thick forest around them was growing quite dark. The waters of the Whynne were still very rough, so they decided to set up a cold camp there for the night.

Dunewell collected an armload of evergreen boughs and laid them out as a bed for the two girls out of the wind. They curled up together into the boughs and looted cloaks against the coming chill of the night. Maloch passed Dunewell a water-skin and a bag of dried fruits that he, in turn, passed to the young girls.

Dunewell strode to the river's edge, where he took another deep draft from the replenishing waters of the Whynne. When he returned to the camp, he accepted a small bag of jerky from Maloch. They ate in silence as the two captives drifted off to sleep.

"I can watch for a while," Maloch whispered to Dunewell. "You get some rest."

"I'm far from needing any rest," Dunewell said honestly. "The waters, flowing water, grants me an energy, a vigor, that is hard to describe."

Maloch nodded, looked to the stars of the sky, and then back to Dunewell. He saw the question forming on Dunewell's face. Their telepathic link had been severed when they moved more than a hundred yards or so from Jonas, the source of the magic. Now Maloch relied on his years, centuries actually, of traveling in the company of warriors.

"Ask," Maloch said simply.

"The mind-link we shared, why was Jonas so set against using it to help the girls?"

"Why ask me?"

"You seem to know far more about him than he would like, and more than anyone else I'm aware of," Dunewell reasoned. "You also seemed to understand his sudden reaction to the idea."

"Were it anyone else, I would tell you that you must ask him," Maloch said as he let his eyes drift back up to the stars; how he'd missed them. "However, your life, and the lives of many others, may be in the balance soon, and it is something you should know. Furthermore, I doubt he would ever tell any-one himself. Almost a hundred years ago, he led a group of soldiers into the lair of a vampire deep within the wastes of Tarborat."

Maloch paused, took a long drink from a waterskin, and continued.

"His brother, Lord Velryk, was among those soldiers. They found a young woman who had been taken by the vam-pire but was not yet turned. Her name was Giselle. Lord Jonas opened his mind to her in hopes of soothing her; instead, he in-fected all those under his command with her fear. Many of them lost their lives in that lair. As to how much of that was due to Jonas's decision, who knows. I can tell you Velryk blamed Jonas, and the girl, Giselle, for the deaths of the soldiers that fell that day. Jonas left the King's service shortly after that and married Giselle. Jonas left his life as a soldier and his brother behind. Velryk blamed him for that too. A few short years later, Giselle was killed by an assassin, a Shadow Blade."

"The vampire was Slythorne," Dunewell said as much as asked. "And he's the one that hired the Shadow Blade."

Maloch nodded thoughtfully and then rolled his cloak around him and propped himself up at the base of a large tree. With another nod, Maloch pulled his hood down over his eyes and was asleep with the practiced ease of a soldier in the field.

Dunewell kept watch the rest of that night, but neither heard nor saw anything that seemed out of place. As the sun began to climb in the east, Dunewell cleaned and oiled his weapons and then took another deep drink from the Whynne. As he was returning to the small camp, Dunewell saw that Maloch was awake and polishing the edge of his fine blades with a whetstone.

"Give me a few hours, and I'll hunt us up some fresh meat," Dunewell said quietly so as not to wake the two girls. "Do you mind waiting here?"

"My guess is they will sleep for as long as we let them," Maloch replied. "No, I don't mind a bit. Although, I don't see a bow or sling."

Dunewell smiled, nodded, turned, and began to jog south, parallel to the Whynne, and about a league west of it. Dunewell was jogging at a pace a swift horse would have had trouble maintaining. An hour into his run, he made two observations. One, the river had become much quieter and would likely be calm enough here to cross. Two, he smelled a small herd of deer up ahead.

Dunewell slowed his pace and began to stalk silently through the dense forest, making sure to stay downwind of the game. He eased himself along, putting aside any thoughts of time or goals and allowing the stalk to take as long as it must. He extended his thoughts, his feelings, and could detect the life-force of the deer, experiencing their heartbeats as his own.

Long before he could see them, Dunewell was able to examine them and make his selection of the right one to take. There was an older buck among them that should be left because he guided the rest and took care of them. There were a few does, several fawns, and two younger bucks. Of the two younger bucks, one was strong, mindful of the others, and quick. The other was smaller, less concerned for the herd, and was eager to get to the waters of the Whynne regardless of possible predators.

As Dunewell decided killing the smaller buck would be better for the herd, and thus better for the forest, the similarities struck him with breathtaking force. He couldn't decide if he was being overly dramatic, seeing this as a metaphor for him and Silas, or if Bolvii, or perhaps Silvor, were trying to tell him something. Perhaps they were trying to show him that when it came to life and death, only the benefits of the greater good mattered. As Arto had once postulated, 'the needs of the many...'

Suddenly the deer were bolting toward the river, and a quick testing of the air told Dunewell why. Wolves.

Dunewell sprinted forward, hurdling huge fallen trees, and leaping to swing from lower limbs fifteen to twenty feet from the ground. As Dunewell tore through the forest, he saw them, the wolf pack, as they moved to encircle the small herd of deer. Not a wolf pack though, at least not what Dunewell had thought. The smell was very similar, and at a distance, they looked like wolves, yet these were something else entirely. Craven-jackals.

Dunewell was no woodsman but knew well enough that wolf packs would hunt, much as he had planned to, only the weakest of a herd thereby feeding their pack and strengthen the herd of deer. Craven-jackals killed and ate everything they encountered. They were already moving to encircle the herd of deer and trap them against the waters of the Whynne. Craven-jackals would kill all the deer, whether they could or would eat them all. Craven-jackals were a curse on the land.

Dunewell leapt from the last limb and hurled himself through the air. He hit the ground running and drew his war hammer as he ran. The craven-jackals saw him coming, but too late. Dunewell charged among them, kicking the first one high into the air, striking the second with his hammer, and punching the third hard enough to break its neck. There were more than a dozen remaining and, had he been mortal man, could have easily killed him. However, they drew back, a few latching their maws onto the fallen of their number. Dunewell at first thought he may have found a redeeming quality in the craven-jackals after all as he watched them drag their wounded from the small glade and back into the cover of the thick forest. He dismissed that thought when he heard them, sensed them, begin to eat the three he had killed.

The small herd of deer bolted dangerously close to the still swift waters of the Whynne but did finally veer south again and ran along the edge of the mighty river toward their escape. He could have given chase and caught them, but somehow felt that would be to disrespect the omen he believed he'd witnessed. Or, perhaps he was hoping to find a means, any means, of excusing his inability to kill Silas and his hesitance to do so even now.

A few hours later, Dunewell returned to the small camp to find Maloch standing guard and the two young girls still sleeping. Dunewell took another deep drink from the river and then approached the lightly snoring children.

Dunewell gently placed a hand on each of the girls' cheeks and began a whisper of a prayer to Bolvii. As he prayed, the familiar blue glow began to build slowly around his hands and then flow into the faces of the wounded children. In a few moments, the soft hue had spread to cover the girls entirely.

Dunewell then pulled back from them and, severely weakened, staggered back toward the Whynne. He took another deep drink from the flowing waters, the symbol of life, and was refreshed.

"Can you do anything for their... state of mind?" Maloch asked as he squatted on his heels next to where Dunewell laid on the riverbank. "In the faith of Time, only priest and clerics have those prayers."

"Not that I know of," Dunewell said, pulling himself up to lean on one elbow. "This... this whole thing is more feeling my way through than studying and learning. It's hard to explain."

"The most pure prayer is not the lengthy and complex prayer of an accomplished priest," Maloch said as he looked back toward the two girls who were beginning to wake. "The purest is the one that comes from the heart in earnest love for one's brothers and sisters. You have a good heart, my friend."

Dunewell thought back over brothers who died in the mud of Tarborat, and of the other brother he allowed to escape. Dunewell was afraid of what else Silas might do, and what acts, what sins, might be heaped upon his own soul. For Dunewell had failed to stop his brother when he had the chance and, even now, wondered if he would have the strength to see to Silas's adjudication when the time came. Perhaps even more concerning than those worries was his sin of omission. The sin that marred his soul. The sin of failing to protect Silas when he was a child. For what man can call himself just when he knows of the torture of a child and takes no action to stop it?

Dunewell rolled over to drink deeply from the river again as Maloch rose to stand next to him.

"I think they will feel better when they've had a chance to bath," Maloch said as he nodded his chin toward the two captives they'd rescued.

"The chill in the air is a bit sharp," Dunewell said as he stood and drew his forearm across his mouth, wiping water from his thick beard and mustache. "There is a good fire going at our next camp, and I have meat cooking that should be ready by the time we arrive."

Maloch nodded again, pointed south, and raised an eyebrow to Dunewell.

"You can't miss it," Dunewell said.

Maloch started off in a light jog, heading south on a game trail parallel to the river. Dunewell returned to the cold camp and extended a hand to the girl with the red hair. She accepted and, without a word, he helped both of them up, and they began their walk south.

Dunewell paused at the edge of their small camp to wrap the rope around his left arm and began dragging their raft along with them. It occurred to him then that he might have been better off waiting to build the raft until they reached a point of the river where he could put it to water, but he dismissed that thought. His muscles enjoyed the labor of pulling the raft, and his mind needed the distraction.

The shorter girl, the one with the brown hair, ran her finger into her mouth and over her tongue many times during their walk. Each time she did this, she would look to the taller girl for confirmation that they had been healed. Their physical wounds had mended, but the wounds on their souls would likely be with them forever.

They walked for two hours when the smell of smoked fish came to them. They walked into the small camp to find that Maloch had built the fire up against the chill of winter and had six fresh fish grilling on the fire apart from the dozen or so that Dunewell had caught and smoked on a hastily constructed chimney nearby.

"We'll eat, rest, and when we're warm and ready, we'll take the raft to the other side of the river," Dunewell said to the girls. "Once over there, we'll get another fire going, and you can bathe in the river. The water will be cold, but I believe you'll find it refreshing."

The girls, still silent and the one with red hair still clutching the looted drow's short sword, both nodded in unison. Then, while keeping a wary eye on Maloch, both girls began eating their fish with a hunger and zest any soldier could recognize.

CHAPTER V
Souls Promised

A few leagues outside Moras, and at least a league underground, Lady Dru was being escorted into Queen Jandanero's throne room. Dru was not without her tricks and used one of them now, silently casting a spell that enhanced her myriad perceptions. She noted the nook, what Silas had called a cully door, concealed in the floor of the room, but more importantly, she confirmed what Silas had suspected, and Lynneare had affirmed; Queen Jandanero was in possession of a Dark Guardian.

Dru berated herself for having missed such an incredible aspect of the drow community. The presence of a Dark Guardian, a suit of armor inhabited with the captured soul of a champion, indicated many troubling possibilities. First and foremost, she had been remiss in assessing the strengths and weaknesses of the drow, and of Queen Jandanero herself. To possess a Dark Guardian was the equivalent of having a dragon at one's beck and call.

It also meant that the Queen of the drow had access to a powerful alchemist, sorcerer, and cleric. Any one of the three could be a significant resource, given the complexity of the spells required to create such a being. However, Queen Jandanero had access, one way or another, to each of the three and held enough sway over them to command of them years of toil to produce this single work.

Furthermore, Dru had learned of the subtle tension among the drow of Dark Hammer Coven owed to the rumor that Maloch of the Black Lance rode from Nolcavanor once more. Dru had never encountered Maloch, but she had heard of his legend. If Queen Jandanero possessed a Dark Guardian, and was still concerned, bordering on fear, about Maloch, then he was a dangerous foe indeed.

Finally, it suggested that Dru had been so focused on her backtrail, watching for signs of Slythorne, she had missed significant potential threats that were very close at hand. For, a Dark Guardian was not something easily defeated. Dru was as well versed on the arcane as just about anyone in all of Stratvs, save perhaps the likes of the Warlock of the Marshes, and she was not aware of any way to destroy such a creation.

Momentarily, the Queen was brought in by her customary guard, carrying her on her large throne. As the constructs, and one Dark Guardian, set the throne in place, the ebony-skinned beauty that was Queen Jandanero allowed her eyes to drift up to Dru briefly, before they returned to some scroll in which she feigned interest.

"You may speak," the Queen said at length.

Dru glanced about the room, noting A'Ilys and several other drow courtiers and counselors.

"Perhaps a more private setting, good Queen," Dru offered.

Speak, Dru heard in the Queen's voice within her mind.

Of course, good Queen, Dru replied, attempting to hide her surprise at yet another indication that she'd been far too ignorant of her surroundings. *I am given to understand that you command a Dark Guardian. I have come to ask what I may offer you that would tempt you to loan me, and my agents, use of such a magnificent creation.*

His soul is not that of a champion, but of a family friend, Jandanero replied. *His soul belongs to one that raised me and saw to my tutelage when I was young. His soul belongs to one that protected me with his life, until the very end.*

I see.

I doubt that you do, Queen Jandanero thought/said. *I wanted you to have an inkling of my investment when I ask of you your Chaos Lord in return.*

Good Queen, I cannot.

Not his indenture, Jandanero replied, actually waving her hand to halt any further reply from Dru. *I simply need him to re-create the ritual he underwent. I want him to assist A'Ilys in becoming my own Lord of Chaos.*

From what I understand, we could not guarantee A'Ilys's safety, good Queen, Dru responded.

No need to guarantee his safety, the Queen continued. *If my Dark Guardian is not returned to me whole, and if A'Ilys does not survive the ritual, then you will give over Silas to me to command as I wish.*

Good Queen, if I may, you seem not surprised by any of this, nor are you surprised by my request. May I ask…

You may ask, but this is the only answer I will grant, Jandanero bluntly interjected. *I have many spies, those that walk on two legs as well as four or eight. I know much. Maloch of the Black Lance has been seen beyond the borders of Nolcavanor; thus, something dark and ominous is afoot. You are an educated creature, for a human. Your curiosity would someday overpower you concerning Leapold, my Dark Guardian. That was only a matter of time. If you think I've been unaware of Slythorne, then you insult me with how foolish you assume I am. If casting you out would change anything, make no mistake I would cast you out in chains of lexxmar with your flesh hanging in rags from your naked body. However, Slythorne would come here just the same to inquire after you, and I am not inclined, at the moment, to tolerate his self-righteous attitude. I reserve the right to change my mind in that regard at any time. Now I grow tired of explaining myself to one barely able to comprehend the intricacies of the drow mind. My Dark Guardian, for a time, in exchange for the services of your Lord of Chaos. I'm risking two servants, whereas you only risk one. Perhaps I grow generous as I age to maturity.*

Silas's services would have to wait until after this threat is quashed, Dru replied, still grappling with all the implications thrust upon her.

Understandably, Queen Jandanero responded. *Your word,*

on your soul and promised before one of my clerics in a minor ritual of binding, is good enough for me.

Dru, for the first time in a long time, felt something unusual. She felt afraid of losing something... someone she loved.

Agreed, Dru answered.

Verkial and Hallgrim, aided by Dru's teleportation spell, were securing their troops in Wodock the day after their meeting with Lynneare. Verkial needed to be with his men on the front in Tarborat, but steps needed to be taken here first. Soldiers fighting in Tarborat needed to know that Wodock was a safe harbor for them. They needed to know that a steady supply of food and reinforcements was virtually guaranteed as long as Verkial controlled the pirate city.

Verkial didn't like the idea of diverting any resource from Tarborat. However, he had been able to turn the building of a fortress in Wodock, or rather in the mountains beyond, into a means of boosting morale. The vast majority of his soldiers, a mix of many races, cultures, and species, were motivated by the idea of having something of their own. They were driven by the possibility of holding land where neither Ingshburn nor Eirsett nor any other puffed up lord or duke could tax them and meddle in their lives. Verkial promised an acre for each year of service in addition to their soldier's pay. The land was harsh and uninviting. It was a land of rough weather and rougher peoples of little or no laws. But, it was also a land where they could live as they chose, and that was enough.

Verkial was smart enough to know that the plan, long term, couldn't survive. He would need a government system of some sort to maintain a relative peace within his lands, to prevent anyone claiming rule as a despot, and to keep a standing army prepared and provisioned. He had decided those were troubles for another day, if he lived that long.

Wodock had gone smoother than he anticipated. He was no fool to let his pride get in the way of sound tactics. He had no doubt that Silas's display of destroying the wizards from the

Blue Tower and Lady Dru's appearance and apparent alliance were key to the locals accepting his rule. Verkial had the troops and means to seize and hold the city, but that would have been much more difficult, and costly. The news that mining operations would begin soon also bolstered his position among the merchants and citizens of the pirate outpost.

Verkial walked out from his keep overlooking Wodock proper and headed toward the secluded shed where his witch, Loucura, spent most of her time. She had been with Verkial for more than five years now and had served him faithfully during that time.

Verkial had been sent by Ingshburn to kill a witch, Loucura, that had been causing trouble among his soldiers in the mountains north of the Stone Throne. It seemed she had been peddling her wares, potions of magical effect, to Ingshburn's army. Some had decided the benefits provided gave them the strength they would need to challenge Ingshburn's rule. A Great Man by the name of Luebek led a hearty group of over seventy warriors with plans to recruit more. Verkial took only Hallgrim with him and put Luebek, and his coup, in the grave. In exchange for sparing their lives, Verkial gained the trust and loyalty of a few good warriors that day, and the fealty of one very talented witch.

That was the day he began building an army in secret. That was the day his plans for Wodock and Tarborat began to take shape. That was the day Verkial took his first step out of the shadow of Ingshburn.

As Verkial exited the gate to his keep, Raven's Nest, Hallgrim rose from a chair nearby where he'd been waiting.

"It's not like you to want to accompany me to the witch's lair," Verkial said, knowing Hallgrim must have something else on his mind.

"No, my lord," Hallgrim said as he took up his huge battle hammer and fell in step just behind and to the left of the warlord.

"Well?"

"I've been wonderin' about somethin'. That Duke of Chaos..."

"Lord of Chaos, go on."

"Yeah, that Lord of Chaos, Silas, what makes them so special? I mean there's nothin' easy about droppin' a champion, fallen or otherwise. But, I've done it. And, I've seen you do it more than once. So, what's the big deal with him?"

Verkial continued up the trail that wound into the foot-hills of the mountains, trying to decide how to explain the little bit that he knew about the abominations. They had been only legend for hundreds, if not thousands, of years, but now some fool had re-opened that can of worms. Actually, not just some fool, but a spoiled brat with a smarmy mouth and likely no head for politics or tactics whatsoever.

"You remember that ox that defeated you in those games during our respite in Dead Horse?"

"Sire, I was drunk, and had been fightin' in games all day that day, and I..."

"Shut up. You remember it, right? The game of Rope-Pull between you two?"

"I do."

"That ox was stronger than you," Verkial held up his hand to stop another protest from Hallgrim. "Just barely, but it still won the Rope-Pull. Tell me, did anyone in that crowd fear the ox?"

"Of course not," Hallgrim said with a confused look on his face. "Why would anyone fear an ox?"

"But they do fear you, right?"

"You're da..., yes, they do, my lord. They fear yourself as well."

"Why, neither of us is as strong as that ox."

"'Cause we're a danger to more than just piled up hay," Hallgrim said with a laugh. "Why, I remember this one time..."

"So, it isn't strength alone that makes something danger-ous, right?" Verkial waited for Hallgrim's nod and then con-tinued. "Champions are powerful, no doubt. They're strong.

But, they don't have any ambition, no drive. Some know how to use weapons, but they only know what they're taught. No champion ever invented a weapon or a new killing technique with blade or hammer. No champion ever devised a plan of battle or set up an ambush. The violence of this world is all man-made. A Chaos Lord, well, that's just a man with the strength of a demon at his disposal."

"So, like if I could teach that ox to swing my hammer..."

"No. It would be similar to you being able to take the strength of the ox and add it to your own, for you to control."

Hallgrim nodded and was quiet for a long time after that as they walked through the winding forest trail. Verkial was glad of the silence, for it gave him the chance to go over what he must say, and how he must say it.

Snow was falling, and winter was coming fast to the northlands, and by the time they reached the witch's shed, both Verkial and Hallgrim had their winter cloaks pulled tight about them. The smell of something cooking touched their noses, and Verkial heard Hallgrim's stomach growl.

"Please, come, my Warlord," Loucura said from within the shack as they entered the clearing before it.

The shack, a rough collection of castoff ship's planks and cargo crates, sat squat against the side of a hill. There were only three wooden walls to the chancy structure as the back side of it had been dug several feet into the side of the hill. It always sent a shiver down Hallgrim's back when the witch knew they were coming before they even arrived. It made him worry about what sort of curse she might put on him if he ever had to kill her for Verkial.

"It's cold, my lord," Hallgrim said when he noticed Verkial giving him a disdainful look, likely after seeing him shiver.

Verkial entered the shack first, followed closely by Hallgrim. The two were very large men and were forced to duck to the point of a near crawl to avoid upsetting the shambling hut. Verkial moved directly to the center of the dirt floor where Loucura sat, bent over a still bloody hide of some unfortunate beast. Hallgrim moved with his liege but kept his eyes moving about the interior of the hovel, as if any one of the various petrified creatures stored and strewn about might come to life and strike at him.

There were, of course, a large number of rats and spiders that scurried about the shack, and Kesstral, Loucura's scaly pangolin that was the size of a large dog. Any one of the living creatures in this abode could cause a stout heart to quail, but Hallgrim had always hated the dead things she kept about.

Loucura, who had appeared as an ancient hag to them on some visits and as a vibrant temptress on others, sat with her back to them, a dirty black shawl pulled up over her head, and leaned over the freshly skinned hide. She chanted under her breath, and Hallgrim felt his lower guts tighten.

Without any hesitation, Verkial walked around her to stand over the witch and the hide. As Loucura chanted, her hands swirled over the hide. She dropped one foul-smelling component after another into the still warm fatty tissue and blood on the animal skin. A small fog began to coalesce over the skin. Soon the fog was rolling at the edges and rotating counterclockwise about a foot above the floor. Verkial looked down into the center of the fog and spoke.

"Daeriv," Verkial said as his voice seemed to vibrate throughout the room and carry through the magical scrying fog Loucura had created. "Daeriv, above you."

Daeriv's fragile and bent form could be seen pacing back and forth in front of his opulent throne. He halted immediately and looked up, squinting his eyes as he did so. Lord Kyhn and Engiyadu, Daeriv's undead bodyguard, could be seen at the edge of the fog, their hands closing on weapon hilts.

Lord Kyhn, a Great Man of almost seven feet in height and weighing close to five hundred stone, was clad in his customary black steel plate armor with his deadly shrou-sheld at his side. His ashen skin seemed stretched tight over the bones of his face. Verkial knew him well enough to know he was very angry about something. Something he wasn't talking about.

Engiyadu, the ever cryptic undead ronin, wore no more than his simple blue silk pants and high black leather boots. His katana sat comfortably in the red sash he wore tied about his waist. Verkial had learned much from Engiyadu over the years; however, the primary lesson he'd taken away from his time studying with Blade Master Engiyadu is that someday he would have to find a way to kill him. Thus far, Verkial hadn't.

"Ah, is it Warlord Verkial now, or still only Captain?" Daeriv said derisively.

"You've squandered what little advantage you held in Lawrec, which will anger Ingshburn," Verkial said, ignoring Daeriv's jabs. "The Prince and his men will likely be pushing you from the land before long. I've seized Wodock, and my soldiers in Tarborat have their orders. My separation from Ingshburn has begun. Your failures will put you in danger, but any association with me after today will certainly set Ingshburn and most of Tarborat against you. There it is. You're down and in need, and I'm walking away from you. If you don't understand that, or hold a grudge, well... I don't care. I'm doing you a courtesy just by letting you know."

"How kind, Warlord Verkial," Daeriv said, managing to sound genuine. "You have saved us from making the tactical error of counting on your support. However, fear not, for we have made contingency plans."

"I never offered you my support," Verkial said flatly. "I offered you a chance to join me. You chose not to. I told you that was the wrong approach for Lawrec. Kyhn, Engiyadu, no hard feelings. Ingshburn understands your value and will know the failures in Lawrec should be laid at Daeriv's feet. This will have to be the last time we speak until the battle lines have settled."

"We understand," Lord Kyhn said with a thoughtful nod. "No need in all of us being exiled at once. Can we count on Wodock to be a friendly port if storms come?"

Verkial smiled.

"Always," Verkial said.

Verkial nodded to Loucura, who, with a quick wave of her hand, dispelled the magical fog.

"It would seem the Warlock was right," Verkial said, rubbing his clean-shaven chin thoughtfully. "Hallgrim, it looks like we have acquired dangerous allies."

"What warlock?" Loucura barked in her harsh, cracked voice.

"Nothing to concern yourself with... yet," Verkial said as he stepped around his witch and toward the single door of the shack. "Just the same, I'll want a few charms ready before the week's end. Some for defense against mental intrusions and some against breath attacks by dragons."

"Fire, frost, acid, water, or lightning?" Loucura asked, unphased.

"What?"

"What type of dragon attack?"

"Oh. I'm not sure, but its name is Isd'Kislota."

Verkial walked alone down a back street of Wodock; his path illuminated only by the full moon and its reflection on the snow-covered ground. He could hear the sounds of revelry echoing from the ships at port and several taverns along Horse Eater's Walk, the main street of the pirate city. The celebration had been going on for four days now.

It had been four days since he'd sent word to his generals at the front and his sea captains with their new orders; four days since he'd made his separation from Ingshburn final and sealed his bargain with his own armies. While his soldiers celebrated their liberation from Ingshburn and the Iron Gauntlet of Tarborat, Verkial waited for the King of the Stone Throne's response.

As Verkial looked up the abandoned street, he saw that his wait for that response would be short indeed. A dozen pirates and cutmen began to ease out of the shadows on both sides of the street ahead of him. A quick glance over his shoulder told him there were at least ten more closing in from behind him and from his flanks. He had been wondering when it would come and who it would be. He wondered no more.

"Captain Norost, I thought you smarter than this," Verkial said as he continued his pace up the street toward the gathering cutmen. "How much is he offering?"

"Seven hundred and fifty gold for your head, but he does want the head," Captain Norost, a huge man of uncommon girth, said as he stopped in the middle of the street. "Apparently, he has a need for displaying the head to discourage any others that might be having disloyal thoughts."

Verkial had known Captain Norost for over two decades. Anyone who laid eyes on Norost could tell he was a man of almost morbid obesity. Only his crew, and those who'd seen him fight and managed to live and tell of it, knew that all that fat hid a mountain of muscle and inhuman strength. Verkial had seen him pop a man's head and crush his skull in just one hand and had seen him tear the arm completely free of another. Norost was as dangerous as he was fat.

"Me and you?" Verkial asked as he continued stepping forward in that constant gait. "No blades or cudgels?"

"Now, why would I give you the chance to pull a rider's pike from a boot to stick me with when I can just have my men here fill you with arrows and bolts?" Norost asked with a laugh as he stretched his arms out wide.

"That's what I was thinking as well," Verkial said, his long stride bringing him ever closer to the twelve men gathered before him.

Verkial unbuckled the belt that secured his shrou-hayn to his back and let the large sword fall to the muddy snow in his wake. As the sword struck the ground, Norost's men began to raise their crossbows. They were, however, behind the curve of reaction time. For, when Verkial's sword hit the ground, the twang of crossbows resounded from the deep shadows and rooftops that surrounded them. In less than a second all but Norost and his bosun, Retten, were dead or dying.

Verkial's pace did not change. He did not slow. He did not speed up. He just kept marching toward Norost. Retten stepped to the side, moving his hands away from the cutlass that hung at his waist and wide out to his sides. Norost's lips pulled back in a smile that revealed a host of broken teeth.

"You really think..." Norost began.

That was all he was able to get out. Verkial had seen this all before. He knew it was only a matter of time before someone made the move, so his counter needed to be devastating. Verkial allowed most of his men free drink and women, for soon enough, they would all be sober and fighting for their lives. There were a carefully chosen few, however, who did not get to spend the previous four days drinking and carousing with tavern girls. Those men, quiet men, had been shadowing the new Warlord constantly.

Now Verkial had to tear down Norost. It was one thing to counter his ambush with an ambush of his own. Now he had to make a vicious example of the pirate captain. Verkial, a large man himself and a full foot and a half taller than Norost, had a deceptively long stride. In one step, he was inside Norost's defenses.

In one swift jab with his left hand, Verkial struck Norost in the throat. The blow wouldn't kill the pirate, although it certainly would have killed a smaller man. As Norost instinctively reached for Verkial's face and neck, Verkial swept his right arm under Norost's, grabbed his thumb, and jerked violently, wrenching the arm out to the side and down.

Verkial moved with the arm, striking the nerves in Norost's left armpit to numb the limb, and then sinking his teeth into the tendons that bound the pirate's forearm to his upper arm. Verkial continued to push Norost to the right, avoiding the pirate captain's right hand, while twisting and biting the left elbow. In the space of fewer than five seconds of terror, Norost's left forearm hung loose and ragged from the fatty and tattooed upper arm. Verkial continued to pace around the pirate in the same direction, kicking him violently in the back of the knee and dropping him to the ground.

Verkial bent, then, and pulled the bone axe from Norost's

belt. The axe had been looted from Zepute warriors Norost had captured many years before. It was the jawbone of some large creature that had been fitted with chips of volcanic glass. It had a vicious edge and was wickedly serrated. In Norost's hands, that axe had slashed many throats.

Verkial continued around Norost until he stood in front of him once more. Now, Norost's blood caking Verkial's face and running down his neck, Verkial addressed Norost and Retten.

"If these wounds don't kill you, then I want you to remember this encounter," Verkial said, the control in his voice barely containing his rage. "I want you both to remember and tell the others. Retten, your right hand."

Retten's face twisted with fear that he tried to mask with mock bravery. However, he was no fool. To leave here without a right hand would be better than not to leave this snow-covered street at all. Retten laid down and held his right hand out, making sure to place his wrist over the haft of a club dropped by one of his dead compatriots. He wanted the cut to be as clean as possible.

Verkial struck without further word or warning. The axe ripped Retten's hand free, and, just as he was beginning his scream, he saw the axe bite into Norost's left knee. Verkial made several quick hacks, during which Norost passed out. Then, taking the unconscious man's right hand, Verkial slowly cut off all but the thumb and smallest finger.

"You'll want to tie that wrist off with a good, strong belt," Verkial said to Retten. "You have some time before you'd bleed to death, but who knows how long it will be before you can find someone in Wodock to take you in. Take him with you, and bind those wounds of his as well. If I hear that you survived and Norost did not, then I will come for you. I will find you. You do not want that."

Retten nodded his head stupidly and began pulling the belt from the fallen man next to him. Verkial signaled to his men, collected his sword from the street, and walked back toward Raven's Nest, Norost's warm blood beginning to cool on his face.

CHAPTER VI
Asunder

"That's the best I can do," Maloch said as he returned to the deep shadows of the underbrush where Dunewell lay. "If I alter the spell any more then the results may become... unpredictable."

"It should be enough," Dunewell whispered back.

Dunewell looked again to the small meadow where he and Jonas first met Maloch and where now a small fire burned. It was perhaps an hour after the sun had set, and the two girls, neither had spoken a word to Dunewell or Maloch the entire time, sat and ate of Dunewell's smoked fish.

They had met Maloch in the afternoon, and Ranoct and his men should have encountered Maloch's time spell while the sun was still high in the sky. Maloch had adjusted the outcome of that spell, a dangerous proposition so that Ranoct would be exiting the spell at night. Dunewell was counting on the drastic change to their surroundings to, at the very least, give Ranoct and his men pause. The girls by the fire should be easy enough for them to see, and perhaps the whole scene would cause enough disorientation that Dunewell and Maloch wouldn't have too much trouble 'commandeering' horses.

"Pass me your rope," Dunewell said as he and Maloch crept around the meadow toward the area where Ranoct would likely emerge. "I have an idea."

Maloch did as Dunewell asked, having to shift one hand from the large tree limb he had procured as a weapon. Dunewell had pointed out that none of Ranoct's troops were to be harmed, and Maloch agreed whole-heartedly. Thus, clubbing weapons were all they carried.

As they stalked through the woods, Dunewell began tying loops in the rope, keeping them about eight feet apart. Once he'd tied more than a dozen loops in a single stretch of rope, he coiled it about one forearm. Dunewell and Maloch waited, both realizing that this time, the time of waiting, was the most dangerous for a soldier. Waiting is when soldiers fell asleep or when they grew too anxious. Waiting sometimes caused them to act too soon. Yet, Dunewell and Maloch were both seasoned warriors and knew the pitfalls of surveillance, and both handled the temptations of the slow moments with the stoicism of professional soldiers.

As they watched, the air before the glade began to shimmer like the air heated about a red-hot stove. The shimmering continued, quickened, until all at once eight stout horses were thrust upon the small grove, making a violent entrance, kicking up dead leaves all around, and stirring the fog of the night with their hot breath.

The experienced soldiers reined in their horses immediately, and weapons slipped from scabbards and rings with little to no effort. Each set of eyes among them scanned their surroundings, pausing only briefly on the two young girls sitting next to the campfire only a few yards away. The air was thick with the smell of cooked meat and freshly boiled stew, an idea suggested by Dunewell, who had traveled the hungry road of one in pursuit before.

There were nine of them, including Ranoct, who was at their lead. Ranoct hauled out his scimitar, a trophy from the deserts of Tarborat, and scanned the area while five of his men slipped from their saddles to encircle the small camp. The girls eyed them dangerously, and the red-headed girl hauled the short sword taken from the drow up from under her cloak. Dunewell stood ready to intervene, even if it meant his death. Fortunately, Ranoct's wisdom won out.

"Hold," Inquisitor Ranoct commanded his men. "Hold. Young ladies, we mean you no harm. We are men of the crown and pursue criminals against the throne. Are you in danger? Do you seek aid?"

"Drow took us," the young girl with the red hair said.

Dunewell's shock was complete when she managed to form the words and utter them. He was even more shocked by her next words.

"We were rescued by men, Great Men," she continued. "They left us here, three days ago, and said you would come. They said you were honorable and would see us back to our homes south of here. Homes only a few leagues north of Dolloth. There's stew, if you're hungry."

Ranoct and the rest of his men dismounted and approached while four took to the shadows around the small camp as scouts and lookouts. The horses were left behind, and ground hitched as war horses were trained to do.

Dunewell crawled on his belly up to each horse in succession, twisting the loops of the rope into figure 8's and slipping them over the front hooves of each horse in order to hobble them. He left three unfettered. The hobbled horses were now all linked to one common length of rope.

Dunewell took the reins of the other three and closed his eyes, saying a quick prayer to Bolvii and Silvor. He knew Ranoct's men would likely hear these three horses' movements through the dead grass and leaves, which made up the winter carpet of the forest. The noise would begin the moment he moved to lead them away from the glade, and he and Maloch would only have a few heartbeats of lead time. Dunewell picked their route through the trees and around a nearby outcropping of rock that would provide some cover should any of the kingsmen loose arrows or slings at them.

Dunewell took one last look toward the campfire and saw something curious. He was too far away to hear exactly what was being said now and could only hear the murmuring of voices. He could see the entire glade clearly, though. He watched as one of the girls, the taller one with red hair, shivered as though she were cold, pulled a pepper weed from near the campfire, and threw the weed into the flames.

Dunewell smiled and mounted the warhorse he was next to, a shining black mare with white mane and tail, wrapped the reins of the third horse around the saddle horn, and urged his own mount forward. Maloch, not one to falter, was in the saddle of his mount, a chestnut gelding, in almost the same moment. As they moved, the flames of the campfire shot up to engulf the entire spread of the pepper weed. The loud crackling sounds of each of the thousands of pepper seeds bursting in the heat masked all surrounding sounds for several seconds. The sudden sound drew the attention of even those scouts that had moved to the edges of the glade as sentries. The sudden bright flame ruined the night vision of all those about for several long moments as well.

Maloch was still recovering from the exertion of manipulating his initial time spell but did manage enough power to whisper a prayer and touch a large stone as they rounded it. Both he and Dunewell were tempted to give their horses their reins and charge from the area at full gallop, but the sound of the pepper seeds bursting was dying off already, and a horseshoe striking a stone would be heard for leagues around in the still winter night. Maloch took the lead and chose a path that took them toward a valley to the north.

Dunewell wondered why they were heading north when their destination was to the west, but, in spite of the fact that Maloch was a drow, Dunewell was coming to trust him. Whitburn had vouched for the paladin, of course, and Dunewell had seen him wield the power of Father Time, no mean feat. Yet, Dunewell had already begun to like Maloch before anything else began to influence his opinion. Dunewell had always had a nose for the true character of a person. He had, time and again, selected the right soldiers for different duties, and picked out the suspect of a crime before most of the evidence was gathered.

Those thoughts led him to think about his brother, Silas. Could he have been so wrong about his brother, or was there something there, something so substantial that it could make up for his sins? Was Dunewell allowing his desire of Silas's redemption to so strongly influence his actions? Is that why he so readily accepted Maloch's hopes of redemption, thinking that, if Maloch could gain forgiveness, then so to might Silas?

Those thoughts swam around in Dunewell's mind while his soldier's soul kept his ears alert for odd noises, and his eyes scanned their surroundings.

They continued north until the sun began to rise, and they were in the midst of a deep valley thick with tall trees. The air was crisp and still, and the strong smell of their warhorses brought memories back to both Maloch and Dunewell. Maloch rode into a small clearing where he dismounted, unsaddled his horse, and began to rub the horse's back and chest, whispering to his mount the whole time. Dunewell rode up next to him and did likewise with his mount and the third horse they'd brought for Jonas.

They unrolled heavy blankets that had been packed on the saddles and wrapped the horses with them. Then they found a sack of dried corn among the 'commandeered' packs and fed a few handfuls to each of the mounts. Once that was done, they hobbled the horses and released them to graze for what forage they could find.

Once the horses were cared for, Dunewell and Maloch sat cross-legged and back to back, as was the Silver Helm custom, and ate some of the smoked fish they had left.

"That was a clever fishing spear you put together by the Whynne," Maloch said, referring to the simple wooden spear Dunewell used to catch the fish he smoked. "I don't think I've ever seen one like it. Where did you learn to make it?"

Dunewell's thoughts went back to the first spear, the only other spear, he made like that. It was a pronged design using the natural fork of a stick that branched. With a small amount of whittling, the prongs were barbed, so once the fish was stabbed, it could not shake free. Lady Belyska had learned to make them from the Zepute when she had traveled to JunTeg, the one city of the jungle tribes.

His thoughts returned to her and his daughter, a daughter that should have been born by this time, in the year of the Wolf. He didn't expect to ever see or hear from Belyska again, much less his daughter, but, against the advice of his brain, his heart continued to hope.

"A woman then," Maloch observed without even having to turn.

"Yes," Dunewell finally managed. "A woman that I love."

"Love? Not loved, past tense?"

"No, not loved. I loved her then and love her still. I will always love her."

"I thought the vows of a Lord of Order forbade..."

"They do."

Dunewell's last words seemed to hit the air with a tone of finality; a cue Maloch did not miss.

"I would imagine you wonder why we rode north through the night," Maloch said, changing the subject promptly. "This valley, although out of the way and a bit more treacherous, leads up the back side of this slope and will allow us to approach our meeting place without silhouetting ourselves on a ridge or peak for our pursuers to see."

"I wondered about it, but I trust you," Dunewell said absently.

"Trust, really?" Maloch's tone made it clear he was surprised by Dunewell's statement, but Dunewell was also confident he'd heard hope in there as well.

"Trust, really," Dunewell replied simply. "We are still a day ahead of when we're to meet Jonas, right?"

"Yes."

"Since we've managed to get behind Inquisitor Ranoct and his troop, we should have some leeway there as well. I say we walk and lead the horses and let them rest as much as possible. Ranoct has pushed them hard to catch up to us as it is, and we may need their speed after we rejoin with Jonas."

"Agreed."

"Why haven't we had any trouble with giants or ogres?"

Dunewell asked, noting a few broken tree limbs indicative of one of the large creatures' passing.

"I'm sure we've been seen, smelled at the very least," Maloch said with a yawn. "But you travel with Maloch the Black Lance, the Knight of Sorrows, as far as they know anyway. We'll not be bothered by any giants or ogres any time soon."

"Get a few hours rest then," Dunewell suggested. "I'll keep watch."

The only response Dunewell perceived from Maloch was his gentle snoring that began after a few moments of silence. Dunewell, still sitting back to back with Maloch, couldn't see the northern horizon, but he could see the horses. These were quality war horses and well trained. They would let him know if any trouble came toward them from an unseen angle.

In the quiet hours of that concealed mountain valley, Dunewell took the time for true introspection. Dunewell's thoughts turned briefly to his mother, Lady Helena. He had loved her, of course, but it had always pained him to see the way she treated Silas, even when he was a young boy, as though his presence reminded her of a curse. That was much easier to understand now, knowing that Silas, through Helena's hand and not his, was a reminder of the fact that she had murdered her husband and Dunewell's father to share the bed of a lesser man. Dunewell had not taken the time to grieve the loss of his mother and certainly had not taken the time to acknowledge her crimes of adultery and mariticide. That led him to think of his brother.

Perhaps Silas was redeemable, Dunewell had to believe that forgiveness existed for any who truly sought it. However, forgiveness did not preclude consequences. Silas had murdered many, and, among that number, several innocents. He must face justice for that, even if forgiveness was asked for and granted. Silas must face adjudication. He had failed Silas; however, his regrets over that failure did nothing to mitigate Silas's culpability.

Dunewell's heart was at ease with this conclusion, and

thus he knew it to be the right one.

That matter settled, or as settled as it could be for now, Dunewell turned his thoughts to Lord Maloch. Of course, Maloch held no lands, nor did he serve the King in any capacity, but, in Dunewell's mind, the title of lord was one of respect that he believed Maloch had earned many times over. If a man's life were a scale, good deeds on one side and evil on the other, Dunewell doubted Maloch could ever tip the scales in his favor. However, Dunewell doubted any man really could. Dunewell himself had taken lives, both in battle and in summary executions. He knew other soldiers and knights who kept a count of those they'd slain. Dunewell never needed to, for he saw the faces of his dead almost daily.

Maloch had come to them, a drow, and a well-known villain to Jonas. He had expected earning a chance even to be heard would be difficult, if not impossible. So, who could Maloch be allied with that Dunewell and Jonas would hold in even greater contempt? Dunewell decided the first night at a campfire after they collected Jonas would be the time to have that talk. He doubted Jonas would let it go any later than that anyway. Dunewell closed that matter in his head as well and moved on to the next item he must consider.

Slythorne. Dunewell had never heard of Slythorne before coming to know Jonas, but he had faced many other vampires during his time in Tarborat. He knew them well enough to know that thralls were difficult for them to enslave much less control at a distance. Furthermore, the wills of soldiers, fighting men, were even more difficult for them to master. Slythorne had mastered half a dozen and manipulated them from leagues away.

If that weren't enough to indicate how truly dangerous Slythorne could be, he only had to think of his new companion, Jonas, aka the Gray Spider, and realize he'd been hunting Slythorne for several decades. It was not luck that kept Slythorne from Jonas's blade for all those years; it was cunning and power.

Dunewell knew Sir Brutis and Lord Velryk regretted letting a vampire, a master vampire, slip away from them in the years they served in Tarborat before Dunewell had joined them. Brutis and Velryk weren't the sort of men you asked about something like that, or anything else for that matter. Dunewell assumed if they didn't elaborate on the failure, there was likely a reason for it, and he had let it go at that. Now, based on what Maloch told him, he understood why it would be a sore subject for Velryk, and for Jonas.

Slythorne would be dangerous, even more so if encountered near the city where he would have such a source of potential thralls. Thus, they would have to lure him away from Moras somehow. They would have to also find a way to confine his movements. Master vampires were dangerous enough with their usual combination of martial prowess and advanced repertoire of magic. They were almost impossible to slay when the battlefield offered room for flight. Fortunately, their curse required a deep, dark place to rest, hidden far from the sun and its killing light. Thus, if a man could find their lair, he stood a chance. If not...

Dunewell knew Moras, her streets, and the mountainous regions around her. He had no doubt there were caverns inhabited by creatures more akin to Slythorne's ways of thinking than his own. The channels of Moras would limit his movements; thus, Dunewell decided it would be best to begin a map of Moras that both Maloch and Jonas could study and on which they all could confer. They would also need weapons of silver or Roarke's Ore, blessed if possible, and Churchwood. Water from an altar from any of the churches would be helpful, though it was not as effective against a master as it was other types of vampires.

Jonas's, or rather Ruble's, resources of House De'Char might be very helpful, but Dunewell couldn't rely on them in his planning. He did want to keep all possibilities on the table, though. Dunewell would have to be disguised because of the King's Warrant. Maloch would have to be disguised because of his race. Dunewell hoped, given Jonas's proclivities regarding stealth and subterfuge, their identities wouldn't be too much a problem. He decided those topics would hold for now until he had a chance to speak with Jonas.

Those items sorted as much as they could be, Dunewell turned his mind to Stewardess Erin and the enchantment she had cast on him. The spell was clearly one to influence him to be romantically involved with her. But why? Dunewell was no rube, and women had tried to ply him before. Furthermore, he had faced the spells of witches and vampires that sought to control his mind and exercise some modicum of control over his actions. Never had he been taken in so thoroughly and unsuspectingly. The spell had been a powerful one.

Erin's motives, and possible cohorts, might not tie into the other problems in Moras, but he must keep the possibility in mind. He must remember there is someone out there who is after him and that someone has access to powerful enchantments. Dunewell wracked his mind but could think of no shadowy enemies of his past that might be lurking and hoping for a chance to ensnare him. No former foes or detractors came to mind.

There were also parts of Erin's history that were a mystery to him. He did know her as a child and was aware that she had been back in Moras for a few months before the murders of Killian and Helena. Yet, now that he thought about it, he had no idea where she had been in the interim. Then his inquisitor's mind finally took hold of a thought. He found it quite suspicious that she should arrive only weeks before her uncle's sudden death and be the only one remaining to inherit House Theald. He knew Silas had killed Rugan, but how could Erin have known that would happen? *Had there been another plan in the offing to murder Rugan and Silas simply beat them to it?*

This, too, would have to keep until he had more information. Thus, Dunewell stirred the components of what he knew and what he guessed into the usual mixture in his mind and let his under-mind work the puzzle. This talent, this ability of his, was among the reasons he was chosen to be an inquisitor and was approached by the Sword Bearers to become part of their brotherhood.

So, Dunewell ate of his smoked fish, had a drink from his waterskin, and enjoyed the quiet beauty of this snowy forest. As the sun passed to the western side of the mountains of Nolcavanor, a shadow stretched across the narrow valley. Dunewell guessed it no later than three hours past luncheon but decided they needed to move. The horses, and Maloch for that matter, had their rest, and it was time to find Jonas.

Dunewell gave a slight shrug and heard Maloch's breathing behind him change immediately.

"Do you need any rest?" Maloch asked in a clear, and surprisingly unmuddled tone.

"No, I can push on."

"Very well then," Maloch said as he rose from the ground and brushed dead leaves and snow from his trousers and cloak.

It was cold, but not so cold as to put out two soldiers the likes of Maloch and Dunewell. With night coming on, it would become colder still, and the horses would fare better if they were on the move.

They rubbed all three horses down and re-saddled them. The warhorses seemed eager to be on their way, so, once mounted, Maloch and Dunewell gave them their heads and allowed them to gallop through the snow and among the trees for the first half-hour. As they neared the point of the valley where it rose sharply, they reined in, and Maloch studied the pass.

"Any chance it is snowed in?" Dunewell asked.

"Very unlikely," Maloch replied, not taking his eyes from the mountainside.

"So, why are we stopped here?"

"I'm giving any ogres or giants along the way a chance to see me," Maloch responded matter-of-factly. "I've no doubt either of us could handle any in this region without too much trouble, but, just the same, I'd rather avoid it if possible."

"There's none up there," Dunewell said, without really

thinking about it. "The way is clear."

"How could you know that?"

Dunewell didn't have an answer to that question. He just *knew*. He suspected it was an aspect of Whitburn, one that he had yet to explore or had the chance to come to understand. Dunewell was beginning to think of being a Lord of Order as much like having a newly purchased and highly trained horse. The horse was usually smarter than the rider, but the rider was in charge. There was also a period during which the rider had to learn the horse's personality, capabilities, and limitations. The horse had to learn the same things about the rider.

Maloch led the way on the chestnut; Dunewell swapped to the third horse, a dappled white mare, and led the black mare, giving her a chance to rest. They were able to ride for the first several hours, however, as they climbed, the trail narrowed and became more treacherous. Furthermore, it was a cloudy night, and there was no light from the moon or any stars, making the path difficult for the horses to find. Thus, Maloch and Dunewell, each with his own means of superior vision in the dark, dismounted and walked the rest of the night, leading the horses behind them.

They snacked on dried fruit and hard bread they'd discovered in one of the packs, their eyes on the rocky outcroppings around them, and their minds on the road they must now walk. Dunewell felt much better about what was to come simply from having had a few hours to collect his thoughts and order them. Now his under-mind could work on those problems freeing his upper-mind of the worry. He knew he would have to make time to grieve the loss of his mother, the news of what she had done, and all that had transpired with Silas. However, having spent years in Tarborat, he knew he could do that in increments, or put it aside until he did have the time. It was one of those tricks that soldiers must learn that cannot be taught.

"He's just up ahead, along a path to the right," Dunewell whispered to Maloch.

Dunewell knew that, other than Jonas nearby, they were

alone, but he didn't want his voice to carry too far in the crisp night air.

"Jonas is?" Maloch asked.

"Yes."

"You see him?"

"No, well, not really."

"What are his intentions?"

"He's planning on following us for a while to make sure that we weren't followed," Dunewell said, not really thinking about it. "Then he'll approach from the dark and try to walk right up on us, so he can make himself seem even more superior to us and keep us guessing as to the true extent of his capabilities."

Dunewell heard Maloch chuckle softly.

"What?" Dunewell asked, a bit loudly.

"You have the *sight*, but you don't know it yet," Maloch said. "Lord Mandergane, the legendary paladin who carried Shrou-sheld Blancet, had it. Only he and the few Lords of Order I knew of possessed the ability."

"I don't follow."

"You know where Jonas is."

"Well, yes, but that's a simple matter of..."

"How do you know what he's thinking?" Maloch interjected.

"I..."

"You don't know, but you feel it," Maloch said. "The *sight* can see a man though he's hidden and can see a man's heart even though his tongue may lie. It will likely take some practice, and time, to learn to use it, but you have it. It could be a powerful ally."

"Be warned, though," Jonas's voice came to them from the dark ahead and still out of Maloch's sight. "It can become a crutch. Never neglect what your eyes see or what your nose smells. Shadow Blades have a way of fooling the magic of the *sight*."

"Magic?" Dunewell asked.

Jonas emerged from the shadows ahead of them and made his way quietly along the treacherous path.

"What do you call your use of the champion's powers?" Jonas asked.

"It seems like more than magic; feels like more than magic," Dunewell said.

"Because it is very close to the arcane source," Maloch chimed. "All enchantments come from the same source, the arcane power. It is a combination of the three types of magic. It is the type of power the gods use, and thus, very close to what you have access to through your champion."

"So, even more potent than the spells of a paladin?" Dunewell asked.

"By far," Maloch and Jonas both answered, unintentionally in unison.

Jonas approached Dunewell and held out a hand for the reins of the third horse. Dunewell passed them over, and Jonas fell into line behind Dunewell and Maloch. Maloch led them on for several long moments before any of them spoke again. They all seemed to realize what must be said between them next was essential to all of them, and as fragile as Jonas's trust in Maloch.

"Your brother also has such power," Maloch said, finally breaking the silence that had fallen on them with such weight in the darkness. "His is a twisted version, but potent just the same. He cannot be permitted to align himself with Slythorne. We don't believe that likely, but it is one possible outcome that could be catastrophic."

"Putting it bluntly, the Lord High Paladin here wants to manipulate you into being a weapon against your brother and the evil he has become," Jonas said, just loud enough to be heard over the sounds of hooves striking stones. "Just as I hope to employ you as a weapon against Slythorne and whatever minions he is able to conjure. We both want to use you, and it would seem that our goals may align. So far as being blunt goes, we have also yet to learn of the drow's mysterious partners."

"This trail will lead us to a high crou-mountva, a small

glade near one of the mountain peaks," Maloch said, waving to the north. "That small grove is surrounded on all sides by high stone walls and thus is protected from the wind and the eyes of the outside world. We could have a fire and perhaps some proper rest for us and the horses. I thought that a good place for our palaver."

"Seems reasonable," Dunewell said, for he too was anxious to get a few problems out in the open. "How did you fare against the drow?"

Dunewell had seen the sword hilt, presumably of Jonas's new Shyeld-Hayn, protruding from the heavy drow cloak Jonas had wrapped it in. What he had seen looked to be a silver, or possibly Roarke's Ore pommel and crosspiece, divided by a hand and a half grip wrapped in a cable of red wire. The cloak had only slipped from the handle briefly, when Jonas had tied it to the saddle of his horse, allowing Dunewell a quick glance.

"I finished my sword," Jonas said without any fanfare or brag. "Credit where credit is due, I miss traveling with a paladin that can manipulate time. However, I've never known any that could manipulate the hours and days as you have. I planted the torn clothing of their captives among one faction and returned the offending dagger to its owner, who was found out shortly thereafter. You wanted in-fighting that diminish their numbers. They are most assuredly on that path. Speaking of..."

"Turned over to Inquisitor Ranoct and his men without trouble," Dunewell answered the unfinished question. "They are safe and should buy us all the time we'll need."

"Should," Maloch echoed, emphasizing the many uncertainties that faced them.

They walked higher up along the trail pointed for the north peak, the only sounds those of the wind through the decreasing trees and the subdued clacks of hooves against stone. As they walked, Dunewell noticed Jonas eating smoked fish and jerky from the pack and draining a waterskin. He felt bad then, for not realizing how hungry Jonas must have been. It had been a few days for Dunewell and Maloch, but to Jonas, thanks to Maloch's time spell, it had been closer to a week and a half.

Near midnight the three tired warriors crested a rise and found the slim crevice that led to Maloch's hidden mountain grove. Dunewell noticed the change in temperature and environment immediately. The air was at least ten degrees warmer, and there were several tall pines and aspens crowded into the crou-mountva that was no more than six or seven acres in size. He had not realized how the north wind had been chilling them until being greeted by the unusual warmth of this small meadow.

Within an hour, they had a comfortable fire going, stew comprised of what was left in their packs was cooking, and the horses had been rubbed down, fed, and were now grazing on winter rye. Jonas poured stew into his cup, even though he'd been taking small bites for hours from their other stores. Dunewell watched as Jonas drank his stew with the evident appreciation of a warm meal that only an old soldier can demonstrate. Dunewell began to order his thoughts and anticipate the different possible arguments Maloch and Jonas might make, and settle his own mind about what he had learned thus far. When he felt ready for this conversation with Jonas and Maloch, Dunewell looked up only to find Jonas quietly snoring as he sat against the base of a tree, empty cup still in his hand.

Dunewell turned to see the smile on Maloch's face.

"He must have been exhausted to choose sleep over his chance to rake me over the coals," Maloch said, still sporting his wry grin. "Give me an hour to meditate, and then I will watch for you both."

Dunewell nodded and took up his hammer and cloak as Maloch sat and pulled his feet to cross in front of him and begin his trance. Dunewell wrapped himself in his heavy cloak, poured himself one more cup of stew, and walked out from the campfire. He kept his eyes and ears trained on the dark that surrounded them, alert for potential dangers, and let his under-mind monitor them. This freed his upper-mind for thought.

He had worked out his plans the day before and knew

the dangers of second-guessing oneself. Thus, he let those rest and sent his mind to thoughts of Lady Belyska. Thinking of her had the same effect as a warm hearth during a winter's gale. He knew it was fruitless, but in the pain of knowing she was lost to him, there was also the comfort of his love for her, and hers for him.

During his walk, Dunewell discovered a small stream that flowed casually from one of the higher points around the crou-mountva, across the back third of the small valley, and disappeared through a tunnel at the base of another cliff face. He drank deeply from the stream, both quenching his thirst and refreshing Whitburn. After another long draft, Dunewell led the horses to the stream and allowed them a good long drink as well.

Dunewell walked the perimeter almost ten times before Maloch offered to assume the watch. Dunewell downed another cup of stew and rolled himself into a heavy blanket taken from one of the warhorses. Peaceful, contented sleep came for him for the first time in a long time.

Dunewell awoke to the smell of roasting meat and boiling coffee; how he had missed the smell, the taste, of good coffee. He rose and rubbed the sleep from his eyes as Maloch handed him what he guessed was a roasted pigeon, and Jonas poured a cup of coffee.

"Are we ready for our palaver, then?" Dunewell asked as he took a sip from the cup.

"It may be shorter than you two anticipate," Jonas said, causing Dunewell some concern about what Jonas presumed might shorten it. "My nephew's wedding you attended earlier this year, he wed Clairenese, did he not?"

Maloch's eyes closed, and he let go a slight sigh. He had hoped to solidify a relationship with these two before they learned of the others with which he was allied. Dunewell's expression made it clear he did not recognize the name, or what it indicated.

"She's the daughter of the Warlock of the Marshes, the Original Betrayer, Lynneare," Jonas said, taking his eyes from Maloch to glance at Dunewell and ensure his news was given its proper weight. "Lynneare, who was once the Supreme Pontiff of Time and priest to this one here. Lynneare, whose absolute vanity brought the Battles of Rending upon our ancestors."

Jonas gestured toward Maloch with his coffee cup upon making that point. Then Jonas paused to take a long drink from the steaming mug and give Maloch time to interject or offer some weak explanation. To his credit, Maloch remained seated and calmly sipped coffee from his cup and waited for Jonas to finish.

"That being the case, and knowing that a few powerful paladins of Time can manipulate it, but only the priests of Time can foretell it, I assume it is Lynneare who has cast those powerful spells. That would mean that he has found a way to somehow repair his relationship with Father Time and, I'm guessing here, that my foolish nephew also gave him the Hourglass that holds the Sands of Time. How am I doing?"

Maloch sipped his coffee and nodded.

"How could you have learned so much in such short time and while surrounded by drow?" Dunewell asked, letting his curiosity get the better of him.

"In my travels, I have discovered other powers of mentalism which very few understand, and even fewer can practice," Jonas said. "Some allow me to communicate over vast distances with my network of spies and informants. Furthermore, the Hourglass of which I spoke was taken from Nolcavanor not long ago by that same nephew of mine. Some of the drow in your hole talked of the day you lost the duel to him and then let him just walk out of your lands. Thus, it is not a terrible leap of reasoning to deduce he offered the Hourglass as a dowry for the hand of Lynneare's youngest daughter. Since Lynneare's other children have all betrayed him in their own ways, it makes his son-in-law heir to whatever cursed treasures rest in his vaults. Thus, Maloch here hopes that my ties to a family member I've never met will influence me to join with them, or at least aid them in securing your help."

Jonas sat back, clearly proud of himself, and believing the matter resolved. His facial expression changed only slightly when he heard what Maloch had to say, but just enough for Dunewell to notice it.

"That is sound reasoning," Maloch admitted. "You would have made a fine drow or treacherous warlock yourself, for you have the outlook and the heart for it. You have hunted assassins and even Shadow Blades. You, Dunewell, have been a King's Inquisitor and a fine one at that. So, watch me now and tell me if you detect any lie in what I'm about to say. Lynneare does have the Hourglass and has used the Sands of Time, a feat only possible if one be in the good graces of Father Time. Your nephew married Lady Clairenese because he loves her and for no other reason. No dowry or offering of any sort was made by either side beyond the vows of love and protection exchanged between the bride and groom. Slythorne is a great evil, and we want to help you destroy him. We will likely need your brother, Silas, to cooperate with us, for we will need his mistress's help. Make no mistake, we will hunt Slythorne no matter what you decide, but our hunt stands the best chance of success if we join together. Otherwise, many will likely die."

Dunewell nodded his agreement and was surprised to hear Jonas scoff. Jonas rose from the camp, quaffed the remainder of his coffee, and stepped away quickly toward the horses. He saddled his horse with practiced speed and efficiency and then rode back toward the small camp.

"I take you're with them?" Jonas asked Dunewell.

"Yes," Dunewell said, not surprised that Jonas disapproved but stunned by his rash and rude behavior.

"Then, luck to you both," Jonas said as he reined his horse from the camp and trotted off into the morning frost.

CHAPTER VII
Fresh Scent

On a moonless night, when the chill in the air cut a man to the bone, a heavy fog rolled over the docks and streets of Moras. The sailors knew the fog wasn't natural. Priests of failing faith quailed in their slumber, unsure what evil troubled their shriveled hearts. The watchmen of Moras instinctively patrolled in pairs this night, and even the boldest of rogues found a crowded hearth or boisterous tavern where they might sulk in the corner, in relative safety. Slythorne, now so far removed from the Master Templar Truthorne that had been, walked the pale marble streets of the city as a roaring lion might stroll unafraid among the rabbits of the field.

Slythorne and Ashdow, sometimes known as Jasper Marshal of Levon and, in another time, called Kelmut the Fierce, arrived together in this great northern city of commerce. Ashdow, owing to a tradition of his guild, refused to make a move within Moras until he had made contact with another of his number there. It seemed a matter of courtesy that they notify one another when operating in an area previously claimed. Furthermore, Ashdow had expressed a desire to meet with this Lady Evalynne before beginning the tasks set before him by Slythorne.

Thus, Slythorne walked these passages alone. The feeble light from the lanterns lining the street seemed to shy away from his charcoal overcoat, and high-top boots of black leather. Even the finely crafted breastplate of mercshyeld he wore all but refused to give off a glint in the close atmosphere. Slythorne walked with his left elbow resting on the hilt of his beautiful longsword, which bore the crest of that all but extinct family that history had forgotten.

He tested the air with his nose and his tongue, seeking signs of his lost and lovely Dru. He could taste the fear in a paladin's sweat, and smell the urine that stained a cleric's vestments. He detected the sweet scent of a maiden virgin's first castoff of blood, signaling her entry to womanhood. He noted the acrid tinge of a hearty inquisitor's adrenaline as his quarry maneuvered nearby.

Slythorne walked past an archway that led to a small garden, covered in snow now. His thoughts, his memories, returned to a time when the roses in that garden, famous roses, were in bloom, and a boy templar walked with a young girl. He thought of a time when this city went by another name. Those memories saddened, darkened, when he thought about the last day he spent in that long-ago city. The last day he walked the surface of Stratvs free of the scorn of the gods. The last day he spent as a man.

Father Time and Mother Fate had seen fit to destroy his House with famine and war. As his thoughts drifted to his lineage, his thumb traced over the crest embossed on the hilt of his dagger; the twin spears behind the two-headed dragon; the meaningless crest of a forgotten family. On that day, the last day of Ivory Rose, the gods smote the last son of that lost line.

Anger welled within him in a flash, a violent rage that he quelled with no small strength of will. He had wasted decades, centuries, pounding the sky and the stone in anger at those now mute deities. He had screamed, wept, raged, and lain fallow.

He would not be taken from again. He would allow no loss. He was Slythorne, master vampire and Lanceilier, once of the Old Code. It was for him, and him alone, to summon and dismiss. It was time to see that his Lady Dru understood that.

Slythorne could smell her too, although very faint. He could feel that she'd spent much time here, or near the city. She had been a wonderful companion, but she never understood how complete her life could be if she would simply obey. She was the most brilliant person Slythorne had ever known, and yet she couldn't understand the basic fact that her obedience would lead to her happiness.

There was another smell, a unique taste, somehow tied to Dru's scent. Slythorne let his nose lead him as he strolled through the dim marble streets of Moras. His feet brought him to a manor, some paltry estate with the name Morosse in twisted iron over the gate. Part of the trail was here, but this was only one branch of this dead tree and was missing something... dark. He had no doubts he could convince some servant to invite him inside but decided that would likely be a waste of time and effort.

Slythorne continued through the byways and alleys of Moras, taking great care to avoid the flowing waters of the channels, of course. Master vampire and Lanceilier he might be, but some laws even he had to obey. The next trace of Dru and this other contaminant he detected was across one of these channels and off to the southwest. He took a moment to memorize his surroundings, although such precautions had become second nature to the well-traveled Slythorne.

Then, in no particular hurry for the long centuries had taught him to be patient, he strolled to the southeast, toward the city wall. The route took him far out of the way, but the wall was no barrier to those as skilled in the use of magic as he. With hardly a glance from Slythorne, the minds of the guards posted along the wall went blank as their jaws hung slack from their faces. Slythorne, already appearing as barely a shadow, faded and faded until his corporeal form was no longer in the plane of the living. In this ethereal state, Slythorne passed through the indomitable marble of the city wall as though it was no more than a vapor.

Slythorne then continued in this non-corporeal state and drifted past the small farms and ranches just outside the city wall. He remained on his southeast course until he was a few leagues into the mountains beyond the city. Once far beyond the stone of Moras, its streets honeycombed with passages and caverns, Slythorne approached the stream that flowed out of the mountain range and became the channel that surged through the marble foundations below. The presence of the symbol of life was poignant, and he could feel its course through the rock of the mountainside.

Slythorne resumed his physical state and summoned only a small portion of his immense power to bring force to bear on a few rocks from above. In short order, there was a tumble, although Slythorne's magic ensured the movement was silent, and several large stones began to dislodge. The stones, caught in the air by the force of Slythorne's will, were lowered to the stream, now much tamer. As the flow of water slowed to a stop, Slythorne stepped across the waterworn surfaces to the west side of the stream. Once secure there, Slythorne turned the stones to dust with barely a thought. The stream began to flow once more, and no one would notice any change in the city far below.

Slythorne took on his non-corporeal form once more and traveled back into the city. After only a few moments, the scent he was following led him to an unusual and confusing sight. The dirt had been turned, but a large structure had burned to the ground here, and within the past year or two. Many had died, most were children, but that was only part of the darkness he sensed here. There was... not torture, not precisely, but some sort of prolonged and intentionally inflicted pain.

Nearby there were traces of an odor he'd not encountered since Nolcavanor was cast down, not since the day of Slythorne's curse. He detected the barest remnants of the Lord of Order's stink. He had teased the boy in Split Town whose mind he'd invaded but didn't really wish to be bogged down with the likes of a Lord of Order. Slythorne had no illusions about their potential. The presence of that smell now confirmed the other dark scent he'd followed, that of a Chaos Lord. Slythorne was also well aware of how dangerous a Chaos Lord could be. Any individual that could master a fallen champion was one worth considering, and not one to underestimate.

Order and Chaos had done battle here. Slythorne didn't understand it, but knew this spot, this location, was somehow important. He took great care in committing the details of this spot to memory.

A Lord of Chaos, it made sense, of course. To his knowledge, there had never been one without another, but there was something different about these two. The fact that they originated in the same city was unusual, for legend had it, they were formed only when separated by great distances. They were, of course, inexorably drawn to one another, but many times that had taken decades. There was something else, something he was missing.

He decided he must put Ashdow on this trail, to learn of this Chaos Lord and his ties to the Lord of Order. Ashdow's tasks were beginning to stack up; however, Slythorne had complete confidence in him. After all, the wily assassin had managed to evade Jonas of Ozur these many years.

Just as he was leaving, just as he was allowing his mind to chew over the implications of Order and Chaos engaged in personal combat, he caught her scent. Her trace was mixed with the more potent smell of young blood; boys, no older than ten or perhaps twelve. He had almost missed the traces of her in the overriding succulence of such young blood. Boys, two, maybe as many as four, had been on her trail; had stood in a location to which she had teleported. The traces of her magic were mingled with the vibrant taste of youth.

As the sun struggled against the cloudy winter morning at the edges of the eastern peaks, Slythorne lowered himself into a cavern beneath the awakening streets of Moras. He drank in the smell, the taste, of Dru's magic that lingered in the air. He now picked up a new smell that only slightly tinted her trail; the smell of drow.

Slythorne had kept himself to a circuit among the western portions of Lethanor, the islands of the Disputed Isles, and the cities of Lavon and Degra these last few centuries. The territories to the northeast held far too many memories for him. Thus, he was not terribly familiar with the territories surrounding Moras. The mountains nearby were prominent, and he was well aware of the elven forest of sectot wood to the south. Being among the originally cursed, and having developed the powers of that curse, Slythorne was troubled by sunlight, but not so much so that he had to avoid it altogether. Young vampires were verily destroyed by Merc's great kiln. Slythorne's skin would turn, and over time develop a rash, from contact with common silver, but the only metal that could slay him was pure Roarke's Ore, and it was rare enough. Weapons of bone and wood were ridiculous, with two distinct exceptions. Churchwood, if prepared properly, could end his existence, and sectot wood, any simple branch of sectot wood, could destroy him. Thus, he was well aware of the vast forest, the only forest, where it grew.

As to the connection to the drow, the mountains surrounding Moras provided plenty of possibilities, an abundance of possibilities, and that thread would have to be explored in another way. Perhaps Ashdow could learn something from the fair Lady Evalynne in that regard as well. The stubborn assassin refused to allow Slythorne to enter his thoughts to communicate with him mentally; thus, Slythorne would have to return to their inn. He took a moment to memorize this place under the dark stone of Moras, and to be certain of the smell of the boys.

Then Slythorne closed his eyes and envisioned his room at Despion's Rest, the inn belonging to House Despion. He saw in his mind's eye the greens and browns of the curtains and bedding, a color scheme in keeping with House Despion's trademark. Slythorne didn't care for the colors, but the innkeepers had taken an extra step in hospitality by placing a wooden shingle upon each door of the inn, which simply read, 'welcome.' To a person in his position, well, he did much prefer being welcomed; his curse required it.

Now he pictured those tacky greens and browns, the dark wood of the door, the exact location of the shaving basin in the room... and he opened his eyes and was there. Ashdow, ever cautious and ready, was sheathing the sliver of a blade he had apparently snatched from his sleeve when Slythorne suddenly appeared in the room.

"I thought you would be in your own room," Slythorne said as he stepped across to close the shutters of the window.

"That's why I'm not in it," Ashdow replied. Then he looked to the window and the morning sun. He watched for a moment as it struggled to defeat the bleary start of the day. After another heartbeat, he said, "I know it's a bit pedestrian, but don't you think it would be better to be seen returning to the inn instead of leaving curious servants to wonder how you returned without them seeing you?"

Slythorne only responded with the toss of his hand as he strode to the side of the bed and laid a blanket on the floor. As he laid the blanket down, he saw Ashdow's eyebrow raised in a silent question.

"There is a Chaos Lord about as well as a Lord of Order," Slythorne said as he began to undress and hang his gear on the provided armor tree nearby. "I don't have an adequate understanding of their capabilities yet, but I don't want either of them to easily determine exactly where I lay my head."

"A Chaos Lord? You don't think either could achieve the Sleeper's Curse, do you?"

"I don't know, but I don't want to find out by encountering them in the halls of my mind. Speaking of, see what you can learn from Lady Evalynne about these Lords of Order and Chaos. There is something... unusual that ties them together. Of course, they always seemed to come in pairs, one of Order and one of Chaos, but usually, when they meet, only one walks away from the encounter. There is also a drow presence in Moras. See what she knows. Surely, I don't need to tell you not to tip your hand..."

It was Ashdow's turn to respond with a gesture, a very subtle, and quite offensive one. Slythorne smiled in return. Ashdow began across the room to the door, and Slythorne stretched out on the blanket he'd placed on the floor.

"There was something significant about a dirt lot near the graveyard," Slythorne said as Ashdow's hand touched the lock. "There'd been a fire there, not too long ago. That may provide the needed clue."

Ashdow's face shifted from the clean-shaven, hawkeyed visage so well known to Slythorne to the rosy and ruddy face of a merchant fond of drink early in the morning. His body also took on weight, making him appear at least eighty stone heavier. His clothing changed to fine silks and leathers of blue and gray, the colors of House Wellborne of Split Town and Ivantis.

"Anything else?" Ashdow asked in a distinct, southern accent.

"The drow are the key, but I'm quite curious about this Chaos Lord. He might prove valuable if we have to face the Lord of Order. Be mindful of potential leverage on that front."

"Always. Also, I'll want my final payment *before* you decide to face either the Chaos Lord or the Lord of Order. Are we clear on that point?"

Slythorne drew himself up to lean on a single elbow.

"You won't consider something more... reasonable?" Slythorne asked.

"I will not."

"Very well," Slythorne said as he reclined onto the heavy blankets. "Very well."

Two hours later, Ashdow, now posing as Danmorgan, a merchant captain of House Wellborne, sat having coffee at a street café near the dock. He had left their signal, the Sign of the Twelve, on the twelfth post on the twelfth dock, north to south, of the city.

The Sign of the Twelve was a simple scrawl easily confused with lude graffiti or the initials of some mischievous, but lettered, child. The Sign changed from month to month, and region to region, with small, seemingly insignificant, scratches, or marks that appeared to be mistakes. These small marks were predetermined by the Shadow Council every few years to coincide with specific details that could be determined by the environment. For example, if it was the month of Setch and you were north of the Whaler's Rest, a tavern in Modins, then the largest of the twelve marks was to be made on the upper righthand area of the pictogram. If you were south of the Whaler's Rest, the mark was to be made on the lower righthand side of the series of marks.

Ashdow had left an invitation to Ramschel. The Shadow Blade, sometimes called Ramaj, claimed Moras as his home, and the place he conducted business. It wasn't exactly a requirement that Shadow Blades notify one another when operating in their staked territory, but it was usually the wise choice. Given their particular method of ascension, Ashdow didn't want Ramschel to discover his presence by accident and jump to the conclusion that Ashdow was in Moras to kill him.

A young woman was selling chunks of wood, driftwood mostly and the scavenged remains of shipping crates, across the street from Ashdow. As he watched, a beggar began an argument with the young woman, asserting his own claims to that particular portion of the public right of way. Ashdow picked up on the man's wild gestures, along with a few keywords that were misused in his berating of the young woman, that confirmed he had received Ashdow's message.

Ashdow responded with his own set of signals, gestures, and postures, all subtle and all deftly communicative. These two men, several yards apart, held a wholly concealed conversation on a busy street in view of dozens of witnesses with no one the wiser.

Here on a job? the beggar asked through their complex language of signs.

Yes, nothing to do with you or me, or our apprentices, Ashdow responded.

Time frame?

Days, maybe weeks. Ashdow signaled. *If it is to go beyond two weeks, I'll let you know.*

My apprentices could use the coin, if you find yourself in need of leg work, leave a message at the Marble Flagon. Leave it with the barkeep addressed to Redding.

Understood.

With that, the two parted ways, the beggar losing his argument with the young woman and Ashdow dropping a coin for his coffee and going about his day. In moments both had vanished from the street.

Ashdow cycled through three different appearances as he walked the next two city blocks, always careful that any view of him was obstructed by crates stacked on the street, or a coach parked and awaiting passenger and driver. Sometimes he merely turned into and then back out of a side street or alley. He had no reason to believe Ramschel would move against him, but Ashdow hadn't made it to the ruling council of the Shadow Blades by making assumptions regarding his safety.

He walked two more blocks until he reached Lower Market Street. Here Ashdow turned among the many street vendors hawking their wares and turned toward the door of a perfume shop built of native stone. Ashdow entered the perfume shop and walked straight to the back of the store toward the alley exit. As his hand touched the knob of the back door, his mind focused on his mental, magical, abilities and he altered his appearance once again to that of Danmorgan of House Wellborne.

Ashdow entered the alleyway with a new appearance, a change in gait, and a cacophony of smells layered over his own. Given the measures implemented, he would have been virtually impossible to follow. Virtually.

A short time later, Ashdow, posing as a House Captain, approached the Keep of Moras with a smile and a forged invitation to speak with Lady Evalynne. He decided that he had made the right choice of roles to play. When guards or watchmen heard he was representing a merchant House from Split Town, their dispositions became much more friendly, and quickly.

Ashdow followed his escort, a pair of sturdy fellows in fine armor who wore their weapons as though they knew how to use them, along a hallway lined with large windows that curved toward the tower of Lady Evalynne's inner chambers. Ashdow noted, with admiration, that anyone walking along this hallway could be easily observed from an obscure window mounted on the inner tower. New arrivals could be watched for several long strides before rounding the corner to approach the doorway. Ashdow was still smiling as he was led to the door of Lady Evalynne's audience hall.

"My Lady, Captain Danmorgan of House Wellborne, arriving upon your invitation," the escort on his right announced as he opened the door to the chamber.

The guard entered the hall carrying Ashdow's forged invitation while he and the other guard politely waited at the doorway. The invitation was handed to a man Ashdow calculated was likely Uriel-Ka of whom he had heard. Of the many sights in the audience hall, not the least of which was Lady Evalynne's enticing figure, Ashdow found his eye drawn to the beautiful longsword propped against the throne at the Lady's right hand.

"Here to pay our respects, and our tariffs," Ashdow said in response to Uriel-Ka's doubting look upon examining the invitation. Ashdow gestured with the leather sack of coin tucked into the front of his belt, "we at House Wellborne understand how important brisk commerce is to the Lady of Moras, and indeed we share her outlook in that regard."

Evalynne revealed the barest of smiles and nodded to the guards. Ashdow stepped forward to stand before her throne as the guards exited the chamber.

"You are?" Uriel-Ka asked, rather bluntly.

"A merchant who expects to conduct some business in your fair city," Ashdow said in a polite and diplomatic tone as he tossed the bag of coins to Ka. "You'll find a few roarkor mixed with the gems and gold within. It is my prayer that it be enough to console your curiosity, garner your disinterest in my activities over the next few days, and perhaps acquire a few pieces of rather delicate information."

"Do you plan an assassination among any of the Houses?" Uriel-Ka asked, maintaining his direct tone and dismissing the vague nature of their conversation.

"I do not," Ashdow replied simply.

"Among any nobility?"

"No."

"What is it you would know?" Ka asked.

"There is a dirt lot near the graveyard; tell me about it."

Uriel-Ka took a brief moment to glance at Evalynne, to which she replied with a slight nod.

"There isn't much to tell about that plot," Ka said. "Although I am happy to tell what I know. It was a hospital of sorts, operated by Silas of House Morosse for a short time. It burned down about this time last year. Ownership of the property is retained by the Stewardess of House Morosse, Lady Delilah, as the property was originally a warehouse belonging to House Morosse."

"So, Silas of House Morosse?"

"He passed, about the same time last year," Uriel-Ka said, however, his quick look to Lady Evalynne was all the confirmation Ashdow needed.

"If I were to have a need to contact a group of elves, perhaps not the sort that live in the forests of the Suthiel..."

"There have been rumors about the mines belonging to House Morosse," Ka began, but Ashdow heard the distinct click of Evalynne's teeth clenching together reflexively. "However, those are not the only goods reputed to be fashioned by elves. We are a major trade city, after all, and see wares from all cultures."

"Am I to understand that your curiosity regarding my brief stay is satisfied?" Ashdow asked as he nodded toward the bag still held by Uriel-Ka.

"We are satisfied and are happy to have you in our fair city."

Ashdow bowed and maintained his polite but slight smile and relatively flat affect. He had learned far more than either Evalynne or Uriel-Ka suspected. They were practiced in the arts of diplomacy and deception, but Ashdow was a master.

Ashdow had learned there was definite drow involvement in the area, and that it was tied to the mines of House Morosse. He also knew that Silas of House Morosse was somehow tied to the drow and this place near the graveyard. He suspected Silas was not dead, and that Lady Evalynne profited from the whole affair.

He needed to investigate Silas of House Morosse, and the Morosse estate. However, he thought his first move should be to look into the mines of Morosse and discern exactly how drow were involved there.

Two streets across from Lady Evalynne's Keep, Ashdow, the Master Shadow Blade, wore the typical garb of a miner from Moras and started toward the mountains that lay just beyond the city walls.

The streets of Moras were no different than the streets of many other large cities. Vendors and merchants crowded about, sailors and mercenaries passed through, farmers bartered, and soldiers sought entertainment. And, just like most other large cities, children, orphans of the harsh life in Stratvs, scrambled for food and shelter. Jaime and Haycen were two such children, although both boys were a year older now and had been wise enough to hide the bulk of the silver gleaned from the physician, Silas.

Now they squatted in the cold dark of a blind alley, trying to merge their shadows with those of the surrounding fishnets and coils of rope piled nearby. The sun had dropped below the western peaks of the surrounding mountains less than an hour before, and now the fish merchants were packing away their carts of fish. Jaime and Haycen knew this was the best time of day to snatch a fish or two from the carts. Many of the hawkers were glad to see the end of the day, either because they were looking forward to returning home with a healthy profit or because business had been so slow that they were just glad to have it over. Either way, they were much less observant during the fifteen to twenty minutes it took them to pack away the remaining fish and prepare the carts to be stored overnight in a warehouse.

Each boy, driven by the growls of their stomachs, selected with their eyes the fish they would take when the time came to make their move. They had learned early on in their endeavors to feed themselves, that it was best to know exactly what you planned to take before even beginning toward your mark. The vendor they were watching turned to step behind his cart for one final article to pack away. The boys made their move.

As they both rocked up onto their toes and leaned toward the street, pale but strong hands wrapped around their heads to cover their mouths. With a single violent jerk, they were both pulled deeper into the shadows of the alley. The merchant across the way looked up and then directly at them. The look gave Haycen a moment of hope. Jaime, having fallen victim to the streets of Moras in more ways than one, had let the last of his hope die months earlier.

With a simple telepathic suggestion, the merchant became sure he had seen a rat scurry among the nets and returned to his work. Slythorne could have used the same power to put both boys at ease, convincing them they were being pulled into the arms of a mother they never knew. However, that was not in his nature. Instead, he fed every fear that pounded through their frantic minds while paralyzing them with a simple mental command.

Slythorne rifled through their thoughts, their memories, just as he had done to thousands of others. He found what he needed rather easily because it seemed that this young physician, Silas of House Morosse, had made a distinct impression upon both boys. An impression that only could be made with silver coins. Slythorne also noted the many sins and sinners that had victimized the boys in one way or another, some by dull apathy and others by far darker means. Slythorne smiled to himself when he realized that neither boy had experienced anything compared to what they would soon face at his hand. When one of them, Haycen was this one's name, tried to call out to Father Time, Slythorne almost giggled.

CHAPTER VIII
The Warlock, the Warrior, and Wizard's Bane

Ashcliff had his own ways of traveling by magical means but was forced to admit that the Warlock of the Marshes was indeed a master of teleportation. Ashcliff could move from one point in a city to another in only seconds by way of his spells, but Lynneare's range appeared to be limitless. With a single spell, they, all three of them, disappeared from a foggy dock in Modins and reappeared on a sharp outcropping of rock, the infamous Blue Tower just within sight.

All three of them; that situation certainly unsettled Ashcliff. Dactlynese, known to Ash as Dawn for the first years he knew her, had hunted the young man, threatened him, enslaved him, tortured him, and tried to kill him and his friends. His friends. Ash's thoughts strayed then to Roland and Eldryn. He indulged those pleasant thoughts for only a moment before returning his focus to Dactlynese. A woman as dangerous and ruthless as her bore watching.

Dactlynese was as beautiful as she was deadly. Her face and figure had halted many a man in mid-stride and cost them their lives for the glance. She was pale and strong, quick and confident. Her black hair was cut short in the style of the Silver Helms and stopped just short of her dangerous blue eyes.

She carried a brace of daggers in her boots and another concealed in her bracers. She wore a mercshyeld falchion at her waist and carried a mace of sectot wood with Roarkor studs on a lanyard that hung from her left hand. It was not lost on Ashcliff that both components of that mace were well known for their most rare property, the ability to slay a vampire. The plate armor that covered her torso, which usually muted the figure of a woman, somehow only accentuated hers.

When he met her, she was in league with Daeriv, the sorcerer attempting to overthrow Lawrec. Lawrec was a land held by Prince Ralston far to the north and west. Lynneare held the area known as the Marshes, an uncontested swamp that occupied several thousand acres in Lawrec. Daeriv hoped to enslave Lawrec, all of it, including the Marshes. The sorcerer, Daeriv, had recruited some powerful, and merciless, allies to that end. Among those allies was Dactlynese. Ashclifff, a budding Shadow Blade at the time, was hired by Lynneare to infiltrate Daeriv's forces to spy on Dactlynese and report to Lynneare on her welfare.

It seemed to Ashcliff that the relationship between Lynneare and Dactlynese, one that he now knew to be that of father to daughter, had been strained in the past, to say the least. Her moniker, Dawn, had apparently been selected as a symbol of Lynneare's chief weakness. Being a master vampire, Lynneare could expose himself to sunlight; however, the experience was, by all accounts, an unpleasant one. However, Lynneare had prevailed and managed to capture Dactlynese.

On that not so long-ago day just outside the city of Modins, Dactlynese and a wizard, Yorketh, also in Daeriv's service, almost killed Ash and his two friends, Roland and Eldryn. Lynneare, with some help from another daughter, Clairenese, had defeated their forces and, as what appeared to be a side effect, saved Ash's life and the lives of his friends as well.

Ashcliff was no fool and was coming to master the fine art of manipulation. He understood, and appreciated, how many victories Lynneare took from the battlefield that day. Lynneare had rescued his daughter, Dactlynese, he had managed to make a Shadow Blade indebted to him, and he had befriended Roland and Eldryn, two young men with the potential for bright, powerful, futures. Since that day, Lynneare had seen Roland married to his youngest daughter, Clairenese, and had apparently come to some sort of reconciliation with Dact-lynese. The Warlock had also managed to arrange for Roland to spearhead the actions against Daeriv in Lawrec, winning him an even more stalwart ally and pushing an established enemy further back without even having to take any direct action. Yes, Ashcliff certainly had an appreciation for the skills of the mighty Lynneare.

Just the same, Ashcliff did not trust Dactlynese, nor did she seem inclined to even feign regret or apology. However, having the Warlock of the Marshes counted among his satisfied clients had done wonders for Ashcliff's career and reputation. It didn't hurt that the old vampire paid in Roarkor coins, either.

Now Ashcliff, a young assassin and spy that had not yet seen his twentieth year, crouched near the top of a rocky outcropping alongside one of the most powerful creatures in Stratvs examining the most impregnable stronghold ever known.

"Not the most impregnable," Lynneare said, not taking his eyes from the Blue Tower far off in the distance. "Although, nothing to take lightly, either."

Ashcliff knew the master vampire could read his thoughts easy enough, but it still bothered him that his mental defenses were so feeble an obstacle against the powers of the old Warlock.

"You really believe they'll let me just walk in?" Ashcliff asked as he studied the surrounding terrain and double-checked the inside pocket of his cloak for the small pouch provided to him by the Warlock.

"Their security measures are all designed to keep their slaves and hoarded knowledge within their walls," Lynneare responded. "You should not be challenged upon entry. If your abilities to alter your appearance and conceal your identity proximate my estimations, you should have no trouble at all. Egress will be a different matter."

Lynneare handed Ashcliff a gold coin, a specific coin the

Warlock had enchanted with a spell of tracking. Ashcliff knew the small pouch, dimensionally altered to carry a number of useful tools, also contained an item with a tracking spell that Lynneare had failed to mention. However, as Ash had no plans to double-cross the likes of the Original Betrayer, it didn't bother him. What did bother him was the prospect of infiltrating and arousing the ire of the fabled Blue Tower. Then Ashcliff noticed something that gave him an idea. He saw a sea-green tint among the shadows of a rocky outcropping southwest of their position.

"The powers of the pouch and the tracking spell on the coin are meager and should be easily camouflaged by the other magical items you will carry," Lynneare said. "Magical items are commonly carried by the masters of yon tower. The entry to the chamber where the Drakestone is held will be somewhere in the master staircase. When you find it, recite the incantation I taught you. A dimensional doorway should appear before you. Enter, perform your tasks, and exit. It should be as simple as that. The outer walls of the keep are warded against teleportation or any such spell. If you can make it beyond the walls on your own, then do so, and we will meet on the western shore two days hence. If not, rub the coin, and we will come to you. It will be difficult to breach the wards of the Blue Tower, but not impossible for one such as myself. Either way, the moment we teleport to you, the wizards of the Blue Tower will be alerted to our presence and will immediately respond. So, if you have to activate the coin, be prepared to act."

"And prepared to stay out of my way," Dactlynese put in from behind them; this being her first contribution since they'd arrived on the island of the Blue Tower.

"You seem confident," Ash said, ignoring Dactlynese and allowing his eyes to drift to the tower of such mystery and legend.

"Thanks to your efforts, I possess the Sands of Time," Lynneare said, following Ash's gaze and also ignoring Dactlynese's comment. "I have foreseen many outcomes of many scenarios. I have seen many of your futures. Your success here is in all of them."

"Then..." Ash began but was cut short by the Warlock's upheld finger.

"The future is like silence," the old spellcaster said. "Once spoken, twice broken."

Ashcliff looked again at the Warlock, trying to display that his youth did not make him a fool.

"Are you familiar with the philosophy that the mere observation of a situation, unnoticed observation, changes its nature?"

"I'm an assassin, true enough, but I'm also a spy," Ash said with a slight bow to Lynneare. "It is sometimes my sole duty to observe and report. If I believed things changed just by watching them, I'd have to change careers."

Lynneare's only response was to return the bow.

"If you two are done, we should be about our mission before I have to kill every spell caster on this rock," Dactlynese said as she turned her eyes on Ashcliff. "And, if I have to begin killing spell casters, there's no telling where I might stop."

"Are you under the impression that your successes in Modins against my friends and I are a result of your prowess?" Ash asked as he began down the embankment toward the hard ground below. "I assure you it had much more to do with the fact that we were outnumbered more than ten to one. If you weren't afraid of my friends, I've no doubt you would not have felt the need to bring a small army with you. Perhaps, then, you are more wise than you seem. You were smart enough to fear Roland and Eldryn, after all."

Ashcliff turned then, just for a moment, to see Dactlynese twist her face and open her mouth to respond only to have that response quelled by a single look from her father, Lynneare. Ashcliff smiled and continued down the rocky slope feeling much better about his day.

Once he reached the base of the small rise, Ashcliff moved off toward another outcropping of rock. This outcropping was less than a league off the trail from his current position to the Blue Tower, but he thought it an essential stop. Ashcliff had marked the outcropping with his eye when he had noticed a slight hue of teal in the shadows of the rocky overhangs. Ashcliff moved from one point of cover to another, making sure that no one keeping watch from the Blue Tower would have an opportunity to see him.

As he closed with the outcropping, Ash reached into the mental powers he'd be trained to manipulate. His appearance began to shift, his face taking on age and his clothing changing color. With each step he took, the alterations continued further from his original form. He was not as skilled in this practice as his master, Ashdow, was, but Ashcliff had improved remarkably. By the time he reached the outcropping, Ashcliff appeared to be a sixty-year-old version of himself, and his clothing had become robes of a distinct blue hue. After a few more minutes of concentrating, Ash was able to add a subtle stitching to the collar and around the sleeves of the robe. Lynneare had described this stitching in great detail because it marked the wearer as a master of the Blue Tower.

For the most part, the way the Shadow Blade Guild was organized was brutally efficient. Twelve masters sat on the council, and each was allowed to train apprentices. Apprentices were allowed to accept employment on the one and only condition that their masters be made aware of who was hiring the apprentice. Beyond that, all operational details were for the apprentice to maintain. This ensured the confidentiality of the client's requests.

There were only two ways of graduating from apprentice to master. Those two pathways to master were for an apprentice to kill a master, or, if one of the twelve died by other means, all apprentices would be invited to participate in a selection process that ensured one of them a seat at the council while ensuring shallow graves for the others. There was no such thing as second place in the process. All new masters took the twelfth seat at the council.

Masters were forbidden to take the life of an apprentice, unless the apprentice moved against that master first. This rule contributed to the ever-honed skills of spotting an ambush or assassination attempt on the part of the council. The only way for a master to advance from his position toward the first seat of the council was for a master above him to die. Whether that death come at his hand or by other means was of little consequence.

Thus, the Council of Shadow remained ever sharp and populated by only the best of their profession. However, the secrecy also provided for the occasional, accidental, opposition. There was no way for apprentice Ashcliff to know that his master, Ashdow, was currently operating at cross-purposes to his own. There was no way for Ashdow to know that his apprentice, a young man whom he had trained since the boy's eighth year, was working against him.

Ashcliff, acutely aware of the nature of the moss he sought, began searching about the rock with tender fingertips. He searched for the teal moss he'd spotted from his scouting position. After several long minutes of searching, Ashcliff found the shaded ledges where the moss grew. This was a rare species of moss that only grew in the northern regions, and only in areas that were protected from exposure to direct sunlight.

Ashcliff held his breath and gently brushed snow away from the edges of the moss. He used a dagger to delicately remove the moss from the stone, and carefully eased it into a leather pouch he carried at his waist. He took every precaution to avoid disturbing its potent spores. Once he'd collected several samples of the valuable component, Ashcliff headed for the main gate of the Blue Tower.

He strode with confidence, attempting to convey a sense of condescension toward the guards posted near the wall and at the gate. Magic could change his appearance and conceal his movements if necessary, but only skill could guide his posture and actions. Now he must play the role of a master of the Blue Tower, a creature with absolute disdain for any, save his most esteemed peers.

Ashcliff kept the hood of his blue robe pulled low over his face, as Lynneare had said this was their custom. Lynneare had also described, in remarkable detail, the layout of the inner structure. Ashcliff had memorized those details and walked, with a patience and calm that he did not feel, toward the fabled tower.

There were aspects of the magical structure that fluctuated in order to prevent anyone from memorizing those places for future teleport spells. Hallways would shift, stairs would loop through dimensional doorways to link two distant passages by only a step or two, and the internal physical size of the structure would shift almost constantly in some specific areas. This was an excellent means of preventing someone from memorizing the location; however, the disorienting shifting only occurred in the vicinity of those hidden vaults. That fact made it quite easy for an outsider to identify precisely where the crucial doors were located.

No one teleported into the Blue Tower. No one teleported out of the Blue Tower. No one stole from the Blue Tower, at least not until today. Deep within the shadows of his hood, Ash's lips curled into a smile.

He walked past the guard tower, then along the paved stone walkway through a remarkable garden. Ash had been trained in the many uses of different herbs, magical and otherwise, and marveled now at the wealth growing within the walls of this secluded place. Of course, he had been careful in selecting the teal moss as it only grew in the wild and was, to his knowledge, impossible to cultivate.

Ash noted something else peculiar during his walk from the outer gate to the tower proper. The weather outside the gate had been a clear winter day of freezing temperatures and sharp winds; however, within the outer walls, he experienced a warm spring day with no hint of the harsh conditions just outside.

As he approached the large, iron-bound doors of the

tower, Ash began to focus his will and imagine it taking on shape and weight. He continued to pour his concentration into this spell of mentalism, forcing it to accumulate power. Lynneare had explained this part might be difficult. The doors were enchanted to open whenever a mage of the tower came close, bearing a magical charm issued to all who studied at the Blue Tower. The charms could be duplicated, but that would mean acquiring one from a mage studying there and keeping said mage locked away somewhere while an alchemist worked to forge a copy.

Pushing with a spell of telekinesis, Ash caused the doors to open ahead of him, mimicking the effect of the charms. As the double doors swung toward him, Ash saw two mages walking side by side coming out of the tower, and directly toward him. Ash began to move, to step aside for them, when one of them noticed him and began to raise his hand.

Ash froze, waiting for the bolt of lightning that was surely forthcoming. The muscles in his gut tightened, as though that would ward off such a vicious attack at that close range. Just as the mage's hand came up, the fingers curled and flipped the edge of the robe. Then the mage forced his companion aside and both of them stumbled as they blundered into the wall together in a sudden move to flee from Ashcliff's path.

"Forgive us, Master," the mage said in a rushed breath.

The young mage had apparently noticed the stitching on Ash's robe and knew that it signified Ashcliff was a member of the ruling council.

"We did not know... we did not see you coming."

Ash, just now realizing he had also been holding his breath, let only a portion of it out in a bit of growl as he moved beyond the two mages without a backward glance. The moment Ashcliff rounded the corner, he stopped to take a breath, and then another. After gathering his courage and wits, he proceeded down the corridor.

As he passed through the halls of the legendary tower, Ash noticed something he found very interesting. He saw that some of the stones, perhaps one out of every twenty, appeared actually to be clear glass, yet filled with a blue light or hue. When he found one of these stones in an alcove, out of view of anyone passing by, he took a moment to study it further. He saw, actually saw, tiny creatures moving around within the stone. Barely perceptible, there were small humanoid figures that seemed to be wailing and casting themselves about within.

Ash made a mental note of this oddity, or despicable imprisonment, and resumed the task at hand. After all, he was destined to be the first to steal from the Blue Tower.

After another half hour of wandering the corridors, Ashcliff found the section of stair where the walls and ceiling drifted back and forth with a dizzying effect. He found the slight shifting in dimensions to be quite disorienting, and could certainly understand how the changes would prevent someone from memorizing the specific location.

Now that he had the right location, it was a matter of finding the doorway. Ash reached out with his mind, imagining the force of his will as tiny tendrils that drifted over the surfaces of the blue stones. He detected the barest of tremors that seemed to change in frequency violently and knew he had the correct stone.

Ash took a moment to check above and below him on the stair, ensuring he was alone, and began the ritual as taught to him by Lynneare. The ritual called upon aspects of magic Ash was yet a virgin to; however, Lynneare assured him his attributes would suffice as long as his execution was perfect. Ashcliff had made perfection his life.

Ash spoke the words, and his hands followed with the prescribed, and exact, gestures. He watched, a bit amazed, as the door began to take form. It began as a speck. The gray quill point folded out, and out again, in rapid succession. Ash took a step back, and, in the time of the step, the speck had folded out to roughly the size of a large barrel. In another two breaths, the portal had folded out to the size of a doorway that would accommodate any man and his horse. He tried to look through the doorway but found it was a gray mist of opaque and charged air. Ash stepped inside.

Lynneare had cautioned him about the mental assault that would come. Ash had raised his defenses in the form of several enchantments of mentalism but was still nearly dropped to his knees by the magical commands to withdraw. He infused his mental defenses with the strength of his will and forced the magical commands from his mind. The struggle was brief, but intense. Sweat began to break out on his brow. Ashcliff could certainly see how this measure would turn away any that were not adequately prepared for it.

It took almost the same amount of self-control to regulate his breathing and prepare his next spell. The room was warded so that anything causing a sound within would be ensnared, so Lynneare had said, with Spider Bonds. Spider Bonds was a potent spell that replicated the nature of a spider's web with the notable exceptions that the tendrils of the web were as thick as a strong man's thumb, could withstand several hundred stone of pressure, and could only be cut by the keenest of blades.

Ash focused his thoughts once again, bringing forth his powers of mentalism, and generated a field of absolute silence that surrounded him and all he carried. He cast a second spell, one that would conceal his aura, his magical presence, as well. Lynneare had not mentioned anything about the wizards monitoring for sentient beings but Ashcliff thought the precaution worthwhile.

The next trial also tested his level of discipline. Never had Ashcliff imagined such a collection of artifacts, rare gems, powerful magic totems, and trophies from exotic beasts. A portion of his training had been learning to identify forgeries and fakes, and assessing the value of a variety of articles. He had been commissioned to assassinate, and to surveil, however, his first significant mission was to retrieve artifacts from Nolcavanor. The success of that mission to Nolcavanor had established his reputation as a professional, and had resulted in a boon of coin as well.

Now, his eyes strayed over artifacts such as the Chalice of C'Lea'yth, a goblet of pure roarkor capable of transforming anything placed in it to holy elven wine. He saw the Locket of Bengyll, a gold locket given to the champion of Time, Mil-lynne, by her human lover, Bengyll. This was the charm that began the jealousy of the gods. He examined Guardian's Bane; a black steel dagger said to be able to destroy the soul of its victims so that no sleuth or cleric could discern the events of the victim's death. He looked over these wonders and many, many more. Lynneare had warned Ashcliff of this danger as well; the temptation to fill his pockets, and, in so doing, getting himself caught. Ash did make a mental note of what was present and how it was secured, though. Someday...

He moved to the massive chunk of black and red emerald that occupied a large area of this treasure room. He could see the design on the inside of the corner piece. It appeared to be the portion of the mold for the dragon's right wing joint.

Ash maneuvered himself carefully around the edge of the great stone to its back side. Once there, he took out his magical pouch and removed a hammer, chisel, and a thick silk pillow. He placed the pillow on the floor before him and positioned the chisel against the back edge of the Drakestone. Then, holding his breath, Ash struck the chisel with the hammer and waited.

No sound had escaped. Ash knew how his spell of silence was supposed to work, but, to his knowledge, no one had ever attempted to operate a hammer and chisel with the spell en-acted. He waited for several more heartbeats and, when there was no response from the residents of the Blue Tower, he con-tinued.

Ash sculpted three stones, roughly the size of a chicken's egg, away from the back portion of the Drakestone, where no one was likely to notice. As he finished the final stone, for Lyn-neare had explicitly stated that he needed three, a sliver the size of a small dagger broke away from the majestic stone and fell to the pillow next to where he had placed the first two pieces. It didn't take Ashcliff long to decide what should be done with the sliver.

Holding his breath once more, Ash removed the teal moss from his other pouch, placed the three egg-sized stones in the bottom of it, and gently laid the moss back over the top of them. Then he slowly secured the top of the pouch. He allowed himself a single, measured breath, and then secured the pouch to his belt.

Next, Ash slipped the hammer, chisel, and pillow back into the magical pouch, which once again shrank the items so that it could be easily concealed in his inner cloak pocket. Finally, he took a piece of leather from his pocket and folded it over the jagged edge of the Drakestone sliver and tucked that into the crotch of his pants. He knew that even when using infravision or ethereal sight, most people tended to shy away from that area of the body.

Ash approached the doorway back to the stairwell and paused for a moment, casting another spell to sense ahead of his position. He needed to determine whether there was anyone on the other side. Sensing no one, Ash eased through the doorway and back into the stair tower. He turned around to find that the doorway had vanished and that the stone where it was hidden had moved.

He moved down the stair, assuming a slow and confident gait. In a few minutes, he was back outside and walking along the paved stone path that wound throughout the inner grounds. He kept his head low and concealed within the hood, but managed to scan the top of the outer wall with one eye. Ashcliff saw his exit in the form of an irregular column of stone in the outer wall. To the casual eye, it would look much like the others, but he noticed the slight pitch and uneven edge of the column that would provide just enough surface for him to make the climb. The wall was thirty feet in height, but Ash thought he could make that climb, with the aid of yet another spell, in less than five seconds. He turned his attention from that spot to the areas that might be able to view...

"Excuse me," came from his side and just behind him, causing Ashcliff to nearly jump out of his skin. "I saw you at the outcropping east of the gate earlier."

"Yes," Ash said, trying to disguise his accent and the timbre of his voice.

This was another area of skill that Ashcliff had only been studying for a few years, whereas his master, Ashdow, had been studying it for decades. Ash turned slowly to see one of the wizards of the Blue Tower standing on the stone path just behind him. He cursed himself for allowing someone, anyone, to get within arm's length of him without him seeing them coming first.

"I don't suppose you were collecting klaatu narkta, were you?"

"In fact, I was," Ash said, wondering if he should rub the tracking coin or stab this mage in the eye first.

Ash considered the fact that the deadly moss might end the life of this wizard for him, but decided against that being very likely. If the mage knew the name for the moss, and where to find it, there was also a high probability that he knew just how deadly the spores of the moss could be.

"May I ask what spell you used to collect it? I've been thinking of collecting a small sample for some time now and haven't devised the proper spell."

"I just used a dagger," Ash said with an unintentional shrug.

"Interesting, a direct approach. I hadn't thought of that. I was hoping to discern at what specific point the spores become poisonous. As I'm sure you know, the moss itself is quite harmless, and the spores are so brutally lethal; thus, I was hoping to learn more about the exact process that generates the poisonous quality. And you?"

Several seconds passed before Ashcliff realized the wizard had asked him a question.

"Oh, I am curious as to the specific size of the spores and thought to test them on different creatures of different sizes, insects primarily, of course, to see if any were small enough to avoid the hazard of inhaling the spore by nature of the size of the portal to their lungs."

Ash cringed inside when the wizard stood up a bit straighter and moved his hood back enough that Ash could see his face. There was a look of profound confusion on that face, and Ash acted on it.

"I don't understand how you would..." the wizard began as Ash moved to put his arm around the wizard's shoulders.

Ash didn't know if it was common for the residents of the Blue Tower to be so familiar with one another, but at this point, he felt he had little choice.

"Please," Ash said as his arm wrapped around the wizard's shoulders. "Come, I'll show you."

"But..." the wizard began, his voice raised a bit.

Ash struck, instantly and viciously, driving his fingertips into the wizard's throat, disrupting his breathing and his ability to speak. This move accomplished two things for Ash. First, it kept the mage from raising the alarm, and, second, it prevented him from casting any spells of the schools of essence or channeling. Ashcliff also needed the wizard upright and walking, so anyone observing them wouldn't think anything of it.

As they walked, Ash felt a needlepoint of pain begin in his forehead that rapidly began to spread throughout his brain. He looked the mage in the face and saw an expression of concentration painted clearly across the man's brow. This wizard had somehow also managed to learn something of the protected arts of mentalism as well.

Ash struck the wizard again, this time breaking his nose. Ash reduced the force of the blow; after all, he didn't want to drive the mage's nose into his brain. The Shadow Blade needed the mage stunned, not dead. Ash knew from hard experience few things in this world could disrupt focus and concentration like a sharp rap on the beak.

A lightning bolt of pain shot from the mage's septum, up his face, through his eyes, and deep into the back of his brain, setting fire to every nerve it encountered along the way. His eyes watered immediately, and his vision blurred to the point that light and shadow were the only details he could discern. For a moment, he forgot his name, forgot who he was, where he was, and why he was here. In that moment, the only thing he knew was the stabbing pain that radiated from the middle of his face.

Ash turned back toward the wall, putting the wizard on his left. Ash dropped his left hand and hooked the four fingers of that hand under the mage's rib cage. Compelled by the automatic response from his nerves and muscles, the learned mage stepped quickly to keep pace with his assailant.

Ashcliff knew the sands were now passing through the hourglass for him. If he could get beyond the wall, he would be in the open. However, each step he must take toward the wall was another chance that he might be discovered. Each step was another moment, another grain of sand, when a wizard might appear from the ether to strike him down with a bolt of lightning or spray of acid; or something much worse. Many had heard the wild tales of curses wizards and sorcerers had used to plague their enemies; Ash had taken the opportunity to study them. Although his steady hand did not reveal it, he was terrified of having his eyes turned to honey or seeing a thousand spiders crawl along his muscles just beneath his skin. The idea of experiencing either threatened to seize his nerves; the notion that those of the Blue Tower could force him to endure such tortures for decades caused his bowels to twitch dangerously. Yet, Ashcliff was no soft prince or wealthy merchant's toff. He was a Shadow Blade and would execute his mission with professionalism, or die trying.

Ash positioned himself, so, to anyone observing them from behind, they would appear to be merely walking close to one another. Ash gestured with his right hand toward the wall a time or two, as though he was pointing out something to his companion while concealing his left hand under their robes and keeping a vicious hold on the mage's lower ribs.

Twice more Ash struck his captive in the nose, maintaining the wizard's stunned state, and once more Ash struck him in the throat. The wizard pawed at Ashcliff's left hand, but the effort was weak and lacked conviction. Ash had no doubt this spell caster was a formidable opponent when he could employ his enchantments; however, in a martial contest, he offered less resistance than a paid tavern girl. Ash had no intention of allowing the mage to regain his casting abilities. No codes of chivalry bound the Shadow Blade.

As he approached the great outer wall, Ash searched its top one final time for guards and mentally probed the stones and mortar for magical resistance. The Warlock had been right, of course. The wall was heavily warded against any teleportation in, or out. Ashcliff selected his path up the wall with a practiced eye and then turned to his companion, the captive mage.

As he turned, Ash saw another mage, not more than thirty strides behind them and gaining on them quickly.

"You two, hold there," the approaching wizard said. "If you're studying the wardings along the walls, you must..."

His voice was cut short by the shock of what he witnessed. Ashcliff, in a single and swift move, palmed a dagger from his right sleeve, and pushed it through his captive's left eye and deep into his brain. As the mage began to fall, Ashcliff hurled the dagger at the wizard approaching him from the tower.

With a quick word and the jerk of a hand, the wizard managed to deflect the path of the thrown dagger harmlessly to the side. Ash hadn't expected the dagger to draw blood, but he did need the wizard distracted for a moment.

In the same moment he let go the dagger, Ashcliff cast a spell. His body, and all that he wore, began to take on the hue of the wall behind him. It wasn't invisibility, that was much more difficult, but it was excellent camouflage. While the wizard was twisting away from the thrown dagger and casting his spell, Ashcliff was scurrying up the wall.

He leapt and hung a toe on a slim ledge for only a moment. He pushed off from that ledge capitalizing on the momentum from his initial leap. He used that momentum to force himself up several more feet to a handhold. Again, he only made contact with the surface briefly, as he continued his ascent. He then threw his hands up above him and slapped out to the left and the right, applying tremendous pressure between the wall and the small corner formed by the irregularity there. As his momentum continued upward, Ash tucked his legs into his chest and then shot them above his head in a final leap for the top ledge of the wall.

Ash's hair stood on end as the air around his body was instantly charged with the harbinger of an inbound lightning bolt. Ash heard the crash as the force of the magical bolt struck. He felt the spray of small projectiles against his lower back and thought, just for a moment, it was the sensation of the bones in that part of his body being blasted apart. As he propelled himself up the wall, he saw that the bolt struck the wall just beneath him and had blasted away a layer of stone in all directions.

Ash extended his body entirely and managed to snag the top edge of the wall with the back of his heel. In a flash, all the muscles from that heel to his shoulders flexed in concert to hurl his body upward and into the air over the wall. As he turned in the air, his head flying forward as he tucked his knees into his chest, another bolt of lightning tore through the small, temporary, space between him and the top of the wall. Ash wondered why he hadn't heard the wizard casting and realized only then that the close strikes of lightning had likely deafened him.

Now he ran along the top of the wall at a full sprint. In moments large bolts from arbalests would be coming his way, not to mention more magical attacks. He took a moment to realize how the defenses of the wall had worked against the powerful mages. None of them could teleport to him, or beyond the wall to intercept him. He just had to survive to get to the other side.

Ash saw the curve he had been looking for and ran all out.

Ash plunged his feet toward the outer side of the wall, making his first and only physical contact with his heels and buttocks. The bolt of a crossbow drove deep into the muscle of his left shoulder then, the tip striking the bone in his upper arm and then scraping along his shoulder blade. However, Ash's maneuver had begun, and his concentration was perfect. Between the outward curve of the wall, and his speed, Ash was able to slide down the wall at an angle. As he struck the ground, Ash dispersed his impetus by tumbling into an acrobatic roll. As he leapt to his feet at the end of that roll, he realized his hearing was beginning to return. He also realized blood was pouring out of his shoulder.

Ashcliff ran. As he did so, he held his breath and popped open the pouch with the teal moss, the klaatu narkta. At each drop of his blood that hit the ground, Ash dropped a piece of the deadly moss. Then, calling on his considerable willpower, he pushed his pain and circumstances out of his head and focused on another spell. His next step sent him stumbling forward as, suddenly, the terrain around him had changed. He had teleported himself four leagues to the west in hopes of leaving any traditional pursuit long behind him. Now, more feverishly than he intended, he began to rub the coin given him by Lynneare.

"You have them?" Lynneare asked from a burst of smoke that appeared just before the beleaguered Shadow Blade.

Ashcliff, his breath coming in rasps, was only able to nod vigorously.

"Excellent work, Shadow Blade," Lynneare said as his right hand extended a coin purse, and his left reached forward, palm open and up.

Ashcliff handed the pouch of Drakestones over and accepted the coin purse. He didn't bother to count it. His line of work was one of word of mouth referrals and repeat business.

"There's a moss in with them, klaatu narkta," Ash said as his breathing slowed. "It's very poisonous."

"I'm familiar with the plant and its spores," Lynneare said as he examined the three stones within the pouch. "This concludes our business, for now. I know you have other matters to see to. Shall I drop you in Modins?"

"Yes, thank you," Ash said as he pulled a poultice from a hidden pocket and applied it to the wound on his shoulder.

The world around them filled with smoke.

CHAPTER IX

Allies?

A'Ilys watched as the drow, or rather the Shadow Blade posing as a drow, made his way throughout the market street of the dark elf complex. The spy was clever, A'Ilys didn't enjoy admitting that fact to himself, but he understood that self-illusion was the most dangerous of pitfalls. The Master of Spies watched the intruder moved from shop to shop, occasionally making purchases and haggling prices from time to time. A'Ilys also noted the way this impostor's eye caught reflections of buildings, guard posts, and the seemingly unprotected balconies of Queen Jandanero's residence in the middle of the vast cavern.

A'Ilys had failed to discover the Shadow Blade's arrival in Moras on his own. However, his carefully crafted network of spies and informants paid for itself one-thousand-fold when they brought him the information of a merchant captain marking dock posts. A'Ilys didn't read the Shadow Blade codes, of course, but he did understand some of how they were communicated from one operative to another.

It was mere chance that A'Ilys had collected this errant bit of information at all. For his watchers on the docks almost failed to mention such an odd, but apparently mundane, act. Three factors played in the Master of Spies favor; one, his expansive network of spies, two, Queen Jandanero made it clear that she was to be alerted the instant the Knight of Sorrows arrived in the area if he was indeed on the move which, in turn, caused A'Ilys to be more fastidious than ever, and three, this Shadow Blade seemed to prefer the guise of this Captain Danmorgan and used it frequently, making him easier to follow.

A'Ilys was also on the alert for any sign of the master vampire, Slythorne. The Master of Spies was confident the mysterious aristocrat accompanying Captain Danmorgan at Despion's Rest was Slythorne, or one of his vampire servants. Each of A'Ilys's informants gave the same account of this curious noble. None could remember what he looked like, or the times he came and went. They could only remember that he was important, and none were to interfere in his business. To A'Ilys, that meant one possibility; the spell known to him as Mind Cloud.

Mind Cloud was a favorite among the drow mentalists, for it obscured details about the casters from any witnesses. For most drow to move about on the surface of Stratvs, a keen disguise was required. However, if one could cast the spell Mind Cloud, no disguise was needed, for none could remember, or truly recognize the spellcaster's actual appearance.

A'Ilys had learned more about Slythorne than the Knight of Sorrows and the Shadow Blade combined. However, much of the research on Slythorne had been done for him. A'Ilys had availed himself of every journal entry; every note, Lady Dru kept on her former companion. She had believed her history with Slythorne her secret, but there are no secrets kept from A'Ilys, certainly not within this drow coven.

From her detailed notes, A'Ilys had no doubts as to the lethality of the master vampire. He was an accomplished practitioner of both incantation and the art of fencing. He had mastered the shrou-sheld and dagger centuries before being endowed with the powers associated with vampirism. Add to that the fact that Slythorne had been living in the open as a vampire for almost three thousand years, and you had an excellent picture of the former Master Templar's capabilities.

However, A'Ilys respected Slythorne for another reason entirely; two reasons, actually. One, he kept his circle very small, reducing the likelihood of betrayal. Two, and more importantly, those he chose to surround himself with were the absolute best in their respective professions. A'Ilys had no doubts about the magical prowess of Lady Dru or how she had contributed to Slythorne's goals. The recruitment of the Shadow Blade, though; that was a masterstroke. For, if you were one who could not enter a place simply because you had not been invited, the greatest way to complement that weakness was to procure the services of one of the best infiltrators in the world. Now, A'Ilys followed that infiltrator.

A'Ilys was no spellcaster himself; however, he did possess a large and varied collection of trinkets, each of which provided a spell or two the Master of Spies found useful. Currently, he employed a silver earring that masked both his body heat and his scent. He wore a black diamond pendant that allowed him, within limits, to alter his physical appearance or to become invisible for short stints. The crafty rogue also wore a set of supple drow chainmail that silenced his movements.

A'Ilys followed as the Shadow Blade started along the winding path that would inexorably take him back to the surface of the mountain above. A'Ilys followed at a respectful distance but made sure to keep the dangerous Shadow Blade within his sight at all times. He had five skilled drow stationed at various locales within Moras watching for any sign of Maloch, Slythorne, and this Shadow Blade; however, if Slythorne had established a camp outside the city, A'Ilys would have to follow the skilled assassin to find it.

The impostor drow shifted his form, although remaining as a drow, several times before reaching the final corridor that led to the surface. A'Ilys almost lost the assassin a few times. However, the Master of Spies had made note of the Shadow Blade's particular gait, something most difficult to alter about one's self. With each change of the assassin's appearance, A'Ilys was able to spot him again within two to three strides.

A'Ilys watched as the impostor skillfully triggered the hidden mechanism to open the outer passage of the drow cavern. A'Ilys moved with absolute silence as he followed the assassin out into the overcast night. The assassin took a path back toward the south and away from Moras; A'Ilys had been hoping for just such a change in direction. This meant the Shadow Blade was indeed headed to a new encampment.

The assassin moved around a large outcropping of rock while A'Ilys, more skilled in traversing mountain trails, ascended above the turn so that he could watch the assassin's movements from a higher vantage point. A'Ilys crept to the crest of the outcropping, careful not to allow his silhouette to give him away. The Master of Spies squatted on his heels, several feet back from the crest, and scanned the area where the assassin would reappear.

"Your thoughts are so loud," a strange voice whispered from behind the drow. "You are skilled; I'll give you that."

A'Ilys began to take in a preparatory breath when he felt the point of a dagger slip around the neck of his fine armor and slightly prick the skin where his collar bone met his throat.

"Now, now," the stranger said. "Let's not be rude. My employer may wish to seize control of the clan of ogres or coven of drow when this is all over. He might find one of your relative skill of service. We are both professionals, so let us not squawk about. The only reason I might let you live is that you provided me quality information such that your remaining alive would be a benefit to my employer and to me."

A'Ilys knew well the area beneath the assassin's dagger tip. There were at least three ways an injury there could disable someone. First, there was the proximity of the large artery in the neck that, once cut, could bleed a warrior dry in less than a minute. Second, there was another artery that ran along the collar bone and injury there could prove just as fatal. Finally, there was a cluster of nerves in the region that, when struck, could cause temporary paralysis. However, if a blade sliced through those nerves, the paralysis might not be quite so temporary.

"Slythorne," A'Ilys whispered in reply. "We are both professionals, so let's not use euphemisms amongst ourselves. Your *employer* is Slythorne."

"Ah, well-spoken," the Shadow Blade responded. "You may call me... oh, it's a bit chilly out, so you just call me Frost."

"Very well, Frost. What would you know?"

"Delightful. It is such a relief dealing with another professional. How committed to Lady Dru's defense is Queen Jandanero? I don't want to hear about her feelings on the matter; I want to know how many soldiers she would lose before she abandoned the effort. I want to know how much loss she would endure before leaving Dru to her own means of defense. I also want to know if there is an amount of coin that might spare us all this nonsense and enlist the good Queen's assistance. Oh, and you will tell me how far along the Chaos Lord is and about the relationship between him and this risen Lord of Order."

"He won't tell you those t'ings," came from a raspy voice off in the rocks. A voice that A'Ilys knew well. "He won't tell you 'cause I'll kill 'im before he does."

"Well now, that's a bit rude," the Shadow Blade, sometimes called Ashdow, said. "You must be afraid of me to hide off in the rocks as you have. Come on down here, and we'll all discuss it."

"I'm afraid, 'tis true," Hellmog said from his high perch. "I'm afraid of my Warlord, Rogash. He wouldn't like the drow tellin' secrets. He wouldn't like the drow dyin' neither, but I'm thinkin' secrets 'er more important."

The assassin twisted the needlepoint of his dagger just a bit as he turned to look in the direction of Hellmog's voice.

"Come on down here, and we'll discuss how your warlord might be rewarded by my employer."

"If you think me dumb 'cause I talk stupid, then you're dumber," Hellmog said, not moving from his concealment. "You'll not twist my pride to make me come within reach of you, assassin. You won't 'cause I got no pride. It costs too much."

"Tell me, friend, why can't I hear you?" the assassin asked, sounding genuinely curious. "I could hear the drow's thoughts clearly. One sneak to another, why can't I hear you?"

"I don't think too much," Hellmog replied flatly. "You move away from the dark-skinned one, and I won't put an arrow in your head. Maybe I'll only put an arrow in your leg."

"I have a different plan..." the assassin began as he twisted his right foot in preparation of a spell assisted leap.

Hellmog loosed his first arrow, and then a second in such quick repetition, the common eye could not even track the movement. Ashdow had no time for the move he'd prepared. The assassin pulled his dagger from A'Ilys's neck in just enough time to slap aside the first of Hellmog's arrows.

However, Ashdow was no novice to quick and deadly combat. As the dagger in his right hand led the way to parry the first arrow, Ashdow pitched his left hand out with the speed and agility of a serpent striking. Before either Hellmog or A'Ilys could blink, Ashdow caught that second arrow, spun, and drove it into the seam of A'Ilys's chainmail shirt at the armpit. The instant the arrowhead punctured the drow's flesh and was driven into his lung, Ashdow summoned his exceptional magical skills and caused a smoke flash to burst at their feet. The flash dulled Hellmog's night vision, and the following smoke obscured the entire area. In that same move, Ashdow cast a spell of teleport that moved him far down the mountainside.

"You can pursue me, Sneak, if you like," Ashdow said from far out in the darkness. "However, your drow will bleed to death long before you catch up to me. Take my employer's offer of coin to your masters. They will be richer, and won't lose nearly as many soldiers."

Hellmog was already moving down the rocky outcropping on nimble hands and feet. He was at A'Ilys's side before the assassin had finished his sentence. Hellmog pulled a wineskin from his pouch and crammed it into A'Ilys's hands.

"Drink," Hellmog commanded.

"What... what is it?" A'Ilys finally managed to say.

Hellmog's only answer was to look over A'Ilys's shoulder and nod to a point in the distance behind him. When the drow turned to look in the direction of Hellmog's nod, Hellmog grabbed the end of the arrow and broke it off less than two inches from the entry wound. A'Ilys gasped in pain, and fresh blood splattered his lips and chin.

"Dwarf potion," Hellmog said as he moved around the drow to take him up under the opposite arm and helped him to stand. "Now, drink."

"Pardon me," came from a rich voice in the darkness just behind the two unlikely partners. "Could you tell your respective potentates to meet me on that peak an hour before sunrise?"

Both turned to see a tall man with a shaved head and pale skin standing before them. A'Ilys's first thought was to note the unusually proper posture the figure maintained. Hellmog first noticed that he'd never seen anyone wear a Shrou-Hayn on a hip-belt before. Both knew they were likely being addressed by the Warlock of the Marshes. Both nodded.

"Oh, and A'Ilys, would you be so kind as to tell your Queen that I would be quite grateful if she were to bring a certain construct to our meeting?"

Three hours later, and an hour before sunrise, Lynneare stood on a mountaintop, looking out over the harshly beautiful valleys that surrounded the area. He could take no action against Slythorne directly; however, he did find the constantly gloomy weather irritating. Thus, with a wave of his hand, the dense fog and overcast sky cleared to reveal crisp stars and a radiant moon.

Dactlynese paced behind her father while Warlord Rogash and Queen Jandanero approached their position from two different trails. Lynneare smiled when he looked upon the suit of animated armor that marched behind Queen Jandanero; the old vampire was glad to see that the drow had indeed brought her Dark Guardian.

"How long will this take?" Dactlynese demanded from behind him. "Every moment I'm away from Wodock, my position with Verkial's troops diminishes."

"'Accept peace when it is offered, enjoy the sun and stars

while you may,'" Lynneare quoted.

"Do not speak to me of platitudes and maxims," Dactlynese snapped back. "If we're to be away from here, then let us be about it!"

"You worry for him," Lynneare said as the realization came over him, surprised him. "He does walk into the path of danger, but I have seen his survival many times over."

"I don't know who you mean."

"Your drow paladin," Lynneare said simply. "I knew he cared for you. I am glad you also care for him."

"Father, you push my temper."

Lynneare smiled and drank in the cold mountain air. He smiled again when he noted the scent of the other two, the two he'd met just a few hours before. They were quite stealthy; there was no doubting that.

"Ah, fair Queen, mighty Warlord, thank you both for coming at my invitation," Lynneare said when the two rulers stepped onto the plateau of the summit. "I hope you understand why we had to meet under Merc's Road."

"We met here 'cause I ain't about to invite *you* into my caverns," Rogash stated flatly.

Lynneare only responded with a smile.

"I have deigned to acquiesce to your request," Jandanero said as her eyes drifted over the horizon and peaks surrounding them.

All there heard Dactlynese's teeth grind and saw her twist the lanyard of her mace around her wrist.

"That was very gracious of you, fair Queen," Lynneare said in his rich voice. "I'll have *him* back to you intact and before the next moon."

"What you gonna do about your bloodsucking buddy down there in the city?" Rogash asked.

"I've done what I can... what I may," Lynneare said with a tired sigh, perhaps revealing a genuine emotion for the first time during this exchange. "Slythorne's fate is sealed, I think. There may be loss. There almost always is. Frost may be another issue."

"What's that supposed to mean?" Rogash asked with an edge in his voice.

"I'm not quite sure," Lynneare responded, clearly unconcerned about the warlord's mood. "Speak to your Lady Dru and your Chaos Lord. Dunewell and Maloch will face Slythorne soon and will need their help. Maloch holds my part of our bargain for her. Please, pass that information along. They must work together, or they will fail. Afterward, well, there are some corners of the future less opaque than others. Soon another will come against you; against all. Be ready, and don't waste time and resources by squabbling."

With that, Lynneare whispered a series of quiet words that generated a thick smoke that engulfed him. In a moment, he, Dactlynese, and the Dark Guardian were gone.

"I hate vampires," Rogash said as he swiped a vast clawed hand through the dissipating smoke.

"I understand your... creature, Hellmog, was somehow involved in the attack on my Master of Spies," Jandanero said, ignoring Rogash's conversational prompt altogether.

"Involved? He saved your skinny drow's life is what he did."

"Perhaps. It is good to have valuable servants."

"Your point?" Rogash asked, growing impatient.

"I may have work for this Hellmog in the near future, should you allow it, of course."

"That will depend on the work."

"Then, perhaps, you will have work for him which will benefit us both," Jandanero said. "I will provide the direction, you the scout. Then we will share in the information learned. Oh, and do tell your creature that I am quite adept at perusing the minds of wizards and sorcerers, I'm sure his mind would be no trouble."

I hope you understand, I mean no intrusion, the voice in her mind startled Lady Dru from her contemplation. *I pray you'll forgive my need for expedience. The Queen of the drow, Jandanero, has held up your end of our bargain, and thus, I am sending your piece of the Drakestone with the Lord High Paladin, Maloch.*

A paladin of Time is going to surrender a Drakestone to me? she asked as she also cast a spell of searching, attempting to ensure she was alone in her chambers while mentally engaged with the likes of the Warlock of the Marshes.

He will. In the days to come, he may have reason to destroy you. However, you both understand that Slythorne must fall. He understands that an even greater threat looms. As to the behavior of this Inquisitor, Dunewell, I can only say that he understands the dangers one such as Slythorne poses. He and your Chaos Lord do have unsettled business. That may pose a problem, assuming they survive the encounter with my old Master Templar. I know something of the bond between master and shyeld. I hope your words of reason will guide him.

I think you misunderstand, Lady Dru replied. *Silas loves his brother.*

Silas entered Lady Dru's rooms in A'Ilys's chambers. He paused in the doorway to bow. Typically, his signs of courtesy were sarcastic at best and usually some subtle means of mocking someone in the room. However, this morning he sincerely hoped to communicate his subservience to his mistress. He doubted any had noticed, but he knew she was frightened.

His curiosity, rarely sated, was burning within him now over the subject of Slythorne. The Warlock of the Marshes, the Original Betrayer, had called on them to face this threat; this threat and some other threat yet to be named. He had called on them to face these threats together. The fact that Dru was afraid, not concerned but afraid, was enough to raise Silas's interest in the person. When one considered both Lynneare and Dru paid Slythorne the respect of their alarm, the unanswered questions became maddening.

Dru sat at her desk, flipping through tomes of powerful spells, yet Silas had the feeling she wasn't really reading any of them. He had sworn his loyalty to the vampire mistress before him as a means of maintaining his independence from the demon princes and because he thought their purposes would be aligned. He had not anticipated finding someone who loved to discover, who loved to learn, as much as he did. He had not anticipated her superior intellect or strong will. He had not anticipated loving her.

"Lady Evalynne's compliance has been without hesitation," Silas said when the silence in the room became more than he could tolerate. "The assassin, said to be a Shadow Blade, has arrived and questioned her and Uriel-Ka at length regarding Stewardess Delilah and the death of Steward Silas of House Morosse. I spoke to Ramaj, the Shadow Blade, previously employed by House Morosse, and he offered nothing about the other Shadow Blade. Also, I'm fairly certain Ramaj is not his actual name, but no matter. In truth, I don't think he knew anything about him. He hid it well, but seemed surprised when I mentioned another of their guild being in Moras, and then seemed eager to be on his way. Interestingly enough, he is posing as merchant captain Danmorgan of the Split Town House Wellborne, technically making his alias a subordinate of my alias, Cambrose of House Wellborne. I thought that quite amusing."

"I offered her you in exchange for the loan of the Dark Guardian," Dru said, not taking her eyes up from her book of spells.

"Understandable, and expected," Silas said. "The Queen has indulged my presence thus far only because of her curiosity about my... current state of being."

"You are to aid A'Ilys in attempting the same ritual," Dru continued, still not willing, or unable, to look at her Chaos Lord. "If that ritual should fail in any way, then you are to become her sworn subject, loyal to only the Queen."

"I understand," Silas said, hoping to sound more dutiful than he felt.

He did not take this as any sort of betrayal; it was simple pragmatism. Given the apparent danger of their current circumstances, Silas understood the necessity. Although, he began to wonder if Lady Dru was keeping her eyes to the pages before her because of some perceived guilt, some sense of shame. That thought touched him profoundly. The idea that her attention, her concern, might be so much so that she experienced a feeling of guilt over him quaked the foundations of his heart.

"I understand that this Slythorne is a vampire," Silas said, hoping to change the subject, and hoping this topic would not again raise the ire of his mistress. "Is there anything you would tell me that might serve to defeat him?"

"He was a Master Templar before he became a vampire," Dru said, with a resigned sigh. She knew this conversation would have to come. "Thus, he's a master of the blade as well as a gifted spell caster. He was there the day Lynneare led them all astray. He was the second to be cursed. Vampires vary in capability and strength. I am more powerful than most because of the arcane magic I've studied and the fact that I was turned by one of the original vampires. We are notoriously difficult to kill. A skilled hand can incapacitate us, but destroying us is another matter altogether."

Silas took a step closer and tried to hide his excitement. Lady Dru had taught him a great deal, but there were a few topics that she rarely discussed. Silas, always hungry for knowledge, had labored to avoid making himself a nuisance but was very eager to learn any detail about the unusual race.

Many had classified the state of vampirism as a curse and others as a disease; however, Silas had classified them as a race, a species, all their own. For he was aware that a few scholars theorized that some were able to produce offspring by coupling with other vampires and, on rare occasions, coupling with humans. This possibility fascinated him, but Lady Dru's reluctance to reveal much about vampirism had frustrated him. He attempted to conceal that frustration, and indeed had much more to learn regarding a myriad of other topics that would occupy his time. Not the least of which was combat with blade and magic.

"Slythorne's alternate form is a knot, or nest of vipers," Dru went on, still not looking up from her book. "We cannot cast spells from our alternate forms, but we are also nearly invulnerable in those forms."

"You mean to say you can, innately, change to another creature, another type of being?"

"Yes. Lord Lynneare's form is, of course, a black dragon; the modern symbol for betrayal."

"Ah, how poetic," Silas said without realizing the light-hearted nature of his tone. "The dragon was once the symbol for undying loyalty as the gods only granted dragons to their most loyal subjects as mounts. When the dragons sided with the humans during the Battles of Rending, that changed the perception. Now the symbol is the dark mark of a betrayer. Interestingly enough, the term dragonslayer can alternately mean…"

"Do you want to hear this or not?"

"Sorry, my Lady."

"As I was saying, the Warlock of the Marshes can become a black dragon, although I'm not aware of any instances of that happening in centuries, not since the death of his first wife. I can shift my physical form to that of a cluster of spiders, Portia to be specific. Our different forms allow us different capabilities. For instance, as a cluster of spiders, I can scatter toward every point on the compass, slip through the slightest of cracks, and virtually vanish. Furthermore, lexxmar can do nothing to inhibit the changing ability."

"An interesting fact about the Portia jumping spider; they have displayed tendencies to learn from…" Silas stopped short when he noticed Dru's jaw muscles begin to clench. "Wouldn't the spiders be easy to kill, though?" Silas asked, as his mind began down a different path, running through possibilities regarding a knot of vipers.

"Individually, I suppose. However, to incapacitate a vampire, you must destroy the entirety of their alternate form. Of course, each one that dies before I change back causes injury, but nothing significant."

"Do you perceive your surroundings through the means these creatures, these forms, normally use?"

"Yes," Dru replied, finally taking her eyes from her book to look at Silas.

She closed the tome and gestured to the seat across from her. Silas bowed again and moved quickly to the chair. He took the liberty of pouring a glass of bloodwine for each of them and then sat quietly, waiting as patiently as he could stand. Lady Dru accepted her glass, favored him with a brief smile, and took a deep drink.

"Understanding the world around you from that perspective takes some practice," Dru continued, clearly more comfortable now. "It took me years to simply move around a room as a cluster of spiders."

Dru took another long drink and then seemed to resolve some inner conflict. Her eyes set with the determination of someone who had decided a vital matter. She sighed again and continued.

"To truly destroy one such as Slythorne, you must first disable him, as I've said. Then he must be decapitated, his mouth stuffed with holy wafers, his body washed in holy water, and his heart spiked with churchwood, sectot wood, or a blade of roarkor. Once that's all been done, his head and his body must be buried underneath two different sources of running water. It is no easy feat to halt the flow of a river, one that you can count on to continue to flow for centuries, so that you may bury the important parts of his corpse."

"If the Warlock is powerful enough to seize all of us the way he did near the Blue Tower, then why doesn't he handle Slythorne on his own?"

Silas had pondered this very question for some time. He had some idea how powerful his mistress was, and Warlord Verkial was no young pup. Lynneare had taken control of all of them without showing the slightest bit of effort. Yet, he had come to them asking for help, or, when Silas thought about it, had come to them demanding they comply with a bargain.

Silas understood some of the unique laws of nature that bound those of the vampiric race and thought that Lynneare's need for a stalking horse must have something to do with those unusual relationships between vampires.

"I don't know, not for certain," Dru said as her eyes drifted up to a dark corner near the ceiling. "I believe it has something to do with their curse. They were both holding the Sands of Time when Father Time struck them, or so Slythorne told me. He only spoke of that day once, and I could tell speaking of it, all these centuries later, still pained him. I do know that, over the decades, they have each sent pawns to disrupt the plans of the other, never acting directly against one another."

"I see," Silas said as he lowered his eyes a bit. "Do you still care for him?"

"Who? Oh, no, of course not. I never really did. What I loved about Slythorne was an idea of who... of what he was. I never loved *him*. I suppose I did him a disservice in that regard. But I don't think he ever really loved me, either. He was attracted to my strength and intellect, but I don't think he ever appreciated where those came from, their origins. Not truly. His pursuit since has been that of a spoiled child who's cast-off toy has been stolen. He didn't want me when he had me and, when I left, he wanted nothing else. He has spent centuries learning to hate the world around him, and decades telling himself that somehow I wronged him. Facing him will be deadly."

"Has there been any word from the Warlock?" Silas asked, wishing to move Lady Dru's thoughts from her once-upon-a-time lover.

"Yes, he has the pieces of Drakestone, he has sent someone to bring one to us and is taking the other to Isd'Kislota," the beautiful vampire said as she gracefully leaned forward and took Silas's hand. "Verkial will be busy with his preparations and would be of little help against the likes of Slythorne anyway. The Warlock and Dactlynese will join Verkial to assist as they can, and Queen Jandanero has sent her Dark Guardian to Lord Lynneare. There is something else. Other allies are coming. Allies that Lord Lynneare says will be necessary to defeat Slythorne."

"And?"

"Among them is your brother."

"We must go immediately," Silas said as he turned to take up his cloak.

"We cannot run from Slythorne," Dru cautioned.

"We're not running," Silas said as he stopped and turned back to his mistress. "They will capture or kill Dunewell. I can't let that happen."

CHAPTER X

Seeing is Believing

Dunewell took in the cold mountain air and enjoyed the peace that only night on a remote peak could bring. Having made a deal with a drow to ally with the Original Betrayer and Silas, Dunewell was striving for peace, outward and inward. His intuition, always strong and always to be trusted, had guided him along this path. Yet, the logic of his mind could not be ignored. Fallen paladin, vampire, and a murderer clothed in a demon's black soul; these were the allies he'd chosen.

Though, of the three, only Silas had been unrepentant. He had seen the evidence of Maloch's contrition and had the paladin's word that this Lynneare had guided him to his road of repentance.

"He is here," Maloch said from behind Dunewell.

"Yes, I know," Dunewell said, sensing the presence that was not black and not white but a mottled gray of morality. He could sense the struggle with Lynneare.

Both warriors turned toward the small grove of snow-covered pines and stepped in among the shadows.

"Dunewell, Lord of Order, son of Stilwell, this is my daughter," the Warlock of the Marshes said as they entered a small clearing within the grove. "Dactlynese has her crimes, as do we all, but now she seeks to redeem those wayward years."

Dunewell looked from the tall, shadow clothed Warlock to the stunning warrior he referred to as his daughter. Her beauty was undeniable, but Dunewell knew a killer's eyes when he saw them. The way she cut those eyes toward Lynneare when he mentioned her quest for redemption indicated to Dunewell that, perhaps, she wasn't as interested in forgiveness as the Original Betrayer implied. However, Dunewell, trusting to his intuition and Whitburn's insights, decided there was more to their hearts than could be seen with the eye.

"So, you will be joining us in our hunt?" Dunewell asked.

"No, our work lies to the west," Lynneare said in a rich, smooth voice. "Maloch here will deliver this to Lady Dru, also known as Stewardess Delilah of House Morosse."

Dunewell opened his mouth but held his tongue when Lynneare raised his hand and nodded apologetically.

"You will no doubt have much business to settle after the threat of Slythorne has passed," Lynneare continued. "However, she is the one he will be drawn to and could prove very useful to you in that regard. Her Chaos Lord, your brother Silas, will likely accompany her. She has given me her word; they will work with you to see Slythorne destroyed."

Lynneare retrieved a jewel of black and red emerald, roughly the size of an egg, from a pouch on his belt. The jewel was mounted in a setting of gold and hung on a thong of black leather. He handed it to Maloch, who tucked it away into his pouch without hesitation.

Drakestone, came from within Dunewell's mind.

"You're also giving this vampire, likely the same one that terrorized Moras, the power to command a dragon?" Dunewell asked, an edge in his voice.

"I am."

"Why?"

"I am not accustomed to explaining myself," Lynneare said, almost reflexively adding a magical weight of suggestion to his words. "This is the best course of action."

Dunewell felt the power of the words rush ashore on his mind as the waves of a violent ocean. Yet, just as those waves, the power receded again.

"Consult your champion," Lynneare said as he rolled the edge of his cloak to the side to reveal a magnificent Shrou-Hayn and a large box of black wood that had somehow been magically concealed beneath the outer garment.

Lynneare reached across with one delicately muscled hand and, even as he did so, Dunewell's hammer leapt to his hand with the speed of lightning traversing a dark storm cloud. Dactlynese quick-stepped to the side and, with the jerk of one wrist, swung her mace into her waiting hand. Maloch, standing near to Dactlynese for just such a reason, stepped between her and Dunewell, and lifted his hands to his sides, ready to catch her mace and pull it off course.

"Calm," Lynneare said as he cast his eye toward his daughter. "Everyone, be calm."

Lynneare unhooked the large box from his belt and handed it to Maloch. Maloch, keeping one eye on Dactlynese, moved over and extended his arms. Lynneare laid the box across Maloch's forearms, unfastened the latches, and opened it to reveal the Hourglass within. Lynneare gestured toward the Hourglass.

"It is dangerous to wield if one does not understand and know its ways," Lynneare said as he took up one side of the Hourglass. "Take the other side, and I will guide you."

Dunewell transferred his hammer to his left hand and took a moment to look at Maloch. The dark paladin nodded, and Dunewell took the other handle of the Hourglass without any further hesitation.

Time and space flew from his reality. Stratvs fell away on all sides, and he was only a specter floating along a solar wind among the fiercely burning stones of the sky. He looked beneath him to see a living maze spiraling and shifting as it swam into view. He saw faces, some he knew, and bright lines of energy that danced between them and contorted around each other.

Lord of Order, I am here.

Dunewell turned to see the Warlock, not as he knew him, but as he must have been, a tall Great Man of sharp features, lush black hair that shined like a crow's wing at midnight, strong hands, and a gentle smile.

Your mind can be easily lost in the flow of Time. Take my

hand, follow my words, and see what may come.

Lord of Order, he knew his name, but it just slipped from his tongue, reached out for the Pontiff. He took his hand and looked back to the maze that continued to re-write itself before him.

Then he saw. Yet, it was more than seeing. He felt, he experienced, each aspect of the tableau in motion beneath him.

Lord of Order saw the wolf pup, his daughter, standing against enemies bearing the symbol of the serpent, and the horn of the huntsman. Her hair was the same color as her mother's. He saw a single branch of the many twisted paths spiral out toward his death and the death of all those he loved at the hands of Slythorne, once known as Truthorne. He saw a young man, a Great Man, fall to a huge beast of bone and black magic. He watched as Ingshburn marshaled his forces under Verkial and Daeriv and marched across the fields of Lethanor in the wake of the UnMaker's greatest weapon. He saw the red raven and white rose crushed in the grip of an unclean serpent. He looked on as Lord Kyhn, bearing another much older Drakestone, sat astride a black dragon and led a cavalry charge against the very walls of Ostbier. He saw a maddened and anguished woman, no, a vampire, rampage throughout a church of Bolvii in the city of Skult. He watched himself hesitate at a fork in his road, a decision between Jonas or Silas.

You have seen. Now, do you understand?

I do, Lord of Order struggled with those two simple words and only now realizing Warlock had been speaking to him for a long time now.

"Catch him," Maloch said to Dactlynese.

He was nodding toward Lord Lynneare while moving to catch Dunewell himself.

Maloch stumbled back under Dunewell's considerable weight. After a few moments of staggering bewilderment, Dunewell regained his senses, and his balance.

"How can so many branches contradict the others?" Dunewell managed to ask.

"They are all possibilities," Lynneare answered in his smooth voice. "The future is always in motion. Our choices, even small ones, cause fluctuations that can be nigh impossible to foresee. The Sands of Time have driven many mad."

"The shadow I saw, and the unclean serpent..."

"Yes, still possibilities, but already less likely. Daeriv and Kyhn have split from Ingshburn, as has Verkial. The black dragon should now be beyond Kyhn's reach. However, if Slythorne should survive to unite them, or ally with any of them..."

"Yes. I see now. The young man crushed by the beast, the vampire attacking the church; you know them?"

"Yes."

"And you love them," Dunewell asked, but realized the truth of it as the question formed on his lips.

"Yes. Their fate is not yet set."

"How can I trust you, or trust what I saw?"

"Don't trust me. That would be foolish. As to trusting what you saw. Well, if your heart doesn't recognize the truth of it, then nothing I can do will persuade you."

Dunewell nodded and looked to Maloch.

"I assume, given your apparent capabilities, that you could transport us with magic to an area close to Moras?"

"Yes."

"Can you also get us some rags, preferably flour sacks from Degra?"

Dunewell expected, and accepted, the confused looks he got from each of the other three.

"Yes... I could do that," Lynneare said, his curiosity plain in his tone.

"Excellent."

Two hours later, only minutes before sunrise, Dunewell rowed a small boat up to the docks of his home, the magnificent city of Moras. He spotted a pair of watchmen patrolling the dock and made for a cleat near to them to tie off the small boat.

Dunewell's hair, now dyed black, hung loosely over his eyes, and he was clad in a pair of ragged trousers and a stained shirt. He wore a battered, and likely stolen, seaman's coat and sat atop a sea-chest that stored his other gear.

Maloch sat across from Dunewell dressed in much the same fashion, his hair and eyebrows also dyed black, with one key exception. Every square inch of Maloch's skin was wrapped in the clothe of old flour sacks and coated with grease. His weapons and armor were also concealed within the sea-chest.

The watchmen, one younger and of lithe build and the other a bit older and a bit heavier, stopped to regard the two-man crew of the small boat drawing near to them. Dunewell knew it would be close to time for them to report back to Blackstone Hall, which is why he chose this time of morning.

"Look here," one of the watchmen, the older of the two, called as Dunewell's small craft drew near to the dock. "What's all that about, then?"

"You mean them wrappings?" Dunewell tried to mimic the accent Jonas had adopted when portraying himself as a pirate captain but feared his performance was less than convincing.

"Well, I don't mean your lordly clothes and regal vessel," the watchman spat back. "Now tell me and be quick about it. It's past time I'm headin' back to Blackstone."

"You know Degra, do ya' good sir? Well, there's been more than one sailor caught somethin' he shouldn't't've from them tavern girls there. My mate here is looking for that young doctor you got here in Moras."

Dunewell was careful not to lie but was still unsettled by the deception of his actions and words. However, he knew it was either this or risk killing a good man over the lies of others.

"Your mate's missed his berth," the watchman said. "That young doctor was kilt little more than a year gone now. There's some that still sells some of his salves and the like, though most of that is spurious. Now, what he's got ain't catchin' is it?"

"No, sir," Dunewell said. "I've been with him a while now and ain't caught nothing from him."

"Quite well, quite well. Get on your way then."

With that, the watchmen resumed their stroll along the docks in the direction of Blackstone Hall. That thought jerked a string of sentiment in Dunewell's heart. He would likely never again walk the passageways of Blackstone Hall nor hear the morning bell from her tower. Thinking of the visions shown him by the Sands of Time, Dunewell felt small indeed for indulging such self-pity.

Dunewell tied the small boat to the cleat and then hopped up to the dock. Maloch tipped the rather heavy seachest up, and Dunewell took hold. Dunewell could have lifted the chest with ease, but to do so might give away his identity and render pointless all their preparations. Dunewell hoisted the chest onto the dock and extended a hand for Maloch. Once Maloch was clear of the boat, Dunewell pulled a piece of parchment and black chalk from his pocket.

"What are you doing?" Maloch asked under his breath.

"I'm leaving a note as to which ship this launch belongs to," Dunewell whispered back. "It's custom and should ensure it gets back to its rightful owners."

Maloch opened his mouth to say something but hesitated and then closed his mouth again. He had enjoyed traveling with a warrior of such good character and high moral standards as Dunewell, but Maloch thought Dunewell could stand to be a bit more mercenary from time to time.

Dunewell scrawled the ship's name, *Cloud Chaser,* onto the scrap of paper and pushed it over a protruding nail on the cleat. Then he stood, nodded to Maloch, and started for the streets he knew so well and had once loved.

"Where are we to go first?" Maloch asked, trying to mask his elven tone and heritage.

"There is a young lady here who I must know more about," Dunewell said, attempting to maintain his sailor's accent.

"I don't think now is the time to pursue... those types of interests," Maloch finally managed to finish.

"She cast a spell on me, a potent one, before I left Moras. The Lord of Order ritual burned the spell away, but it was very subtle and quite powerful. I am no novice to witchcraft, but this enchantment enslaved my thoughts without me even realizing it. Before we face Slythorne, she is an unknown that needs to be resolved."

"Could she be with the Archives of the Arcana? Or, perhaps an agent of the Blue Tower? I think you mentioned the vampire trouble might somehow be linked to the wizards there."

"Anything is possible, but she is now the Stewardess of House Theald."

Seeing Maloch's confused expression, Dunewell continued.

"The merchant Houses wield the same influence as nobility in the major trade cities and beyond. A Steward, or Stewardess in this case, is the head of that House. She commands an army of guards and dockworkers, and a navy of merchant vessels and sailors. The Houses are also known to employ their own spies and assassins from time to time."

"Merchants flaunting an authority that should only be granted by the Supreme Pontiff or King?" Maloch asked, unable to hide his disgust at such a notion. "How could such unbridled debauchery not result in absolute chaos?"

"Do you think there is no greed involved when a king grants lands or awards titles? Do you think greed has no place among the clerics and priests who demand collection of tithes? I've spent many hours pondering the nature of this system. If nothing else, it recognizes the greed of men and seeks to incorporate that into its function rather than ignore it. In Moras, the coin is mightier than the sword."

"I think, perhaps, you've traveled too long with your sour friend, Lord Jonas."

"Now, now," Dunewell chided with a smile curling the

edge of his lips. "Glass castles and catapults and all that. All kidding aside, though, perhaps my time with him broadened my view of the world. You haven't exactly led a life free of malicious acts."

"True enough," Maloch responded thoughtfully. "However, I never, not on a single occasion, pretended to be something I was not."

"So, of the seven sins, today is the first day you've committed the sin of deception?"

Maloch's only answer was to look down at his wrappings and disheveled clothing, and then to chuckle and nod.

Twelve hours later, as Merc's kiln was setting in the west, Dunewell and Maloch eased their way through the deepening shadows. They were edging their way around the manor of House Theald, careful to avoid alerting any of the staff to their presence.

Dunewell, who had led more than his share of stealth missions in Tarborat, had developed a new understanding of the Quiet Step in his time with Jonas. He moved as silently as the shades that concealed him. His *sight* allowed him to survey the area around them without so much as having to turn his head.

Dunewell extended his thoughts, his intuition, out from his mind in search of other sentient beings. Thus far, he'd encountered four staff members whose surface thoughts were trivial. However, as he approached the kitchen, he noted the thoughts of two young women who labored to prepared for the following morning's breakfast. He noted that both were upset that only the staff and guests of House Theald were the only ones to actually eat a meal there. Both worried for their frail Stewardess, who was rarely seen to take any sort of a meal.

As the two warriors crept through the cold twilight air toward the stable, Dunewell sensed the thoughts of the coachman. This poor fellow was lamenting the loss of the young doctor, so famous for his treatment of unusual ailments. It seemed the coach driver, a young man of no more than twenty-five, perhaps thirty, was suffering from acute memory loss. Dunewell, uncertain of how to go about it, attempted to push his mind deeper into the thoughts of the young coachman.

The coachman was afraid of his Stewardess, Lady Erin. That fact was plain to Dunewell, who sensed the emotion immediately. However, he also found areas of *fog* in the young man's mind. Dunewell delved into those tangles of thoughts, areas that reminded Dunewell of dark clouds with interrupted flashes of lightning spasming within.

Dunewell pushed through the outer border and examined the memories they held. He saw the coach drive through the low streets of Moras in the black hours of the night. He saw Erin exit the coach and take men, women, and children, sometimes two at a time, into the coach with her. He listened as the coach rolled forward and screams erupted from the unwitting passengers. His skin tightened, and his stomach turned at the sounds of the children screaming. Within the safety of the estate walls, he saw Erin step from the coach with blood on her lips and on her breath. He heard her tell the coachman to clean the hansom carefully, and then to *tou-gurr*, to *forget*. He saw, through the coachman's eyes, the remains of her victims, most notably a blood-soaked stocking and shoe belonging to a child no older than six or seven years.

Dunewell caught his breath and realized that he had physically jerked back as a reflex to distance himself from the magical suggestion. Dunewell recognized the word and knew the meaning, and the power, of the command. It was a word, a command, used by champions, and fallen champions, to wipe the memories of mortals.

Dunewell reasoned that Erin was somehow possessed or controlled by a fallen champion. Champions could, of course, also use the power, but champions didn't often eat the living flesh of women and children.

Dunewell motioned for Maloch to follow and moved silently across the stone path. He made his way into the hedge maze that sprawled before the vast estate and followed several twists and turns until they were deep enough to avoid being overheard.

"Stewardess Erin is possessed by a demon," Dunewell whispered to Maloch. "A powerful demon. I looked into the mind of her coachman. She's mesmerized him on several occasions to drive her about the city at night so she can... so she can feed; vagabonds, but women and children as well."

"Has she used him for anything else? Has she used him to recruit soldiers, or weapons, or magical charms of any sort?"

"Not that I saw. From what I gather from the staff, her nightly rides with the poor coachman are about the only times she ventures from the estate."

"That would explain a great deal," Maloch replied in the same hushed tone.

"How does that explain anything?"

"Chaos Lords and Lords of Order always appear in pairs," Maloch said as his mind continued to piece together what Dunewell had told him. "It usually requires years of forging their character before they are ready for the ritual, but there are always at least two. Those two are always drawn to one another. Just as good men will always clash against men of evil."

"So, she was drawn to me because she, or it, went through the ritual and is a Chaos Lord? It somehow knew I would become a Lord of Order and sought to obstruct my path?"

"I think so," Maloch said. "But there is something else, I think. Champions, fallen or otherwise, tend to be ponies of only one trick. They were created to carry out specific tasks and thus tend to be very good at that task and little else. That's part of what makes combining them with flesh so powerful. You or I might find a dozen ways to make use of their powers to solve a single problem or vanquish a foe, whereas the celestials only know the one."

"I'm not sure that's accurate. Whitburn, the champion bonded to me, is very clever and is a remarkable tactician."

"That's odd, for I assure you that is not the norm. Anyway, it sounds to me as though she seems satisfied feasting at night, but has made no other preparations nor ambitious moves. Nothing beyond her single move against you all those months ago. You said she came to Moras from afar?"

"Yes," Dunewell said, struggling to put together the puzzle before him even though Maloch hadn't yet revealed all the pieces. "What are you thinking?"

"In the process, the ritual, you are given command of the champion that is bound to you. With Chaos Lords, they must conquer the demon that they bind. They must master them in order to control them. If the subject of the ritual fails to do so, and the fallen champion is not mastered, then they continue to take orders from their prince or god."

"So?"

"So, I think your Lady Erin was the subject of a failed ritual. She was sent here by her demon prince to prevent you from completing your ritual and to ensure that your brother also faced the trial. Lords of Order and Chaos Lords are drawn toward one another, to be sure, but only after they have completed the ritual. The only way she could have known that it was in your future is if one of the three demon princes had looked into the future and seen the possibility. Prechii, the fallen champion of Hate and Murder, was formerly a servant of Father Time. He likely knows of another Lord of Order and hoped your brother would fail to master the demon that he bound. Then, Prechii would have two servants in Moras, well placed, when Slythorne arrived. As it is, I think he only has one, and the other has the power to stand against him."

"So, there is another Lord of Order out there," Dunewell said. "Shouldn't we seek him or her out then?"

Maloch furrowed his brow and gave Dunewell a questioning look.

"My mother was a mighty warrior in her own right, and my... the woman I love is as well."

"If time, and Time, allow, then yes, we should seek them out," Maloch replied. "However, I don't think we'll have that luxury. Lords of Order and Chaos are placed by the gods and the demons who serve the UnMaker. They are as pawns on a board not unlike a game of Scepters and Swords. If he, or she, is to be involved in this or to come to our aid, I think their deity would have already arranged it."

"So, what does all this mean? What does it change?"

"Nothing, really," Maloch whispered plainly. "Supposition only. Killing her, it, would be the same whether she is possessed by the demon or she is doing the possessing. Only weapons blessed by the gods, or of pure Roarke's Ore or sectot will injure it. It will be tough to defeat. Furthermore..."

Maloch paused for a long time, as though he was trying to make up his mind about something.

"Furthermore, she's not the one we came for," the dark paladin finally finished. "I'm only guessing that she's here to bolster Slythorne. And, even if that is so, we can't lose focus on the master vampire."

"This Slythorne, he likes his traps and his ploys, right?"

"Yes. He's a remarkable tactician and quite skilled at manipulating his surroundings to his favor."

"The plan, our plan, was to use this female vampire he's after to draw him out. He is likely trying to get to her first. He's also likely expecting us to attempt to use her in just such a fashion. That means he probably has eyes on her waiting on us. She has to be in a protected place because, if she weren't, he would have left with her already. So, he's watching her and waiting for our move. If our first move is to take down an ally of his, I think it will put him off balance. I think this has to be our first move."

"You don't think we'll be tipping our pieces?"

"No, I think he probably already knows we're in the city. If he doesn't, he will soon. He spotted Jonas and me in Split Town before either of us even caught wind of him. Furthermore, the longer we're here, it becomes more likely there will be innocent casualties."

"Very well," Maloch said with a shrug. "Battlefield planning was my forte; this sort of intrigue is not in my area of expertise."

"It wasn't in mine either," Dunewell said with a smile. "I suppose we all have to move beyond the skills we're comfortable with if we seek to truly make a change."

"So, what do you have in mind?"

"The coach house," Dunewell said. "There is only one way in and one way out, and the only innocent about will be the coachman. If we can surprise it in there, I think we have a good chance."

Maloch nodded, drew one of his shrou-shelds, and gestured with the other hand for Dunewell to lead. Dunewell led them unerringly from the maze back to the stone bench, where he once spoke to a demon about the possibilities of marriage. He eased his way around the outer hedge and saw the coachman, still at work hitching up his horses. Fortunately, the coachman was a large fellow, though not as large as Dunewell, and wore an all-encompassing black cloak.

CHAPTER XI

Unwelcome Guests

Steam rose from the nostrils of the horses, their senses having alerted them to danger long before this situation approached its climax. Stewardess Erin, wearing nothing more than a provocative evening gown, strolled through the snow on bare feet with a smile twisted across her face. The gown was new and would likely be thrown into a fire by evening's end, but House Theald could afford many such gowns.

She sniffed the air and caught several scents among the freezing drafts of the night. Each smell excited her, or, rather, the thing in her. Although she was not holding the reins of her body, she did volunteer for the ritual to become a Chaos Lord. Among her fellow cultists, she was deemed the most likely to succeed in completing the mastery of a demon of Prechii. Thus, the smell of blood about to be spilled pleased the trapped Erin within as much as it did the fallen champion without.

She entered the coach house with a slight bounce in her step, careful to walk around to the side opposite the figure wearing her coachman's cloak.

"Why, Inquisitor Dunewell," the demon said with Erin's voice. "What are you doing wearing my coachman's clothing? Were you hoping to proffer your services as my driver?"

Dunewell, knowing his disguise was of no more use, tossed the cloak from his shoulders to reveal his glowing war hammer in one hand and his rider's pike in the other.

"You'd so willingly cut down the body of this beautiful young girl? It seems like a waste. Furthermore, it doesn't seem like you to be so willing to take the life of an innocent."

"Innocent? Young Erin volunteered for the vile ritual that brought you to this plane; of that, I have no doubt. As to why, who is to say?"

"You'd not take my word for her reasons?" the demon asked in Erin's voice, managing a coquettish giggle. "You'd not hear of the cultists of Prechii that discovered and then violated a temple of Merc? You'd not hear the tale of how Silver Helms aided me in my escape? You'd not hear me explain the pain and suffering that drove young Erin to such lengths?"

"No pain, no suffering can justify treating with demons."

"Yet you seek to do just that. You seek to justify your brother's actions; do you not? And I'm not the one in league with the Original Betrayer. I'm not the one traveling with the Knight of Sorrows."

"Your nights of preying on the people of the street have come to a conclusion," Dunewell said, tired of this demon's games.

Dunewell, with a single hop, cleared the coach and descended upon the demon-possessed Erin with his war hammer at the ready. He was prepared for a partial parry or a full out attack with claw or fang from the demon. He was not prepared for what happened next.

As Dunewell descended, Erin screamed in terror and fled the coach house for the front door of her estate. Maloch, also caught off guard by the surprising turn of events, moved from the shadows near the door to cut off her escape, but too late. As Dunewell and Maloch both turned toward the manor, their surprise was complete when they heard a voice call to them from the darkness. Dunewell then knew why the demon had engaged him in conversation. The creature had been stalling.

"Throw down your arms, and you'll be taken without injury," King's Inquisitor Ranoct said as he stepped from the other side of the hedge maze. "Out of respect for your record and your service, you will not be harmed if you surrender."

Dunewell and Maloch watched as Erin, who took only a moment to look back at them and toss them a sly wink, ran to

Ranoct's side. Several more warriors, and at least three paladins by Dunewell's count, also stepped out with him. Crossbowmen leaned out from the corners of the vast manor and silhouetted themselves over the stone fence that surrounded the front yard.

In spite of the odds against them, Dunewell thought he and Maloch would have a decent chance; however, that would mean putting the lives of these good men in peril; that he could not tolerate.

"You don't understand what's happening here, Ran," Dunewell said, pleading with his friend. "You couldn't."

"Let me guess," Ranoct replied. "Young Stewardess Erin here is a demon, and you have an excellent reason for traveling with a drow. Not just any drow for that matter, but the Knight of Sorrows, himself."

"How did you..."

"One of Medaci's informants came across with the details not long ago," Ranoct said, his elbow still resting on his sword. "As luck, or rather Fate, would have it, one of the local priests also had a vision. Many witnesses know you attempted to court the young Stewardess before you murdered the Reeve here. Some suspected that, if you should return, you might try to coerce her to lend you aid and speak on your behalf with Lady Evalynne. I knew you once. I'm willing to accept your surrender only because of the man I once knew. I can't say that I recognize the man before me now."

"Informants prompted by Slythorne's tongue, no doubt," Maloch whispered to Dunewell.

"This is foolishness!" came from one of the Paladins of Fate standing just behind Inquisitor Ranoct. "Why do we waste time speaking when there's a cursed drow in there before us?"

The paladin drew his short sword and moved to shove past Erin and Ranoct. Then Fate intervened.

The paladin's shield, more importantly, the holy symbol on the paladin's shield, brushed against Stewardess Erin's exposed shoulder as she feigned fear of Dunewell and huddled next to Ranoct. In a burst of motion, Erin's skin began to sizzle, the demon within her cried out to Muersoruem the UnMaker, the paladin screamed and leapt away, and Ranoct pivoted on his toes and drew his longsword and companion hand-axe with reflexive speed.

The creature that had been Erin of House Theald lashed out with claws that sprouted from the flesh at the ends of its fingers. Ranoct parried the first swipe with his sword, but the second was too quick and slashed through plate armor, skin, and muscle with equal ease. Ranoct gasped but still managed a cut across, his axe traveling in just behind Erin's attacking swing. The common steel of the axe struck the uncommon flesh of Erin's side just below her right breast. The hardened surface of her skin easily turned the axe aside.

Some of the crossbowmen, apparently confused as to what had just transpired, loosed their bolts and quarrels at Dunewell and Maloch. Dunewell dove behind the coach while Maloch twisted and spun behind the cover of the coach house wall. Somewhere in the darkness, a sergeant had the wherewithal to yell the command, "reload!"

A quick glance showed Dunewell that the paladins flanking Ranoct had fallen away, and the Inquisitor parried frantically to keep the demon's claws from finding the flesh of his neck and face. Dunewell, knowing he would have several heartbeats before the crossbows would be reloaded and ready for another volley, ran to Ranoct's aid. As he dug his toes in to leap, he saw Maloch, swords in hand, roll out from the wall and charge toward Ranoct's position as well.

Dunewell's vault, a feat that stunned all who saw it, carried him across the vast yard of the estate to land at Ranoct's side. He thrust his hammer forward to drive aside the demon's claw bound for Ranoct's scalp and then stabbed hard with his rider's pike. The stiletto, aimed for the gap of the demon's armpit, missed its mark and struck Erin in the shoulder instead. Boiling blood, cursed steam, and unworldly screams erupted from the foul creature as it thrashed to the side.

R.J. HANSON

Just as Maloch was building speed in his charge, the fallen champion leapt from the yard to the second balcony of the manor in a single bound. Maloch skidded to a stop in the snow and gravel, giving no thought to the inquisitor, paladins, or the crossbowmen. All eyes watched, mesmerized, as the creature leapt again to the rooftop and then again to bound to the outer estate wall. No more than half a heartbeat behind, Dunewell pursued.

Maloch sheathed the shrou-sheld from his right hand, pulled his hourglass pendant from his shirt, and called a quick prayer to Father Time. His prayer was answered when he noted the slowing flight of Dunewell from rooftop to wall. Maloch turned and ran after the demon while the rest of the world decelerated around him. He heard Ranoct shouting orders to the paladins and other soldiers he'd marshaled, but Maloch had no time for such trivial concerns. It had been nearly three thousand years since he'd been on the opposite side of the likes of the demon he chased. He was not going to allow this chance to slip his grasp.

Dunewell was gaining on his prey, but not fast enough. She would cover a great distance and possibly put a number of civilians in jeopardy if he could not stop her soon. He had one distinct advantage; he knew this city. The buildings gained in grandeur and height as one moved from the edges of the city toward the center. Erin was moving in a straight-line west by southwest. Dunewell veered northward toward the taller buildings.

While Erin was slowing to pick where she would jump to next, Dunewell knew the exact route he was taking. As Dunewell vaulted from balcony to steeple to rooftop, the demon was running along rooftops, stopping at each edge, and then leaping to another building. Dunewell was gaining on the creature, but they would soon be running out of high structures to bolster their speed; they were reaching the southwest corner of Moras. Dunewell closed and saw Maloch running after Erin at a remarkable pace. Then Dunewell saw the walls of Nobles' Rest; he saw the trap, but too late.

Maloch ran on. Aided by powers vested in him by Father Time, Maloch sprinted along the city streets of Moras with incredible speed. He wasn't able to leap from roof to roof like Erin or Dunewell, but he ran with enchanted haste. As he ran, he gripped his hourglass symbol with his right hand, whispering another prayer. As this prayer flowed from his lips, a holy aura began to surround the Paladin of Time and the weapons he carried.

He felt his own vanity rear its ugly head, but there was little he could do to stop such a sin. He had not whispered this prayer in millennia, and it had been even longer since he had been graced with this much of Time's power. Now, to feel it flowing throughout his nerves and muscles, Maloch felt invulnerable.

Maloch saw the demon leap over an iron fence mounted to marble posts and half-walls, and he was closing on it fast. He stuck his right hand out as he jumped, caught the top of the railing and vaulted the tall iron fence. His shrou-sheld flew from its scabbard on his side to his right hand as he landed. Maloch looked up and saw the demon standing only a few yards away in the rows of stones ahead of him. Rows of headstones. He watched as Slythorne stepped from behind a mausoleum, a smile quirked at the edge of his mouth.

"Come to your master, serve my command," Slythorne shouted as he stretched his hands forth and then upward toward the night sky. "*Kuyon Hammesh Teh!*"

Maloch saw, felt, the stirrings of corpses all around him. He heard the grinding of stone upon stone as tombs, hundreds of tombs, began to slide open. The wretched smell of graves being turned out violated his nose and mouth.

Maloch thrust his sword into the ground, grabbed the hourglass symbol that hung around his neck, and began another prayer. He worked his lips and tongue feverishly through the complex pronunciations needed for the prayer, and, while he did so, the dead marched forth.

As he reached the final phrase of the prayer, the diseased nails of a fleshless hand clawed at his exposed neck. The sharp pain from the nails dissipated quickly, and the rot carried in them burned away as the holy aura that encompassed him served its role in his protection. A protection that would endure a few of the risen, but not the hundreds.

"*Vesliosh!*" Maloch shouted the last word of the prayer as he reached for the pommel of his sword.

A blast of celestial blue fire surged out in all directions from the Paladin of Time in waves that struck down dozens of the awakened dead. The blast continued out for several yards until it washed upon the feet of the master vampire. There the power of the spell winked out with a heartbreaking whimper.

Maloch reached his right hand for one sword while he cut a sweeping arc around him with his left. The swing of his second shrou-sheld drove back the few undead creatures that were able to weather his spell of repulsion. The drow paladin then spun the tips of both shrou-shelds up before him and began an oft practiced routine as one blade cut across, its companion thrust forward, both aglow in holy light. He took only a moment to examine the sea of undead creatures that shambled into the lane separating him from Slythorne. He watched as crypts in the distance slowly erupted with skeletons wearing armor and wielding the weapons their hands knew in life. These were no mere undead, mindless in their quest for living flesh. These were Captains of the Abyss, intelligent, skilled, and deadly, and only the most adept in the arts of necromancy could summon or hope to control them. The mighty Paladin of Time felt despair prick his heart.

Dunewell summoned the powers at his command and vaulted toward the graveyard. He landed dozens of yards inside the fence, several yards behind the front lines of undead. He called upon the powers of the champion within him, and blue holy fire burned all about his body and his weapons. Great wings of blue flame burst forth from his shoulders, and his eyes shone with the same dominating blue hue.

The forces of un-life burned away around him like the leaves of fall before a great fire. The bodies, animated by dark powers, burst apart and were consumed in Bolvii's sacred blue flames. Dunewell swung his hammer and thrust his rider's pike with the brutal efficiency of a skilled warrior as he cut his way through the waves of risen corpses.

As his hammer swiped the head from another undead's shoulders, the lane before the Lord of Order cleared. Four Captains of the Abyss stood awaiting him. Two wielded the mighty Shrou-Hayns of old, another a great axe, and the last a longsword paired with a shield of absolute black; all wore well-crafted plate armor and stood a full foot taller than Dunewell.

The four stepped forward, and two stepped around Dunewell to his back and his flank. Dunewell's multi-spectrum view of his surroundings revealed the dark aura that drifted around these beings and their weapons like the black smoke that poured from a fresh-lit coal oil lamp. Dunewell also noticed how they gripped their weapons and positioned their feet. They were not only powerfully enchanted, by the look of it they were skilled in combat as well.

The great axe swiped toward his head in a fat arc. As Dunewell side-stepped and punched up with his hammer to knock the heavy weapon wide, he saw the thrust of the longsword coming in opposite. Dunewell followed his hammer toward the huge skeletal fiend, driving the pommel up to strike it in the chest. None of the creatures expected such a bold move by any man, confident in their superior strength and their adroit handling of the cursed weapons they bore.

The thrusting longsword fell short of its mark, while Dunewell drove the pommel of his hammer from the chest of master undead up into the bones of its face. The head burst in sacred blue flame as Dunewell's blessed war hammer continued its thrust past the creature's shoulders. Dunewell followed, stepping on the undead's chest, hopping, and spinning in the air to face the other three that closed in from behind him.

Dunewell watched as the two with the Shrou-Hayns pulled the large swords up into a fighting stance that Dunewell had only heard about a few times, but had never actually seen in use. They grabbed the pommels of their greatswords in a reverse grip and wrapped the fingers of their off hands around the blade, almost two-thirds along the length of it. This was the ancient style of the Raven Wing.

As Dunewell was assessing the dangers surrounding him, he heard Maloch call out for aid. Dunewell drew upon Whitburn's powers once again, turned, and leapt high into the air, flying over dozens of undead. His landing was a crash that blasted many of the clawing hands and biting teeth back several yards.

Maloch, taking advantage of the brief reprieve, dropped to one knee, sucked in a deep breath, and whispered another prayer to Father Time. The combination of holy power from the Lord of Order and the Paladin of Time reverberated out from the duo, causing many of the risen dead to collapse and many more to burst apart. However, in that moment of triumph, they saw their doom. Dozen, perhaps hundreds more of the creatures shuffled in while the remaining Captains of the Abyss took up three points of the compass around them and the fallen champion the fourth.

It became clear to the Lord of Order and the Paladin of Time that the four were somehow controlling, maneuvering, the horde of undead before them. Both Dunewell and Maloch had faced their end many times. Both had faced insurmountable odds in their violent lives. Both were now committed to killing as many of the enemy as possible before death took them.

"Her?" Dunewell asked as he nodded toward the demon-possessed Erin.

"As good a start as any, I suppose," Maloch said between heavy breaths.

The two started toward the fallen champion, working their weapons in an exquisite concert of complementary strikes, parries, and thrusts. Each time Dunewell struck out high with his hammer, it was followed with a low cut by one of Maloch's fine blades. Each time Maloch parried aside a biting maw, it was followed by a thrust from Dunewell's rider's pike. The undead fell before them as wheat before the sickle. Each worked hard to keep the raking claws and biting teeth from their flesh while trying to maintain their drive toward the demon. Both heard chanting and looked up to see Slythorne in the air above them.

"*Kellun ka belleo!*" the master vampire shouted the last words of his incantation.

The undead about them swelled and twisted in response to the dark spell. Serrated horns grew from their foreheads, shoulders, and elbows while their legs took on additional joints and lengthened another yard.

Now Dunewell and Maloch worked feverishly to parry the many attacks slicing in at them from all angles. Dunewell tried a few thrusts with his rider's pike but found the horns that had sprouted from the heads of these creatures more than adequate to parry his short blade. Maloch attempted to slash and thrust at those closing in on them but found his blades caught in a hellish forest. A nest of horns that had grown from the elbows and shoulders of the beasts. These enhanced abominations no longer cowered from their holy auras, nor were they even slowed by them.

As the frenzy of cursed claws, teeth, and serrated horns lashed about them, Dunewell and Maloch each suffered dozens of nicks, gouges, and slashes. The volume of the sharp ringing of steel against hardened bone continued to rise. Blood streamed from wounds on every square inch of skin not covered by plate armor and their breathing was now coming in rasps as even their enchanted speed was not enough to keep pace with the many attackers.

Dunewell caught a glimpse beyond the fray of a templar, one that he knew. A templar he once threatened to arrest for beating a man in the street for the crime of stealing Church-wood. Dunewell thought the man's name was Fladeen. The templar's facial expression was hard to read as he sneered and dropped his upheld arm in a gesture of command. A command to loose.

"Back, back to the churches!" Paladin Illiech yelled as he staggered back from the sight of Stewardess Erin's flesh singed by the symbol of Merc, the ever-burning flame, upon his shield.

Men in service to the churches of Fate, Merc, and of Silvor faltered as many of them stepped back from their posts and ex-changed looks of uncertainty. Many swords and axes dipped; many crossbows lowered as the men looked about in confusion.

"Hold!" Inquisitor Ranoct, known to many as Siege-Breaker and others as Dragon-Slayer, yelled. "Hold, curse you!"

"Merc, by means of our Supreme Pontiff, calls for the head of the pretender, Dunewell, and the cursed drow only," Il-liech retorted. "This... this creature, whatever it may be, is not the mission we of the church were sent here to execute. This monster is a matter for the inquisitors and watchmen."

There were Templar Captains and Sergeants among the ranks from the churches, and many of them from the church of Fate; however, the most senior Paladin among them was Il-liech. Although Fate outranked all other churches except for Time, Paladins always held a higher position than Templars of any rank. Paladins were able to cast spells with their prayers, whereas Templars were not, thus, Paladins were considered closer to their gods than Templars and recognized as having command in any situation where Priests were absent. Priest and Clerics, their spells being even more powerful than those of Paladins, were considered to be even closer to the gods. Thus, they were often considered as the direct conduit for the will of their chosen deity. However, it was rare that a Priest or Cleric was found in the field.

"That creature is a demon," Ranoct said at the very edge of his self-control. "If that isn't the business of the church, I don't know what is. Sergeant!"

"Yes, Inquisitor," Sergeant Lisban of the Moras contingent of watchmen responded promptly.

"Take note of every man here," Ranoct continued. "Take down the names of each templar, paladin, and officer. Any that do not follow, and follow immediately, will be tried for cowardice once this demon is put down, and this business is sorted out."

"Yes, Inquisitor."

"Now, move out!" Ranoct commanded.

Ranoct began at a jog in the direction the demon, and Dunewell and Maloch, had been headed last. Given their incredible speed, Ranoct had no hope of catching them unless they were somehow delayed. However, that would not slow the determined inquisitor.

"Paladin Illiech," Sergeant Lisban said with a tip of his helmet in the motion of the common greeting. "Templar Captain Fladeen. Paladin Mylo."

Sergeant Lisban motioned to his watchmen and jogged after Inquisitor Ranoct, making sure to call out the names of paladins and templars present, in greeting of course, as he passed them. He made sure they understood he knew their names. As the watchmen assembled and began down the street in their traditional grouping of three men to a squad, a few templars and paladins started down the street at a walk. As the sound of boots pounding on stone rose, so did the blood of warriors. By the time Ranoct had gone a full city block, the whole of the contingent followed, pacing him.

Ranoct signaled for his runners, men designated to scout ahead of any troop movement. He sent three to fan out in front of them since they'd lost sight of Dunewell and Maloch. Each scout carried a torch in one hand and signal horn in the other. In minutes a signal horn to the west and south of their position could be clearly heard. Ranoct stepped up the pace of the men who were now all running in step behind him.

"Instruct your men," Paladin Illiech said between

breaths to Templar Fladeen, who ran at his side. "Their first volley is to be aimed at Dunewell. The second volley is for the demon."

Templar Captain Fladeen nodded and signaled for his crossbowmen to break away from the group as he led them down a parallel street. He could hear the sounds of combat carried to them by the echoes off the stone buildings of the streets. The echoes seemed to come from the graveyard, Nobles' Rest, and must be magnifying the actual combat, he thought. For it sounded as though dozens, if not hundreds, were fighting instead of the three that he knew to be their quarry.

Fladeen led his men along the wall of a stable that concealed their approach to the graveyard.

"From here, we'll crawl along the half-wall of the fence until each man has room to loose," Fladeen whispered to his troops. "Stay low and out of sight until I give the command. Upon my command, you will rise and loose. Your first target is to be the pretender, Dunewell. Your second volley is to be aimed at the Stewardess, for she does show all signs of being possessed."

Fladeen belly crawled across the street and along the outside of the marble half-wall. The sounds of battle seemed more intense than they should have; however, he was hard-pressed to hear anything over the sound of the armor and weapons of his men scraping the stone upon which they crawled. He reached a point nearly seventy yards from where they had first crossed the street and looked back to his men. The last of them were securing their places, crouched behind the short wall of stone. Fladeen took a moment to enjoy this time. He was about to order the death of that prideful inquisitor and garner himself the Shyeld's Crown, a prestigious medal awarded for meritorious service, in the process.

Fladeen rose, his mind already creating the scene he would find before him. He fixed his expression to one of triumph mixed with elation. He looked down the line and saw that his men were on task, just as ordered. Each man among them rose, shouldered his crossbow... but then none of them looked to their leader, not one. Fladeen turned and was stricken virtually immobile by the horror of the bloody display. Several long seconds passed while his mind, trying to refuse the sight he beheld, struggled to move beyond this shock.

"Sir?"

The word seemed to come from far away, although it was spoken by the templar at his side.

"Sir, what..."

Fladeen just continued to stare forward. He was locked in just that position for several more heartbeats until one of the undead, catching the smell of living flesh just outside the fence, turned its maw toward him. When the creature snarled and opened its maggot-ridden mouth, Fladeen whimpered and gave the signal to loose.

None of the templars, including their valiant captain, had ever encountered an undead creature before. All had been taught about the many varieties; all had been trained in how to slay the different types. However, none of their preparations steeled their nerves enough for the scene before them.

Crossbow bolts flew into the horde of undead, less than a dozen fell, and cries of alarm rose from the mouth of each templar there. Some ran for the church to argue later that they had gone for re-enforcements. Some fumbled at reloading their crossbows while spitting curses mixed with hurried prayers. However, some were warriors. These last climbed the fence and hit the ground on the other side with a weapon in hand and the name of their goddess on their lips. These last made Fate proud in Her high temple. These last would be welcomed into Her garden.

Illiech, from his vantage a few blocks to the east, was only able to see less than a third of the army of undead that clamored about in the graveyard. He also saw what he perceived to be the leading edge of Fladeen's charge. Not to be outdone, for he had begun his mission this night with thoughts of claiming Shyeld's Crown for himself, ordered his own charge.

Other Paladins and Templars of Merc shouted to their deity and burst through the gates of Nobles' Rest in what they hoped would appear to be a valiant effort.

Ranoct, understanding that his men would need their wind when they arrived, kept his troops to a light pace and was only just arriving as the last of Illiech's men topped the fence and charged the wall of undead. Ranoct's heart quailed at the sight, but his actions reflected his years in Tarborat and service to the King. The command of "charge" burst from Ranoct's throat without any sign of hesitation. His watchmen, hand-picked for this night's work if not this exact mission, obeyed that order without question.

Ranoct, sometimes called Ranoct Arrow-Eater, cut his way toward one of the Captains of the Abyss.

Dunewell was pleasantly surprised when the first volley from the templars on the fence dropped several of the undead on the outer edge of the throng. He was shocked when he saw them climbing the fence in full charge, the name of Fate on their lips as they came on. He also heard the charge from the Paladins of Merc, although they were behind him and beyond one of the Captains of the Abyss.

Dunewell and Maloch felt more than saw the change in the battle when the forces of Fate and Merc collided with the army of the undead. In the space of a few sword strokes, the enemies surrounding them thinned, and the claws, teeth, and horns gouging for their flesh were lessened by half. Still breathing in violent rasps, Dunewell and Maloch were able to strike almost as often as they parried now.

The tide of the battle turned, and Dunewell and Maloch were once again on the offensive. Both heard the command of *Vesliosh* shouted from different points on the battlefield. Both could see the Captains of the Abyss and Erin above the undead. Dunewell and Maloch both noticed they were no longer the focus of those wretched creatures.

The ground quaked again, and Dunewell saw Slythorne,

perched on his heels high up in a dead tree, smiling down at them. The battle raged on for several more minutes before Dunewell understood what Slythorne had done.

As he cut down another of the undead raised from the graveyard, Dunewell caught a glimpse of the iron gates leading into Nobles' Rest. He also caught a glimpse of the dead that had been called from the watery graves of the river and channels of Moras. Hundreds of them.

Illiech, surrounded and losing men every few seconds, called to Fladeen and Ranoct only to discover Fladeen was nowhere to be found on the battlefield. Ranoct, however, answered the call and, after several vicious moments of hacking and slashing, joined his troop with the soldiers of Merc. Seeing this, the remaining contingent of the church of Fate also pushed to join with Ranoct and Illiech's forces.

Sergeant Lisban assumed command of the young soldiers from the church of Fate. Ranoct began to bark orders for overlapping support and preparations for maneuvers. All pride suspended, Illiech accepted Ranoct's position of command and signaled as much to his troops. In the span of a few heartbeats, the combined force had hemmed the undead throng into a semi-circle and was pushing the army toward one corner of the graveyard. Ranoct could see Dunewell and Maloch at the center of the undead horde, but had no means of reaching them, not yet. He reasoned that, if his friend and the dark paladin could hold the undead off for just a bit longer, his force could draw the full attention of the abominations.

Just as lines were being established and soldiers with shields were linking up and forming a solid defense, a cry went up from the northern edge of their line. Ranoct leapt atop a nearby headstone, and his heart sank at what he saw. Hundreds more of the undead creatures were marching on the gates of Nobles' Rest.

The seasoned warrior scanned the graveyard and selected the area where they would make their stand. He had hoped to cut through and cut down the undead army and re-capture Dunewell and Maloch. Now he hoped they could hold out long enough for Lady Evalynne's troops and the soldiers at Blackstone Hall and the Silver Helm academy to heed the call of their signal horns.

Ranoct commanded his troops to fall back in a series of bounding or leap-frog maneuvers that allowed one group to provide cover for another as they retreated to defensible positions. Then, the roles would reverse, and the second group would provide protection while the first would fall back. Ranoct had spotted a set of mausoleums that provided solid walls on three sides and a narrow alley of access between them. That is where they would make their stand.

The combined force worked their way backward, struggling to hold the ends of their line. Ranoct set four men to stand and boost their few remaining crossbowmen up onto the roofs of the mausoleums. Once in place, they began raining bolts and quarrels onto the undead army while the troops still on the ground formed a tight shield wall across the short expanse between the stone buildings.

Ranoct climbed to the roof of the tallest building to survey the field before him. His heart sank again when the nearest channel transformed into a swirling hellscape of acid spouts and flaming waters. They were now completely cut off from the rest of Moras. Furthermore, and the true reason for his new concern, with the water perverted by such a spell, the undead could cross into the city unhindered.

CHAPTER XII
Brothers Stand

"Nobles' Rest, of course," Lady Dru said as she opened her eyes and let her concentration on her most recent spell dissipate. "We should…"

"Not we, my Lady," Silas said, in a rare moment of defiance as he cut her statement short. "Only I."

Dru only raised a single eyebrow, but the wrath dancing behind her eyes was a clear warning to Silas.

"My Lady, if you go, then Slythorne might take you," Silas continued quickly, hoping to make his point before he had to discover precisely how Dru might express that wrath. "A'Ilys reports that Slythorne's man scouted the cavern already. If they could move against you here, they would have. He hopes to draw you out by drawing me out. He knows, or at least suspects, that I must go because of Dunewell. He likely also hopes that we will attempt to strike him down while he faces Dunewell and whatever other allies the Warlock has mustered. Don't you see? All he has to do is escape with you, and he's won; gone and leaving us no way of pursuing him. Please, if I have garnered any value in your eyes, allow me to do this alone."

"No," Dru said simply as she rose from her chair and walked to the door. "Not alone."

Silas stepped through the cluster of swirling smoke and, as one boot was lifting from the cavern floor of the drow complex, the other struck the stone of a walkway in Nobles' Rest. He took a moment to reflect on how much had transpired in his life since his boots trod the stone of these pathways last.

In that same moment of reflection, he drew his family's shrou-sheld with his right hand and called forth Dreg Zelche, the icy scimitar of drake claw. Silas sprinted for the horde of undead and selected one of the Captains of the Abyss as his first target. Silas leapt.

The creature's surprise was complete when the Chaos Lord landed next to him, driving a wicked-cold blade through the gap between the monster's breastplate and girth. Silas continued the thrust, angling the blade upward and slicing through what had once been the risen creature's kidney, spleen, lower lung, and intestines. With a single vicious stroke, Silas cut the unsuspecting abomination nearly in two. Silas examined the dropped shield, smiled, and sheathed his shrou-sheld.

As one the other two huge skeletal creatures and the fallen champion looked toward Silas. Then, they looked beyond him.

The three remaining commanders of Slythorne's army hesitated when they saw a small force of ogres and giants pour out of a dark cloud of teleportation alongside two dozen armed and armored drow soldiers. The soldiers sent by Rogash and Jandanero waded into the undead with abandon, cutting down the first three rows of raised creatures before there was any response from those mastering them.

Silas watched as the three commanding the undead throng exchanged a look and then began to move. The two Captains from the Abyss marched toward the center of the horde, toward Dunewell. The fallen champion took flight and hovered above the mass of undead, where she focused all her might on controlling and directing the mindless force.

In a single bound, Silas leapt again to land within the tight circle Dunewell and Maloch had carved out around them. Silas, looted shield on one arm and Dreg Zelche paired with it, moved in alongside his brother, striking down two undead with one great slash from his evil blade.

Maloch wheeled, bringing his swords to bear instinctively.

"Hold," Dunewell called as he drove his glowing rider's pike into the empty eye socket of another undead, dropping it. "It's Silas."

"Aye," Maloch said, unease clear in his tone.

"It's good to see you, Dune," Silas struggled to maintain a light tone while shoving back a snapping maw with the shield and slashing across to take the hands from another raised corpse. "You're looking well."

"When this is over..."

"Yes, yes," Silas said, finding it easy to interrupt Dunewell, given his heavy breathing. "Although there are some facts I would like to point out."

Several heartbeats passed while the undead around them seemed to surge with power. A quick glance up revealed the source of that power. Erin was hovering directly above them, lines of concentration carved deeply across her forehead. Each of the three parried and struck, Dunewell and Silas making four or five strikes for every one of Maloch's.

"I have killed," Silas continued after a few moments of desperate fighting. "However, those you call brothers-in-arms have also killed. I would like to point out that I have saved lives as well. How many of your so-called noble friends can say that? In fact, by my calculations, I have saved seven lives for every life I've taken. Not even you, gallant brother, can say that."

"If you... can't comprehend... the difference... the murder of children... the murder of our mother... then I cannot... explain it," Dunewell finally managed as he struck and parried with both ends of his enchanted war hammer, destroying six of the undead creatures in the time it took him to speak the sentence.

"What about your dark-skinned friend?" Silas asked, his breath beginning to sound labored. "How many thousands of deaths is he responsible for, and yet you fight at his side."

"He's repented," Dunewell said as he jerked his head back to dodge a diseased claw. "He's trying to make reparation."

"Are you saying I should repent? Repent to who, and

why? Repent to the silly gods that so betrayed these lands? Repent to a church that tortures children for their own sick amusement? Perhaps repent to the law that raises up the likes of Reeve Sevynn and Lord High Inquisitor Gyllorn? I think not, brother."

"Repent to me," Dunewell pleaded. "Repent to me, brother. Let me show you a better way, a way to heal your wounded soul."

Silas's responding laughter broke Dunewell's heart.

Under Ranoct's command, the forces of the churches, coupled with the watchmen, had managed to hedge in the southern side of the undead horde. He could see from his vantage point atop the mausoleum that the newly arrived ogres, giants, and drow were doing an excellent job of corralling the new wave of undead that had come from the river and the channels. The newly arrived monsters were successfully dividing those throngs and cutting them down. The impromptu commander saw the two remaining Captains of the Abyss marching in toward the three gathered in the middle of the horde. Ranoct turned to the west, raising his signal horn to redirect his crossbowmen. As his lips touched the horn a Muerso blade, this one fashioned into longsword, glided under his shoulder blade, between his ribs, and severed his heart. Ranoct Dragon Slayer, Ranoct Siege Breaker and Arrow Eater, fell dead.

Ashdow squatted low behind him and pulled the fallen warrior out of sight from the others under his command. Once in seclusion, the assassin took a moment to study the visage of the famous warrior. As Ashdow looked upon the brave man, the face of the Shadow Blade began to shift. In another moment, Ashdow, sometimes called Jasper and once known as Kelmut the Fierce, had assumed the exact appearance of Inquisitor Ranoct.

Ashdow was tempted to do more, but there was no time. The master assassin's life had been structured around self-control; he had forged his body in the fires of his will. Now that control served him well.

"Form up!" Ashdow, now as Ranoct, commanded.

The Shadow Blade hopped from the roof of the stone building to stand amongst the remaining templars and watchmen on the ground.

"Form up! We are going to push through to Dunewell! You, you, and you three, form the tip of the spear! Paladin Illiech, you'll lead them!"

The soldiers followed without hesitation, except for Illiech, who did hesitate a bit. This group of loyal men unwittingly obeyed the commands of a murderer.

The two Captains of the Abyss waded into the three defenders with a level of skill none had encountered before. Both skeletal creatures took up their Shrou-Hayns in a stance Maloch knew from ancient days. It was the stance of the Raven Wing.

Using minimal movement, the two undead masters jabbed with pommel, slashed with crosspiece, and then gouged with sword tip in a single, fluid motion. In the time Dunewell or Silas could strike twice, or Maloch four times, these masters of the Shrou-Hayn struck out with eight attacks each.

"Please, brother," Dunewell pleaded, worried that Silas might be cut down before his soul could be given a chance. "Surely, you understand the difference between killing and murder. It is about defending the weak... fighting for those that can't fight for themselves."

Dunewell, Maloch, and Silas parried, called upon spells to turn the blades, and lurched violently to keep from being mortally wounded. Dunewell had seen the Shrou-Hayn wielded in battle, but never like this. Maloch understood the secrets of Raven Wing, but it had been eons since he'd had to defend against it.

"Who was there to defend me?" Silas screamed his retort in a rare moment of raw emotion. "I was a child once too! I can tell you I suffered far more than those in my Sanctum did in their last moments of life!"

Despite his best efforts, the cursed tip of a Shrou-Hayn bit through Maloch's armor and deep into the muscle of his chest. As he was reeling from that wound, the crosspiece of the great sword slammed down to crush his collarbone. The holy shrou-sheld dropped from Maloch's feeble grip.

Silas took a blow to the face from the pommel of one of the Shrou-Hayns that staggered him and, as Dunewell moved for a low strike, the other end of the same Shrou-Hayn cut a deep furrow through Dunewell's right thigh. Dunewell's leg collapsed, but not before he was able to drive the point of his rider's pike deep into the undead master's knee.

Maloch was battered to the side by the sheer weight and force of a crosscut by the other Captain. The mighty drow Paladin was knocked to the ground. Silas, stumbling backward, fell over Maloch, both of them tangling together in a heap. Dunewell's rider's pike was ripped from his hand as the creature from the Abyss twisted away from him and then was struck down from behind. Dunewell looked up in disbelief as he was relieved to see Paladin Illiech standing over him, sword in hand.

Slythorne, seeing the ogres, giants, and drow cutting through his forces, closed his eyes in a moment's concentration. He called upon the innate powers of a master vampire and sent a compelling command throughout their ranks. In another heartbeat, ogre turned on giant, and drow against drow.

Slythorne then divided his attention between those recently mastered and the demon-possessed Erin. *The one called Silas must be kept to torture; he is the bait for Lady Dru.*

The fallen champion sent the command to the undead beneath her, who began to fight with a renewed vigor.

The templars and watchmen were all about them then, striking and thrusting at the two Captains of the Abyss and driving back the surrounding horde. Dunewell's heart was gladdened upon seeing his friend, Ranoct, suddenly appear at his side.

"Form up!" Ranoct commanded the soldiers of the church and the watch. "Form up, I say!"

Dunewell smiled and reached out for the hand offered to

him by his friend, his brother-in-arms. Ranoct took his hand and began to pull Dunewell from the ground. Then, seeing the cursed longsword in Ranoct's other hand, Dunewell had just enough time to wonder, *why*?

Ashdow stabbed the Muerso blade into Dunewell's chest. Maloch and Silas both cried out, but none could hear them. As the blade entered his flesh, Dunewell felt the flower that he wore, the white rose pinned to his breast, wilt.

"NO!" The command, the plea, erupted from Silas's throat.

Ashdow let go Dunewell's hand and drew a long knife, another cursed blade. Ashdow aimed the knife for Dunewell's eye. As the dagger plunged in, Silas called upon his powers of shifting and his command of the demon within him. Silas propelled his body between the knife and his brother. The knife plunged into Silas's breast.

Completely piercing Silas's body, the tip of the knife slipped deep into Dunewell's left eye, slick with his brother's blood. Dunewell cried out, in pain and loss.

"Shezmupaulauk Erruk!" Slythorne spoke in an unworldly voice of command. "Depart!"

Slythorne, invoking the true name of the demon Silas had mastered, broke the bonds of slavery with those few syllables. Shezmu, no longer bound by Silas's will, wasted no time in escaping to his home plane to seek his place at Prechii's side. Silas's body slouched to the ground, limp and devoid of power.

"Dune... brother..." was the last faint whisper that passed Silas's already bluing lips.

"Whitburn of Bolvii!" Slythorne then called. "Depart!"

Dunewell felt the strength of an ancient oath take hold within him. He felt Whitburn swell in his soul in a defiant shout against the command. The power of the rose closed the wound in his chest, but his eye burned with a pain that struck him to the core of his being. Dunewell's will, fed by Whitburn's rage, captured that pain and pushed it far from his mind.

Slythorne, once called Truthorne, you cannot command me

thus, Slythorne and Dunewell both heard in their minds. *I am Ivant the Second, father of Jonas and Velryk, descendant of King Ivant, and you cannot command me thus!*

Dunewell felt the power of the fading rose flow into him. He felt the strength of a thousand generations rise and swell within his breast. He felt the sting of the Muerso blade diminish and fade. Dunewell, conditioned from a young age to fight, to always fight, struck out with the head of his hammer and crushed the knee of his assailant. Ashdow collapsed to the ground.

I looked to the place of justice, and there I saw wickedness reign, Dunewell heard in his mind. He understood that it was Slythorne quoting to him from the book of Bolvii. *I looked upon the sons of sinners, and saw their father's sin upon them. Those are the words of your Bolvii, your great and majestic god. Let go this need to please those who are so possessed of vanity and pride. Let go your faith in an empty name.*

It was not a command, not a proclamation of Bolvii's, Dunewell retorted. *It was an observation, a warning, for he had seen the hearts of man. To stand for the weak, to defend the defenseless, those are the tenets of my faith. You cannot turn my heart with your weak words.*

Dunewell looked up to the trees, not with his eye, but with his *sight.*

Be not proud, oh slave to your vanity, Dunewell thought/said. *For your sins have come due.*

As Dunewell thought those words, Jonas struck out with his Shyeld-Hayn, his Lanceilier's blade. The blessed weapon sheared through bone, undead flesh, and a blackened heart. Slythorne gasped, an unbelieving look upon his face. The master vampire fell unceremoniously from his perch in the high tree, his body striking several limbs before finally colliding with the white marble of path below.

The horde of undead collapsed just as quickly, falling back to the dust from whence they came. Jonas hopped from branch to branch, making his way deftly to the ground in pursuit of the fallen Slythorne.

Dunewell crawled over and took Silas into his arms. Weeping, he began to kiss Silas's still cheek and cold forehead. Dunewell summoned the power of Whitburn, now known to him as Ivant II, and his hands took on a blue hue. He pushed the healing energy into Silas's body but felt no response. Dunewell also reached out to Maloch and summoned the power within him once again. A blue hue began to build around Dunewell's hand and flowed from his palm into Maloch's wound. Maloch slumped to the ground, unconscious, but breathing easily.

The fallen champion that possessed Erin was at a loss. Champions, fallen and otherwise, were conceived to take orders and direction, deciding their own plans was a feat beyond most of them. After hesitating for several moments, the demon fled the killing field of Nobles' Rest.

A terrified Illiech screamed, "form up!" and then ran to the aid of Ranoct, or the man he thought was Ranoct. The inquisitor was the only man Illiech could think of that might salvage some of this nightmarish scene.

Dunewell cried out as Illiech took Ranoct, or rather Ashdow wearing Ranoct's face, under the arm, and helped him to stand. The remaining dozen templars and watchmen fell into a loose defensive semi-circle around the Paladin and the assassin.

Jonas dropped to the ground next to Slythorne. The master vampire looked up at him and smiled.

"You think this will be a salve to your heart?" Slythorne asked as his black blood oozed over the brim of his lips. "Do you believe you will sleep soundly this night? I have avenged myself on this world for thousands of years, and I can tell you..."

His words were cut short when Jonas struck Slythorne's head from his body in one brisk stroke. Jonas pulled a sack from his waist and shoved Slythorne's severed head into it. Then he tied the end of the sack to his belt and pulled forth a flask marked with the owl and gauntlet, the holy symbol of Bolvii.

Jonas poured the contents of the flask onto Slythorne's corpse, which burst into a blue-black flame at once. The magical flame consumed Slythorne's body at a rapid pace. Jonas looked from the vampire to Dunewell and then ran to his side.

"Bait?" Dunewell asked.

"Bait," Jonas said, smiling and nodding.

Then both looked to the smoke flash that burst at the feet of Illiech and Ashdow. Jonas, knowing this spell, began to scan the horizon and spotted the duo on a rooftop over a hundred yards away. Dunewell struggled to his feet, blood still flowing from his left eye, and eased Silas's head to the ground. He stood over his brother for another heartbeat and then looked back toward the man he thought was his friend. Both warriors ignored the contingent of ogres, giants, and drow that now gathered at the far edge of the graveyard.

"It's not Ranoct," Jonas said as he jerked his chin to the mausoleum where Ranoct's body lay, lifeless. "It's Slythorne's errand boy."

Dunewell's shock was complete when Silas's body was snatched out from under him with supernatural speed. He caught that something was also taken from Maloch's pocket, but couldn't tell what. He scanned about and saw a woman of exotic beauty clad in an elegant Ussa gown crouched over Silas almost fifty yards away. Dunewell had no doubt this was the vampire Medaci had hunted those many months ago.

"You can chase your assassin, or chase your need to make up for failing your brother," Lady Dru said as she kneeled over Silas's fallen body. "I care not."

With that, she, along with Silas, vanished into the ether.

Dunewell looked to where Maloch had fallen and saw the ghostly image of Dactlynese taking him into her arms and vanishing. Then Dunewell looked in the direction Ashdow had flown. He turned back toward the tendrils of smoke that still floated in the air about the area Silas had so recently been. Jonas grasped Dunewell's arm and jerked him violently.

"We have a mission yet to finish," Jonas said.

Dunewell nodded and wiped the blood from his face.

EPILOGUE
Dark Guardian

"Why don't we face the thing ourselves?" Dactlynese asked as she looked over Maloch's wounds again.

Maloch sat on a rock stripped to the waist and enjoying the icy wind that lashed at his black skin. Dactlynese had brought Maloch to this high mountain top in northern Lawrec, where Lynneare studied the Dark Guardian provided by Queen Jandanero. Lynneare had repaired Maloch's many injuries, but Dactlynese still insisted on inspecting the dark Paladin to make sure he was healing properly.

"As I've said, my dear, I have seen the defeat of Elvvleth," the Warlock of the Marshes replied while he inspected runes carved into the Dark Guardian. "The urn, the phylactery, must be destroyed, but that is still beyond my sight. The physical beast must also be destroyed and that I have seen. There was no mistaking it. It is defeated by a Dark Guardian."

"Your visions have been wrong before," Dactlynese said as she turned her attention back toward her father.

"Not wrong," Lynneare corrected as he raised and rocked his king finger from side to side. "I misinterpreted a few, yes. Sometimes multiple possible outcomes are difficult to foresee, yes. However, the visions themselves are never *wrong*."

"What of this Frost that you mentioned?" Maloch asked as he pulled his shirt on over his head. "That was something new."

"Yes, that was new," Lynneare said, briefly turning his eyes from the enchanted armor to the Paladin of Time. "We see only what we are meant to see."

"You've sometimes contemplated my anger and its source," Dactlynese said with an edge in her voice. "It's vague statements like that!"

****

"Your Paladin friend from the Church of Merc made good on his promise," Jonas said as he squatted next to Dunewell on the banks of the Olithyn. "He petitioned Lady Evalynne on your behalf, and she has sent word to the King requesting your pardon. Pardon, you understand. Not reinstatement."

Dunewell lifted his head from the river's edge and wiped water from his beard. The long drinks of cold, flowing water had revived him considerably. However, his wounds had been deep, and his eye, poisoned not only by Ashdow's blade but also by Silas's blood, was worse than it had been. Jonas winced at the sight of Dunewell's split and blackening iris when he turned to face him.

"I'm surprised saving his life from Ashdow was enough to convince Illiech to testify for me," Dunewell said as he pulled the makeshift patch over his gnarled eye.

"He may have had the idea that he could present the outcome of events in his own favor."

"'May have?'"

"Perhaps Illiech realized he could tell the Lady he'd been looking into the possibility of a demon that was actually responsible for the deaths of her Reeve and Lord High Inquisitor," Jonas said as he kneeled on the bank to fill their waterskins. "Perhaps it was better than admitted a fallen champion had been operating freely in Moras for almost a year. A year in which none in the church knew anything about it. Perhaps the battle of Nobles' Rest sells better to the congregations as a trap laid by the Churches of Merc and Fate rather than a debacle they were lucky to survive."

"That's a remarkable display of imagination and initiative for Illiech," Dunewell said, smiling and not taking his eye from Jonas.

Dunewell was confident he knew who had reached those conclusions, and was sure Illiech was encouraged to latch onto them as his own.

"Well, he's smarter than he looks, I suppose," Jonas said, not taking his attention from the waterskins.

"How did you find us at the graveyard?" Dunewell asked, pointedly. "The battle moved there too quickly for you to have followed. You were set too well to have pursued us there."

"I knew when Ashdow arrived in Moras, he would wish to make contact with any local Shadow Blades. They're courteous in that way, and it is one of the few things relatively predictable about them. So, I made sure to intercept his message and meeting request. I posed as one of their own in a conversation of sorts with him, and then followed him. I stayed with him until he led me to Slythorne. Both scouted the graveyard, which made sense. So, I waited."

"No word of Silas?"

"None, nor of his vampiric friend," Jonas said as he rose and walked back to their horses. "How... how are you?"

"If he is dead, then the world is a better place," Dunewell said after a pause to reflect. "I just wish I could have done... something."

"Chaos Lords do not die easily," Jonas said as he stepped into the saddle. "Do not make the mistake of assuming him destroyed."

Dunewell wrapped his hands around his saddle horn and leaned against his horse. After a few moments, he lowered his head and nodded.

"I'm a bit surprised at your calm state," Dunewell said as he mounted. "I gather Slythorne was only the first name on your list, and this Ashdow is the second. Why are we not pounding the trail in pursuit?"

"If you want to win a race, go to the finish line," Jonas said as he reined his horse back toward Moras. "In my surveillance, I learned something that confirms other information I'd received. I believe our quarry also poses as Jasper."

"Why do I know that name?"

"Perhaps you've heard of the Marshal of Lavon?"

****

"His body is all but dead," the drow warlock said as he turned from the silk bed where Silas's ashen form lay still. "His mind, however, is remarkable."

"So, there is a chance?" Lady Dru asked, struggling not to reveal her feelings, her need for Silas's recovery.

"All things are possible," Queen Jandanero said from her plush seat in the corner of the temple chamber. "For a price, that is."

"What would you ask?" Dru asked, almost pleading.

Jandanero cast a glance at the warlock, a drow schooled in the arts of all three realms of magic.

"His mind is strong," the warlock said, taking his cue from his Queen. "If you had the true name of a demon, absolute control of it, you could command it to possess him. It would have to be a demon of repute. Your man would have to master it on his own, but that would give him a fighting chance."

"Obtaining the true name of a fallen champion, one of renown, is no mean feat," Jandanero said as she stirred her wine with her queen finger and then licked the sweet liquid from her fingertip. "I will expend my resources on your behalf. However, I do have demands of my own."

Dru took a moment to get her thirst under control. She knew when a master vampire died, it had one of two effects on those close to him that he'd turned. Either they were released from the curse of unlife, or they found their inherent powers dramatically increased as the apprentice became the master. She had anticipated the new, potent abilities she now found at her disposal. She had not prepared for the increased need of blood. A need that was driving her emotions to the radical ends of the spectrum.

"I can bring you one," Dru said, thinking of the Door of Will and the Stewardess Erin. "I will pay whatever I must."

If you enjoyed any of our works, please leave a review on Amazon, Bookbub, or GoodReads.

You can learn more on our website for the Bloodlines Reforged Saga at www.bloodlinesreforged.com or on Instagram @r.j.hanson, Twitter @rjhanson5, or on Facebook at www.facebook.com/rolandsquest or www.amazon.com/author/rjhanson

You can also follow me at https://www.bookbub.com/profile/r-j-hanson
or
https://www.goodreads.com/author/
show/18992415.R_J_Hanson
You can sign up for our newsletter on our website, www.bloodlinesreforged.com, and by doing so, you will get an email notification when new books are released and details about promotional offers as well as emails with exclusive content and short stories of high adventure in the world of Stratvs!

We always love hearing from our fans, so please feel free to email us at rj@bloodlinesreforged.com or contact us through the website if you have any comments, concerns, suggestions, or questions. Thank you, RJ

ABOUT THE AUTHOR

R. J. Hanson

RJ Hanson has been a cop for over two decades. In that time, he accumulated a number of real-world experiences that have
served to give him a unique understanding
of the human condition and a perspective
that gives his writing an honest grit. He has
also benefited from years of training ran-
ging from interview and interrogation
techniques to hand to hand combat to
SWAT tactics. RJ is a certified Firearms In-
structor and Linguistic Statement Ana-
lyst. He currently serves as a Lieutenant in the Criminal Inves-
tigations Division of a small Texas police department where he
specializes in crimes against persons.

He also enjoys the distinction of having scored a touch, or
'touche', against an Olympic fencer during a pickup match in
college. He's really too proud of it.

In his youth he worked as a cowboy having grown up on a
small ranch in north Texas. At the age of 16 he was selected for
the TAMS (Texas Academy of Mathematics and Science) project
at the University of North Texas where his young eyes were
opened to the world.

In his spare time, RJ has studied medieval combat and military
tactics as well as arms and armaments of various cultures and
times.

RJ plays in a weekly pen and paper RPG game (Rolemaster) with

some close family and friends and some of the characters played have been around since 1996!

RJ and his wife, Michelle, live on a small ranch where they maintain a modest heard of cattle, two dogs, a variety of barn cats, a peacock named Henry and a peahen named Margaret (aka Ferd).

BOOKS BY THIS AUTHOR

Roland's Path

When two spies escape during young Roland's watch, they begin a chain of events not intended by Fate that may threaten a kingdom. Roland is driven by his shame to take up his axes and track them down. Raised on the rural edges of Gallhallad, can he survive the dangers of the road ahead? Can his ideals of right and wrong weather the complexities of the path before him?

With the help of his lifelong friend Eldryn, the Cavalier hopeful, and an uneasy bargain with a dagger wielding cutpurse, Roland pursues a wizard of unknown powers and a woman of uncommon beauty and deadly skill.

Will Roland's vanity not only doom him, but his friends and a king he hoped to one day serve as well?

In Roland's world of Stratvs, vanity has a high price. A price paid with the blood of the innocent and the guilty. Around him, swords once pledged to justice rust on the altars of the self-righteous.

Roland's Vow

The Warlock of the Marshes is a man marked and cursed by a past of horrible deeds. Will Roland hear his plea?

Can Roland trust the daughter of such a man, or will his own de-

sires betray his reason?

Roland and Eldryn take to the seas of Stratvs, alongside their new Slandik friends, and discover an exotic city that exists in the shadow of harsh laws and savage practices. Lavon is home to every type of trade and pleasure. However, such riches place its very soul in peril.In the distant land of Lawrec, Roland will face trials that will test not only his physical strength, but his own code of honor as well.

Roland's constitution continues to be forged as he struggles against the evils of the world and his own pride. But will his efforts be enough to save a land besieged by raiding armies and a people starved of hope?Join Roland as he takes Swift Blood in hand to battle pirates, fallen champions, and worse.

Roland's quest to earn his father's approval continues in Roland's Vow, Book II of the Heirs of Vanity series.

Roland's Triumph

An unseen evil gathers just beyond perception. In the quiet mornings jaundiced eyes peer out from imagined shadows.

Daeriv's forces have withdrawn, but his pall touch still lurks in Lawrec. Its presence stirs Roland's every nerve. Will he understand its nature before it's too late?

Roland faces a choice. He struggles to fulfill two vows, one to his lord and another to his betrothed. Will he ignore the wisdom offered by his father? If he does, what will it cost?

An army that curses the very ground it walks upon puts the future of Lawrec at stake and threatens a bloodline. How does a knight weigh the life of a single child against the possible desolation of thousands of families?

Bound by his struggle between oaths, Roland may fail to see Claire's own dilemma. As she risks what may be fatal rejection, will her love for Roland be enough to see them through?

Roland's journey continues in Roland's Triumph, the third book of the Heirs of Vanity Series.

Fires That Forge

Murder. Lies. Betrayal. Magic? Can one inquisitor's quest for the truth in a city bound for chaos save its soul? A serial killer roams the shining streets and dark alleys of the great trade city. How can you count yourself safe against a murderer that may wield magic as a weapon? As the body count rises, those in power demand someone pay for the heinous crimes. What if the one that stands accused is innocent? Is there still such a thing as innocence in Moras?

When he learns that his life-long friend is the sole suspect, the decorated veteran turned King's Inquisitor takes it upon himself to save his friend and root out the murderer. Already struggling to keep the doors open to his hospital for those the city has forgotten, the young physician must now also find a way to prove his innocence and dodge the hangman's noose.

Can the Inquisitor find the elusive killer before the executioner calls?

If you enjoy murder mysteries, psychological thrillers, and epic swords and sorcery fantasy tales, then this story is for you!

Charged with tension and intrigue, this thrilling tale of murder and betrayal will leave you second-guessing your own suspicions... and perhaps your perceptions of right and wrong as well.

Return to the exciting world of Stratvs and the adventure of the Bloodlines Reforged Saga! www.bloodlinesreforged.com

Bloom Of Blood And Bone

The murders are solved, but justice has yet to be served. While the killers have been loosed, they are not free. Both are bound by chains of their own forging.

Dunewell, sentenced to discharge his next mission in the company of a harsh, battle-worn companion, must find his way in a world where the system he once vowed to protect has betrayed him. Can a man change his life, himself, after a life in service to a Code he is only now coming to truly understand? Is there a future for him if he fails the secret brotherhood, the Sword Bearers?

Follow as they strive against hidden powers beyond their understanding, and as they seek to unravel which is the hero and which is the villain.

Join us for another tale of high adventure in the world of Stratvs as the Bloodlines Reforged Saga continues!

Made in the USA
Columbia, SC
03 July 2022

62688179R00148